Running Home

Nancy Arey Cohen

Running Home
Copyright © 2022 Nancy Arey Cohen

ISBN: 978-1-954517-45-5

Designed and produced by:
Indie Author Books
12 High Street, Thomaston, Maine
www.indieauthorbooks.com

Printed in the United States of America

To my sons, Robert and Andrew.
Without you, my life would be a blank page.

Chapter One

"I swear to God I'm going to run away from home one of these days!" Susan muttered as she dragged the cooler filled with Gatorade behind her with one hand while balancing a big tray of home-baked brownies in the other, her bag chair slung over one shoulder, and her purse hanging from her elbow. A strand of hair fell over one eye, and she absent-mindedly blew it away as she struggled with her load. When she reached the Little League field, she left the cooler by the dugout and carried the brownies to the bleachers. Opening her bag chair and sinking into its canvas comfort, she shut her eyes and sighed.

"Are we having fun yet?" asked one of the moms.

Susan laughed and repeated, "I swear to God I'm going to run away from home one of these days. Am I too old to run away from home?" All the other moms sitting there in their designer jeans laughed and agreed that it was a great idea. Looking for a topic of conversation during their sons' game, they mused on how they could run away, where they would go, what their families would think about it, and how good it would feel. One said her dream was to disappear to a beach somewhere with a tall cocktail. Another thought hibernating in a lakeside cabin sounded heavenly. One by one they each shared their secret fantasies of running away from home.

Hmm, Susan thought, *I guess I'm not the only one who feels that way.* Before she had a chance to continue her thought, Meg, a practicing psychiatrist, shared that the reason women yearn to run away is because they feel too needed. Suddenly the women in the stands looked like bobblehead dolls, their heads shaking up and down in agreement. "When a person feels deeply rooted in his or her life and family, sometimes she can feel trapped." The bobbleheads agreed. "The excessive love and need can become stifling."

1

"*Exactly!*" Susan exclaimed. The other moms laughed conspiratorially at her exuberance as Susan's Irish heritage blossomed on her cheeks.

Looking all around, Susan, in hushed tones, told the others it was fun to fantasize, but that she really was thinking about doing it. She just wanted a break for a while. Every time she thought about it, though, she looked at her life and felt guilty. She really did have it all. She lived in Greenwich, Connecticut. Her husband was a big-shot lawyer in New York and was not bad on the eyes to boot. Her three sons had never gotten into any serious trouble and made good grades at their swanky private school. She had friends, volunteered for the schools, the Make-A-Wish Foundation, and was a member of the Junior League. She got her hair trimmed every three weeks and had a standing manicure/pedicure appointment and massage at the local spa.

Still, she was uneasy and unfulfilled. With her fortieth birthday approaching, she was thinking more about her life, the consequences of decisions she had made, and the career that she had given up. Some might consider her a rich snob who had no right feeling unfulfilled or unappreciated. But she hadn't always been this woman. She used to be a woman living in New York City inching her way to the top in the publishing field. Even earlier, she had been a girl who lived in a tiny town on the coast of Maine and truly enjoyed the simple pleasures in life, like sitting on the rocks by the side of the water reading a good book or going sailing with friends. When had she become so entitled? She really didn't like herself much these days. Sometimes she just wanted to be a teenager again with no responsibilities and her whole life in front of her. As the other women continued to chat and a bat cracked, sending the ball into the outfield, Susan shut her eyes behind her sunglasses and visited her past....

The sun toasted her shoulders as she sat on the float in her halter top and shorts, making tiny rainbows as she splashed her feet in the water. Friends motored a small sailboat up to the dock to pick her up as, from out of her canvas bag, Otis Redding crooned about sitting on the dock of the bay. She hopped up, grabbed the bag, and leaped effortlessly across a stretch of water onto the bow of the boat as it approached. Her friends commented that she never could wait for them to pull up to the dock, and she laughingly agreed.

"It's too nice a day to be 'sittin' on the dock of the bay, watchin' the tide roll away,'" she dramatically sang, eliciting loud laughter and jeers from her friends.

Susie effortlessly walked from bow to stern where she was grabbed by her high school sweetheart, Bill, who kissed her, to the howls of the other teens on the boat.

"There they go again!"

"Way to go, Billy boy!"

Susie and Bill laughed and found a place to sit amid the coolers, beach blankets, and water toys scattered on the deck.

"Doug, just shut up and get us out into the bay," ordered Susie, with mock seriousness. Her friend Doug replied with a "Whatever you say," and expertly maneuvered the nineteen-foot lightning that he and Bill had found washed up after a nor'easter last fall. No one had claimed it, so Doug and his girlfriend, Jeannie, and Bill and Susie had worked all winter and spring in Doug's parents' cold barn fixing it up, pooling their finances to get new sails, and making it seaworthy again. Now they were enjoying the fruits of their labors whenever they could.

"What did we do before we had *Windfall*?" Susie mused.

"Well, we sat on the beach a lot," answered her best friend, Jeannie, laughing.

"This is sooooooooo much better!" Susie enthusiastically replied, and she leaned back against Bill's chest on the starboard banquette, savoring the sun and the sea breeze.

"We're almost out of the cove, Susie. Get your lazy bones up on the deck and raise the jib, will ya?" directed Doug as he sailed past a power boat sitting still in the water so its people could swim off the rear deck. "We're almost out of the cove and will be picking up some wind."

"Why can't Bill do it," Susie whined. Turning to Bill and raising her face, giving him a sweet smile and a kiss, she was rebuffed.

"Suz, you know the jib is your job," Bill said, and he continued to sit, sipping his cold drink. He then repeated, "jib-job-jib-job-jib-job" several times until he was howling with laughter. "Have any of you ever noticed how funny words sound if you repeat them?" His friends just smiled since they were used to Bill's musings.

When they had been working on the boat, they had come to an agreement on what responsibilities they each would have. Doug would be responsible for getting her into the water and out, storing her in his barn each winter, and skippering. After all, he had found the boat. Bill would maintain the sails and work the spinnaker. Bill also would help Doug with any regular maintenance. Susie would handle the jib and bring treats her mother baked. Susie's mom was known around town by all of the kids as the brownie lady because of her gooey, chewy, chocolatey brownies. Jeannie would clean the boat when they returned to shore and make sure nothing was left behind each time. It was a system that worked, and they stuck to it. Doug said that having everyone's responsibilities laid out would keep them from having arguments about who should do what.

Now, here they were on a perfect summer day enjoying a day sail out to an uninhabited island with a great beach. It was a popular spot, and they knew they would meet up with lots of friends out there. Susie reluctantly lifted her head from Bill's shoulder and grabbed the line to raise the jib. As the small foresail grabbed the new air, she felt the little boat surge through the water, the wind blowing her hair from her face. Her muscles taut, she trimmed the sail and hiked out over the side of the boat, exhilarated by the new speed and salty spray. In that moment, she couldn't imagine ever wanting to be anywhere else.

One of the other moms was poking her shoulder. "Susan, the game is over. The kids want their snacks." She jumped up and realized that a team of seven-year-olds were greedily eyeing the tray of brownies next to her.

4

"Well, come and get 'em, kids!" she called out a little too loudly, shrugging her shoulders in the direction of her friends and leaving the salty sea behind.

With the game over, and cheeks puffed out with a too-big bite, her son Sam grabbed his baseball bag and headed for the car while Susan packed up the remaining brownies, stuffed her chair back into its bag, picked up her purse and the handle of the cooler, and trudged back to her SUV where the seven-year-old waited impatiently for her.

As she loaded everything into the Mercedes, Sam excitedly relived the high points of the game, asking her if she had seen his hit and his great play on the field. She told him that, of course, she had, and they were great. His excitement was balm for her soul. She really loved her little guy. She couldn't understand how her husband could keep disappointing the kids by putting his work over their needs. Susan thought about all Ted was missing in his sons' young lives and was happy that she was there to see it all. As she was thinking this, she heard a disappointed voice from the back asking, "Mommy, why wasn't Daddy at the game? He promised he'd be there."

Her heart breaking for her little guy who wanted nothing more than for his dad to be at his games, she cheerily answered, "I know, sweetie, but he must have had something important come up at work. You know he wanted to be there. You can tell him all about it when he gets home."

Susan was getting tired of always making excuses for Ted. She knew that he loved the boys with all his heart, but he seemed to love his job more. She would have to think of a way to help him see how important it was to spend more time with his sons. Maybe she could think of some way to help him see what he was missing with her too. As she was thinking this, she looked in her rearview mirror and saw little Sam sulking in the backseat, his excitement about the game drowned by his disappointment that his father had missed his hit and the out he made on the field.

As they drove home, Susan's thoughts drifted. Lately, her dissatisfaction with her life seemed to be growing, and she couldn't really explain why. Trying to pinpoint a reason, she thought of the night before, replaying it in her mind....

As she drove her three sons to their after-school rehearsals and practices, Susan contemplated her options. She could simply be quiet and let the CD player continue to blare, her sons continue to argue about what they wanted to listen to, and her blood pressure continue to rise as she got more and more angry with them. She could quietly turn off the CD player, say simply, "We are going to be quiet for a while," and continue driving. Or she could choose the guilt angle that never worked, almost always made her feel worse, and that she was hearing herself use more and more frequently lately.

She glanced at fifteen-year-old Ben, sitting in the passenger seat next to her. As usual, he was lording his age over his two younger brothers, telling them that he could choose what to listen to as long as he was in the car. Peeking in the rearview mirror, she saw David and Sam, her twelve- and seven-year-olds, whining and complaining that it wasn't fair. She had been through this a million times before.

She chose option four—at least for now. She began daydreaming about the upcoming summer vacation. It was only two months away. As her mind drifted, she began to smile. She was excited and optimistic about the fun-filled summertime. It was a time when she and the boys could share carefree days and make some happy memories. It had been a long school year, with lots of hard work and dedication displayed by each of her sons, hundreds of miles of driving done by her, and it was time for a break.

Actually, she was certain that she was looking forward to the school year ending even more than her boys. Although they would be getting time off from school, she would be getting a break from being the constant nag about homework, assorted practice schedules, and bedtimes. She would be getting a break from rousing sleeping, grumpy children out of bed early in the morning, forcing them to get dressed, arguing over who eats what for breakfast, packing school lunches, making sure everything is in backpacks ready to go, and rushing off to drop them at their schools—all before eight in the morning.

A particularly loud wail from Sam because David punched him brought her out of her reverie. She abruptly turned off the radio, which got the boys' attention. Her voice rising with each word, she said, "Last week I drove this SUV over three hundred miles, and *I* never even went anywhere. All I did was take *you*," she looked over at Ben, "back and forth to track practice, play rehearsals, to meet up with friends, and school." The boys in the backseat laughed because their big brother was getting into trouble. *Oh no. You're not getting off that easily,* she thought. Looking into her rearview mirror, she glared at twelve-year-old David.

"And I took *you* back and forth to play rehearsals, environmental club meetings, chorus rehearsals, baseball practices, friends' houses, and your school." David momentarily was quieted. Little Sam felt pretty smug about now. His big brothers were both in trouble. Seconds later, though, he realized that he wasn't off the hook.

"And I took you," she looked squarely at Sam in her mirror, "to baseball practices, and friends' houses, and school. Three hundred miles in one week, and I never even left the house except to run errands and ferry you three around so that you could have fun and get an education!"

Her voice was rising now. "I have been doing this every day for the past fifteen years, and what do I get for thanks? Arguments and complaints. I get to listen to you fight about the dumbest stuff. I get to listen to you hurt each other's feelings. All I want out of life is for the three of you to be best friends, and can you do that for me? No. Well, we can go the rest of the way in silence. I don't care who wants to listen to what. I am turning off *all* music, and you can just sit there and think about what you want to say to me when you get out of this car. I'll give you a hint. It starts with 'Thanks' and ends with 'Mom!'"

After another five minutes of Sam arguing unsuccessfully that he always said thank you and Ben rolling his eyes, there was silence in the car. Susan listened to the sound of the tires on the pavement, the wind blowing through the sunroof, and wondered how it had come to this. She used to get along so well with her boys. They hardly ever argued. They played games in the car, sang, and made up stories. They asked each other trivia questions and tried to see who could stump the others with an obscure query. Even Sam had occasionally won the trivia game by asking a Disney question or something he had just learned in school that the rest of them had already learned and forgotten. They liked listening to her music and all sang along.

Recently, though, all they seemed to do was argue. They couldn't agree on what to listen to for music. Each of them had different tastes and would threaten to puke if other music was played. Lately, Ben had begun lording his age over the other two as he had never done before. He had always enjoyed being the older brother, the protector of the little guys. Since turning fifteen, though, he had begun to think of himself as too cool to be seen in their presence. He threatened and intimidated them, and generally set himself up as the alpha dog in the pack. David was the typical middle child. He tried to be the peacemaker, coming up with reasonable schemes to please everyone, but generally having them shot down by his brothers. His sense of fairness was advanced for his age, and he always tried to make everything even. In fact, this morning he had tried to suggest that Ben pick a song and then he pick one and then Sam pick one. That way, he argued, everyone would have a fair chance to listen to what they liked. Ben had said simply that he was the oldest and he was in charge. Susan began wondering where she had disappeared in this equation. She thought *she* was the oldest and in charge.

She felt guilty for getting angry with her sons, but she was so weary. She was tired of listening to their incessant arguing. *Maybe I'll just drop them off and keep riding off into the sunset,* she thought. *I could just disappear.* In her mind, she could see warm beaches, poolside loungers, and sailing at sunset. She could see tall drinks with umbrellas and exotic sounding names. As she drove, she was on autopilot.

Pulling up in front of Ben's school, she returned to reality. *I wonder if the boys realize how lucky they are.* She looked up at the imposing facade. Kids in khakis and jeans were sitting on the wall by the front steps. The school cost a fortune every year, but she and her husband, Ted, thought it would give the kids the education they needed to succeed in life. It was an investment in their futures. *If I let them live that long,* she thought, smiling. This upper school (*Why couldn't they just call it a* high school? *That's what it is.*) was across town, only ten minutes from their home, but until Ben got his driver's license, she drove back and forth at least twice a day. If she had to be at school for a PTA meeting, or if Ben had an activity at night, as he often did, she could log an extra twenty miles of driving that day. Add to that, her driving to the middle school and lower school campus, which was three miles away, and she did a lot of driving around.

Hmm. Upper, Middle, Lower. Their schools sound like Hogwarts or the three worlds of a science fiction best seller. Susan's imagination started to engage.

"Mom!" Ben was yelling at her.

"What?!" she yelled back before she had a chance to check herself.

"I was trying to say thank you for driving me, but you weren't even listening. You complain when we don't thank you and then don't even listen when we do."

"Ben, I'm sorry." *Wait. Why am I apologizing to him? He should be apologizing to me.* "Ben, I will pick you up in two hours. That's how long rehearsal is tonight, right?"

He mumbled, "Yeah, whatever" and was out of the car in a flash, slamming the car door and jogging off to greet some friends standing on the steps of the school. Suddenly, her sullen teenager had morphed into a happy, smiling, handsome young man. Susan hadn't really noticed how old he looked now. Gone was the gangly teen. He was developing muscles, and his face was taking on the look of a man instead of a boy. The girls standing on the steps surely noticed. She watched him run up the stairs, roughhousing with a buddy, the girls following, giggling and whispering to each other. It wouldn't be too long before he went off to college. He'd meet a nice girl, get married, and probably move somewhere across the country. *Where in the world have the years gone?* She sighed. With a smile and a wave to his back, she headed off to the next school, determined to make it a peaceful drive.

Mustering up some cheerfulness, she announced in a train conductor voice, "Next stop on the Mom Express is David's school," and pulled out of the circle and back onto the road. She opted to take the scenic route to David's school, about three miles closer to home. It was 5:20 when she pulled up in front. David informed her that he was five minutes late for a chorus rehearsal for an upcoming competition. He was never going to get a solo if he got there late. She just glanced in her rearview mirror and said as cheerfully as she could, "I'll pick you up in one and a half hours, okay, sweetie?" He was already running from the car, annoyed that he was late.

"Yeah, sure. Thanks, Mom!" he yelled over his shoulder.

I'll take it. At least he thanked me.

She pulled out and drove down the long, tree-lined drive to the entrance of the school grounds. She turned and said to her youngest, slouched in the backseat, "Well, it's just you and me, kid. How about we listen to some music? Your choice." Much to her surprise, her little guy told her it was okay. She could have some quiet. They could just talk. Susan felt like she had been given a gift.

"Well, okay then. What should we talk about?" she asked her rearview mirror.

"Baseball," Sam answered. "At practice tonight, I'm gonna get to play shortstop. Coach says he thinks I can do it. I know I can. David showed me how."

Susan was so happy just to be relaxing and talking with him, that she didn't even correct his enunciation. She just said, "Well, that was nice of David. I bet you'll be the best shortstop ever."

Sam thought for a while and asked timidly, "But what if I'm not? Is that okay too?"

Susan felt like she had been punched in the gut. *Do I make these guys feel as though they must be the best at everything they do? I hope not. I just want them to have lots of opportunities so they can decide what they like and what they want to do.* She quickly answered, "Well, Sam, if you're not the best shortstop, I bet you'll be the best one you can be. And, if you don't like playing shortstop, I bet you can try another position until you find the one you really like." She hoped she had said it right. She wanted him to know she was okay with whatever he chose. Since he was smiling back at her, she guessed that she had done okay.

Soon, they arrived at the elementary school where his baseball practice was held.

"Hey, kiddo, it's only five thirty-two. You're only two minutes late. That's okay. I'll bet they're not even warming up yet. Do you want me to come watch practice? I can cheer you on at shortstop."

Even at the age of seven, Ben was appalled at the idea that his mother would cheer him on at a practice. The other guys would really tease him about that. He quickly told her that he liked it when she came to his games, but it was okay not to go to practices.

"Well, okay then. I'll be back in one hour, okay? Have fun!" She tried to sound cheerful because it wasn't his fault that she was still annoyed. He was only seven years old. His older brothers should know better, but he was just a little guy. She knew that she always made excuses for him because, after all, he was her baby.

As she tried to smile at him, he looked up at her with those innocent brown eyes of his and said, "It's okay, Mom. If the coach gets mad, I'll just tell him you were busy yelling at us and we got a little late." With that, he jumped out of the car, grabbed his bag, and headed toward the field, seemingly undaunted by her tantrum and her attempt at making peace. Almost as an afterthought, he dropped his bag and ran back to the car. He jumped into the front seat, leaned over, and gave her a hug. "Thanks for the ride, Mom," he called over his shoulder as he got out of the car. He was gone before she had a chance to register what he had said.

Did he just thank me? And hug me? In front of his friends?

She was feeling a little ashamed of herself now for yelling at her kids. After all, if they didn't thank her, it was as much her fault as theirs. Wasn't she the one who was supposed to teach them those things? Suddenly she felt the weight of the world on her shoulders. She knew that if she didn't pull away from the field, she was going to embarrass herself and her son. The tears began welling in her eyes as she sat there. Through a blurry haze, she slowly pulled away from the curb, drove to the opposite end of the empty parking lot, faced the car toward the trees, and cried.

When did life become so mundane? When did I get so irritable all the time? Whatever happened to the carefree girl who would sit contentedly for hours on the dock looking out over the cove, watching the boats come and go? Whatever happened to the girl who always looked so happy,

11

always had a smile for everyone? I just want to kick a rock down the road or swing in a hammock. I just want to dangle my feet in the cold water and splash and look at the clouds. I just want to go for a sunset sail with my boyfriend and my friends. Mmm. We could have a picnic on the island or just sip cold beers on the boat. We could eat lobsters and corn on the cob, and I wouldn't be responsible for anyone.

Chapter Two

"Mom! Mom! Practice is over. Are you going to let me in or what?" Susan heard the pounding on the door and quickly hit the unlock button. Sam loaded his baseball bag into the back end of the SUV and then climbed into his seat. "I waited for you in front of the field and then I saw you way over here. What are you doing?"

Gathering her wits and realizing she had been daydreaming, Susan apologized to her little man. "I'm so sorry, sweetie. Mommy's just a little tired, I guess. I fell asleep in the car while I was waiting for you. And I had a really nice dream. So how'd practice go?" As she spoke, she glanced at the dashboard, realizing she was going to be late picking up her other two sons now too.

She pulled into the middle school parking lot almost twenty minutes late and was, as expected, chastised by twelve-year-old, David. "Mom," he whined, "I've been waiting out here for twenty-five minutes. All the other moms were waiting for their kids. Even the teachers are gone."

"I'm really sorry, honey," she answered. "I guess we're just having a bad day all around, aren't we?" Then she got a little mad at his expectation that she should be at his beck and call, never a minute late. She could wait forever for her children to come out, but heaven forbid she was five minutes late. Now annoyed, she grumbled, "I do the best I can. And don't I always tell you to wait inside until you see me?"

"How could I wait inside when everyone is gone?" he challenged and sank down into his seat, grousing under his breath.

Susan then raced across town to pick up the eldest who also was angrily waiting, pacing up and down the sidewalk. *Wow! He looks just like his father,* Susan thought.

"Mom! Where have you been?" chastised fifteen-year-old Ben. Rehearsal got over early, and everyone left except me. I tried to call you, but you didn't even pick up your phone. Geez, I'll be glad when I can drive and don't have to wait for you like a little kid."

Susan glared at him and said, "Well, I'll be glad when you can drive and I don't have to drive you all over the place, so we're even." She added in a mock appreciative tone, "Oh, and thank you Mom for coming to get me. I really appreciate it. Gosh I could have to take a bus or not take part in activities, but I can do all kinds of things because I have such a great mom who is willing to drive me. Gee, I'm lucky." He glared at her for a few seconds as she drove silently on, pretending not to notice. Surreptitiously, she glanced down at her phone. She had forgotten to plug it in and the battery was dead.

Susan drove for a couple of minutes in relative silence. She then tried to ask each of them questions about their practices and rehearsals and got one-word responses until she finally gave up.

When they got home, she instructed each of them to go inside and work on their homework while she made dinner. "And I mean it," she added for emphasis.

As she was slamming around the kitchen, preparing dinner, Ted, her husband of sixteen years, arrived home from work. With a perfunctory peck on her cheek and a "What's for dinner?" he mixed himself a gin and tonic and headed for their room to change out of his suit, not waiting for her response.

At eight o'clock sharp, Susan called out that dinner was ready. She put the food on the nicely set table, and the boys raced from all directions to eat. Her husband followed, refreshed from changing and sipping his drink, which he brought to the table. "Looks good," he said in exactly the same tone he used every night. Susan thought she could put dog food on his plate, and he would automatically say, "Looks good." There was no thought or real appreciation in the words.

When Susan finally sat down, she didn't even want to eat. She was exhausted from both chauffeuring the boys and the emotional drain of getting upset with her children. She hated it when she yelled at them. Now she looked from one to the other as they gobbled up the food she had prepared for them, their heads down, not meeting her gaze.

Unaware of the events of the past few hours and oblivious to the cues everyone was sending out, Ted smiled at his family and asked, "So how was everyone's day?"

Bewildered by their responses, or lack thereof, he looked at each boy in turn as Susan glared at him. She suggested through clenched teeth that the boys tell their father about their days. After a long, uncomfortable silence, Susan announced, "I'm not really hungry. I'm going to take a hot bath. Please clear the table when you're all finished. And," she added, "you know where the dishwasher is. Use it." With that, she left the four surprised males at the table and plodded upstairs to run a bath. In sixteen years of marriage, she had always assumed responsibility for clearing the table and doing the dishes, and her abrupt departure left her husband confused, annoyed, and in silence.

Behind the closed bathroom door, she put extra bubble bath in the tub, told Alexa to play easy listening music, lit a candle, and lay back to relax. As she sank down into the warm, bubbly water, the scent of lavender bubble bath calmed her. She listened to the music and, as Christopher Cross sang about being free while sailing, she was instantly taken away to floating on a boat in a moonlit bay of coastal Maine, the sails luffing lazily in the evening breeze....

Suddenly there was a banging on the bathroom door, and Susan had to get off the boat and leave her teenaged self behind.

"Mooooooom, when are you coming out?" Sam wanted her to tuck him in. She should have been happy that, at seven, he still wanted her to go through a bedtime ritual, but tonight she couldn't muster any happiness.

"How long have I been here?" she yelled from the tub, trying to be heard over the music.

"You've been in there a loooong time," he wailed. "We finished eating dinner already, and you're still in there." She glanced at the clock on the counter and realized that it had been fourteen minutes.

"Sam, you're just going to have to get Daddy to tuck you in tonight. Mommy's tired and I'm not finished with my bath yet," she yelled through the door.

15

"Aw, Mom, Daddy doesn't sing to me like you do. He sings dumb little kid songs. Come on, Mom, I'll wait for you." And, with that, she heard him sit down against the bathroom door. He started talking about school and baseball and singing to himself and making nonsense noises until she realized that she might as well get out. Quiet time was over.

She wrapped herself in her towel, turned off the music, and called to him as pleasantly as she could, "Go to bed, Sammy. Mommy will be right there."

She donned a pair of cotton pajamas, an old chenille robe, and a pair of fuzzy slippers and scuffed into his room. Once she saw him lying in his bed, face shining up at her, she relaxed a little. She smiled at him, kissed him on the forehead, and asked, "So what will it be tonight?"

"Sing our song, Mom. You haven't sang that in a long time."

"Sung," she corrected. "Mommy hasn't sung that song for a long time."

"Yeah, that's what I said."

She smiled, sat down in the rocking chair next to his window, and quietly sang the Carol King song into the dark room, listening to the lyrics as she sang about running to see her son again if he ever called out her name.

As she finished the song, her mind drifted back to her teen years in Maine and the boy who once sang the song to her as they were getting ready to head off to college. She remembered lying in his arms as they drifted on the *Windfall* at sunset. It was just the two of them since their friends Doug and Jeannie were busy that night. Actually, Bill had asked Doug to be busy somewhere else with Jeannie because he wanted some time alone with Susie. They had sailed out of the cove and into the bay, where they just drifted as the sun painted the water orange and red. Bill softly sang to her in his deep baritone, his way of letting her know that even though she was going away to Smith College, and he was going to the University of Southern Maine, they would only be three hours apart, and if she called, he'd be there.

Susie wondered, though. She wondered if it would ever be as good as it was at this moment. A late summer nip in the evening air tingled their skin and they snuggled in their sweatshirts and shorts, drawing a Hudson Bay blanket over them both.

Her reverie was interrupted by a sleepy boy saying, "Mommy, nobody sings that like you do. I love you, Mommy." Her sleepy little man was too tired to remember that he didn't call her Mommy anymore. She loved these moments.

"I love you too, sweetie," she answered and smiled down at his already sleeping form, cuddling his well-loved teddy bear, Marshmallow.

She padded downstairs to see her teenager sitting at the kitchen table doing homework and her middle son sitting on the couch, leaning against her husband as they watched a sitcom and laughed together.

"This is what it's all about, I guess," she sighed, not unhappily. She smiled, but as she sank into the overstuffed chair in the family room, she noticed that on the television, a group of teenagers was discussing what to do on Saturday night. Her mind drifted away again, as it was doing with increasing frequency....

"So what are you going to do tonight?" she asked her best friend, Jeannie. Jeannie replied that she and Doug, her boyfriend, were just going to hang out, and Susie told her that she and Bill were going to the drive-in to see *Romeo and Juliet*.

"Oh, I could spend a night staring at Leonardo DiCaprio," Jeannie said with a sigh.

"Yeah, I know what you mean, but I think Bill is just as handsome."

"You're a big fat liar," Jeannie laughed. "Bill is handsome, but *no one* is as gorgeous as Leo.

"Oh, so you think my Bill is handsome, huh?" Susan teased.

'You know what I mean," Jeannie quickly added. "At any rate, I'm answering for Doug and me. We'd love to go."

"Okay then. We'll pick you up at seven. We don't have too much summer left." She jumped up, dialed Bill, and told him that Jeannie and Doug were going with them. Jeannie had been Susan's best friend since they'd sat next to each other in kindergarten. They had a history that included everything from losing baby teeth to falling in love with their high school sweethearts.

Even their relationships were similar. Jeannie had decided that Doug was for her after having known him all her life, and the same had happened for Susie. She and Bill had gone to school together since kindergarten but had barely noticed each other. By the time they got to junior high, they started noticing, and Bill had asked Susie to go to the eighth grade Valentine's Day dance with him. Of course, at thirteen that meant that his mother drove him to the dance and hers drove her and when they got there they awkwardly danced together. But Susie would always think of it as their first date. Soon Bill was walking her home from school and, before too long, they were boyfriend and girlfriend—officially.

For the next four years, Bill and Susie were inseparable. What was nice for Susie was that Jeannie and she were best friends and Bill and Doug were best friends. That meant they could double-date all the time. Tonight was different, though. Pretty soon, she and Bill would be heading off to college, Doug was heading to the Army for four years, and Jeannie's plans were to work at the diner and wait for Doug to return so that they could get married.

Thinking about the different paths she and Jeannie were taking, Susie hoped they would still remain friends. She quickly changed into Bill's favorite white sundress with the thin shoulder straps that showed off her tan, slipped her feet into her white strappy sandals, brushed her hair, tied it back with a bright pink ribbon, and admired the result in the mirror. *I really did get a great tan this summer. I hope Bill notices that I wore his favorite dress.* He always told her that the dress turned him on, and she knew it was because of the princess neckline that showed her cleavage. Her father hated her to wear the dress, so she usually put a sweater on when she left the house. She didn't want to wear a sweater tonight, though, because she wanted Bill to get the full effect of the dress when he saw her. She scampered out of her bedroom and down the back stairs to the kitchen to avoid her father's judgmental eyes.

"Bye, Ma! Bye, Daddy!" she called to her parents who were sitting in the living room reading the evening paper. "Bill and I are going to the movies with Jeannie and Doug!"

Her father called out his usual, "Have fun. Be good," and then heard the back screen door slam shut.

Susie raced around the house, out onto the front lawn, up the front steps, and sat on the porch swing to wait for Bill. Soon, he pulled up in his old VW van, and she ran out to hop in practically before he even had time to stop. She leaned over, gave him a kiss, and smiled radiantly. "Let's go," she cooed. "I promised we'd pick them up at seven, and it's almost seven now.

"Okay, Suz," he said, but his loving smile had been replaced by lust. "Boy, you look great tonight! Do they have to come with us?" As he said the last, his eyes fell to the slight rise of tanned flesh visible above the low neckline of her dress. Taking one hand off the steering wheel, he traced the top edge of her dress with the tips of his fingers, sending shivers down her spine. With that, he flashed an innocent smile, wrapped his arm around her, and drove off down the tree-lined road, placing his errant hand firmly on her shoulder.

"You're teasing me, aren't you, Bill Deering? You want us to go alone tonight, right? Summer's almost over and you want to have some fun at the drive-in, don't you?" She glanced over her shoulder and saw the blankets lying on the carpeted floor of the van. "Pretty sure of yourself, aren't you, mister?" She giggled and snuggled a little deeper into his side. "Well, it's okay with me," she whispered in his ear, "but you have to be the one to tell Jeannie and Doug. I already told Jeannie they could go with us."

"Fine with me. Doug won't care. He probably wants to spend the night alone with Jeannie anyway. He'll be heading off to basic training soon." Bill's fingers began their slow descent down Amy's shoulder and under the thin white fabric.

When they pulled up in front of Jeannie's house, they could see Doug and Jeannie arguing on her front porch. As Bill beeped the horn, they stopped, looked over, and Jeannie pointed at the van. Doug sauntered over to Bill's side, whispered something to him, and Bill threw back his head and laughed.

"Well, it seems that we were all on the same page tonight, Suz. Jeannie and Doug wanted to be alone tonight too, but Jeannie didn't want to hurt your feelings, so she said they'd come with us." By this time, Jeannie had leaned into the passenger side window and was whispering with Suzie. Bill saw a look of surprise on Susie's face as Jeannie blushed, but they both were smiling.

"Well, let's get going or we'll miss the cartoon," Susie cheerfully said to Bill as she waved to Jeannie and Doug and winked at Jeannie. "Be careful!" she called out to her friend as they pulled away.

"You too," Jeannie replied, giggling and grabbing hold of Doug.

"Be careful?" Bill asked.

"Oh, never mind. It's just girl stuff." They drove along in comfortable silence, the radio playing softly and the sun setting over the water. Within a few minutes, they pulled into the drive-in, and Bill chose a spot in the back row by the trees. After hooking up the speaker to his window, he pushed the front seats down flat, and he and Susie climbed into the back of the van to get comfortable for the movie.

"This is the life, huh, Suz? I sure am glad I bought this piece of junk." Susie snuggled into his arms, and he pulled one of the blankets over them to ward off the cool end-of-summer air. She gazed up into Bill's strong, angular face and he leaned down to tenderly kiss her. That was one of her favorite things about Bill. She could kiss him all night. He never rushed her. He would just kiss if that's what she wanted. But tonight she wanted more. They were alone. They were in the back row of the drive-in. Jeannie had told her that she planned to go all the way with Doug tonight. After all, they were engaged and getting married when Doug had put in his four years in the Army, anyway. Susie thought that maybe tonight would be her night too. She wanted Bill to remember her when she left for college. What better way for him to remember her than this?

Darkness enveloped the van. With the sounds of Bugs Bunny coming from the speaker on the front window, she reached for his hand on her face and slowly moved it down until she placed it on the bare skin above the edge of her dress.

"Isn't this where you left off?" she whispered as she wiggled closer to Bill and started unbuttoning his shirt.

A few weeks later, while Susie was packing her things to leave for Smith, Jeannie arrived at her house. She knocked on the screen door and Susie's mom quickly answered it.

"Mrs. Ward, is Susie here?" Jeannie asked, a touch of desperation in her voice but a smile on her face.

"Well, hi, Jeannie. She's upstairs in her room. Go on up. Is everything okay?"

"Oh yeah. I just need to talk with her."

Jeannie ran up the stairs. Not even bothering to knock, she burst into Susie's room, taking Susie by surprise.

"Hey! What's up?" Susie had been taking a break from packing for college, just reading in the window seat, and was happy to see her best friend. One look, though, told her that this was not going to be a pleasant visit.

"Oh, Susie," Jeannie wailed, and broke into tears. Sobbing, she told Susie that after letting Doug go all the way she was pregnant."

"Are you sure?" the ever-practical Susie asked.

"Oh, I'm sure. I got one of those tests. That was fun, by the way. Now everyone in town probably knows I'm a slut."

"Whoa!" Susie tried not to laugh. "I will not have you calling my best friend names, especially names that don't apply." Eliciting a tiny smile from her friend, Susie continued, "Slow down and tell me everything."

Jeannie blew her nose and sat cross-legged on Susie's bed. Susie climbed up and sat across from her. If her mother had walked in at that moment, she would have been reminded of the two of them as little girls chatting endlessly about their heartthrobs and friends.

"Well, remember the night that you and Bill wanted us to go to the drive-in with you, but we didn't want to go? Remember I told you that I was going to let Doug go all the way that night?" Susie nodded. "Well, we drove up to Clark's Pond, and Doug laid a blanket on the grass by the pond. It was wicked romantic. At first we just laid on the blanket and looked at the stars, but then we started kissing, and one thing led to another, and it was over before I knew it. In fact, I remember being surprised that was all there was to it. It hurt and wasn't fun like they make it look in the movies." Susie gave her a look that asked her to get on with her story. Jeannie had already told her this part. "Well, we just laid there on the blanket looking at the stars, and pretty soon, Doug started up again. That time he was really gentle and nice and it felt sooooo good. It didn't hurt the second time, so I kind of liked it. It wasn't until after that I realized we hadn't used a condom." Susie looked shocked. The first time Jeannie told her, she hadn't mentioned the part about not using protection. "Well, apparently, I'm one of the lucky ones who can get pregnant easy, because I figure I'm about three weeks pregnant."

As Jeannie leaned back on the bed, Susie sat looking at her friend. They had followed the same path since they were five years old, and had been more like sisters than just friends. Now Jeannie was telling her that she was going to have a baby while Susie was about to begin her first year of college. Susie could feel their paths diverging and didn't want to lose her best friend.

"Jeannine Elizabeth Porter, you listen to me." Jeannie looked up at her. "You didn't do anything that the rest of us haven't done. You know that Bill and I did it that night too. It was weird but nice. Does Doug know?"

Jeannie just nodded her head.

"What did he say?" asked Susie.

"He wants to get married before he reports for duty and for us to keep the baby. Susie," Jeannie wailed, "I'm too young to have a baby, and I don't want to have a quickie wedding and then not be with Doug. I do want to marry him, and I do want to have his babies—just not right now." Jeannie blew her nose and Susie thought about what she should say.

"Jeannie," Susie began quietly and calmly, in contrast to Jeannie's hysteria, "have you seen a doctor? Are you positive that you're pregnant?"

Jeannie stopped crying. "I told you I got a test!" She began breathing quickly.

"Jeannine Elizabeth Porter, right now all you have to think about is yourself." Susie thought for a minute before asking, "Jeannie, when you got the test from the drug store, what did you do and what did it say?"

"Oh, my gawd! I didn't get it from the drug store. My mother knows them. I went to Dollar General. I picked it up right at the checkout and ran out with it. The date on the box was last month but the girl said they're good way after that."

Susie began to wonder if her friend really was pregnant after all. "Jeannie, you need to see a doctor before you assume you're pregnant. We could drive to a walk-in clinic in Bath where no one knows you. All you need is a test. What if I drive you tomorrow? Oh, stop shaking your head no at me. You need to know for sure before you get all upset about it."

"It's too late. I'm already upset."

After a few minutes, Jeannie pulled herself together and left to go talk with Doug. A couple of hours later she called Susie to tell her that, after a lot of crying and yelling and apologizing and crying some more, she and Doug had decided that she would go to the walk-in clinic and get a test. She insisted that if she were going to do it, it had to be immediately, so they made plans to drive down the next day. Doug had to withdraw money from his savings account, since he insisted on paying for it. They didn't want it going on her parents' insurance. If she had to endure it, he figured the least he could do was pay for it. He would take her himself, and it would be okay.

The next day Doug and Jeannie drove to Bath to the walk-in clinic where Jeannie had a pregnancy test. Doug waited in the waiting room and when Jeannie came out he didn't have to ask her the results. She was beaming and shaking her head.

"The doctor said that the test I got at the General was expired and gave me a false positive. She said I was just emotional about you going away to Basic Training and my best friend going away to college, and the stress made me think I was pregnant."

Chapter Three

"Mom! Did you fall asleep? Come on, I really need help. Dad helped me with my math, but I need you to quiz me for the history test."

"What?" she asked groggily. "I'm not asleep—just thinking about stuff from long ago." Standing before her was her five-foot-ten, fifteen-year-old son, Ben, asking for help. Where had her friend Jeannie gone? She got up, heard the antique grandfather clock striking ten, and trudged to the kitchen table to ask history questions.

"Ted, he really needs to go to bed now," she called back to the family room where she heard her middle son pleading to be allowed to watch one more show. She heard a negotiation beginning and yelled, "I said now! You should have been in bed an hour ago." Her husband answered that he was going up to bed too, so he'd tuck David in. David stumbled sleepily into the kitchen, reluctantly walked over to her, and leaned down to give her a perfunctory hug and kiss goodnight.

"Oh, come on," she teased. "It's not like you were going to get away with staying up late on a school night. Give me a real hug." With that, her twelve-year-old hugged her tightly and even smiled. "I love you, you little stinker," she said, and off went her son and her husband up the stairs.

"Well, it's just you and me, kid," she said to her teenager as she tousled his perfectly brushed hair. He grimaced, smoothed his hair, and she began asking the questions, which he effortlessly answered. After a couple of minutes, she declared that he knew it cold and sent him off to bed too.

"Why don't you go to bed and read for a little while," she suggested. That elicited a huge, braces-filled grin.

"Thanks, Mom. I've been dying to get back into the Tom Clancy book Dad gave me." He gave her a genuine hug, a kiss on the cheek, and ran up the stairs two at a time. She sat listening to the house, smiling, as the grandfather clock struck quarter past the hour.

Slowly getting up from the table, she decided a cup of tea would be nice. It was times like this that she really appreciated the Insta-Hot her husband had installed when they moved into this house. He knew how much she liked to have hot tea at all hours of the day and night and had, ostensibly, added it as a little surprise for her. As it turned out, he used it more than she did. Now, though, she thought, *it will never cease to amaze me that I can make a cup of hot tea without even waiting for the water to boil.*

With that thought, she curled up on the couch to watch whatever happened to be on television. She didn't care what it was. The beauty of the moment was that she was alone. She hadn't been alone since five thirty in the morning unless you counted her daydreaming time. It had been a particularly long day, and she hadn't handled its tribulations very well. She had drifted back into her past frequently during the day, and she hadn't been very nice to the boys.

She leaned her head against the back of the sofa as the ten o'clock news droned on, and her mind wandered sleepily. Her glance fell on the pictures in the room that told her life story. She and Ted had never bought expensive art for their home, although some very nice pieces had stayed in his parents' home when Ted inherited it a few years before. Now she thought about the pictures she and Ted had bought— the things that had meaning for them. Her wandering eyes landed on a watercolor painting that Ted had paid a friend of his to paint for her early in their marriage. It was a scene of a cove in Maine, the lobster boats tied up, and the traps stacked on the docks. It wasn't the view the tourists would see, but the backside of Main Street, the working docks where lobstermen brought in their catch each day, brightly colored lobster buoys hanging on the shingled back walls of the shops.

The painting always reminded her of her carefree youth, of a time before everything got so complicated. She smiled at the sweetness in him that had prompted him to ask a friend to paint this from a photograph Susan had taken—especially since it was a picture of a time in her life when he didn't even know her. *If only he could still let me see that sweet, thoughtful side of him. If only he could show a little vulnerability and kindness in his daily comments and expressions. I wonder if he still feels that way. I wonder if he still loves me, or if we have just fallen into the roles of parents, never again to be anything else. We certainly don't do anything together, talk about anything other than the kids, or have romantic times anymore. Sometimes I feel utterly invisible.*

Susan still remembered the day he had given her that painting as though it were yesterday. As she had unwrapped the picture, he glowed, camera ready to take her picture as she saw it for the first time. They didn't have much money then. Ben was just a baby, and they were trying to make ends meet on just Ted's salary, having jointly decided that she would quit her job when Ben was born. They had both agreed that a child needs his mother, and she had jumped into motherhood the way she jumped into everything else—with both feet. Even though she had been promoted to assistant editor and was on her way to her dream job of being an editor at a big publishing house, she had decided it could wait. She would stay at home with her baby, keep up her contacts in the industry, and when Ben went to school, she could return to the business. In the meantime, with all her free time at home, she would write.

The decision to leave her job meant adjusting to a life surrounded by babies and young mothers. No more office parties, heated discussions about books or world issues, or business lunches. No more commuting to New York each day, feeling proud to be among the crowd of people who were living what she viewed as significant lives. But she had adjusted and loved being a mom. She loved talking to her son, reading to him, or singing to him. She loved the way he looked at her with those big brown eyes and seemed to always want to know more.

On her first birthday after Ben was born, Ted had planned a special adults-only dinner. Susan had put Ben to sleep and had come into the kitchen of their Connecticut colonial to find the table set with a tablecloth, their wedding china, and candles. Her husband stood by the stove taking something out of the oven that smelled wonderful. He had bought dinner at a local restaurant on his way home from the train station and reheated it in the oven. This meant as much to her as if he had worked all day preparing it. She was touched that he wanted to make her birthday special, and he had never made a meal for her before (or since, if she was honest with herself).

After dinner, they had held hands leaving the table and strolled into the living room where he excitedly told her to sit on the couch. He then raced from the room and came back holding a package. It was gift wrapped and was obviously some sort of picture. It was large, maybe thirty inches across and twenty-four inches high. She couldn't imagine what it could be. Ted had handed it to her and whipped out a camera from the drawer of the side table to commemorate her seeing whatever it was for the first time. As she unwrapped the large present, she felt a guilty pleasure in receiving something that was just for her. It had been a long time since she'd bought anything for herself. She assumed it would be a picture of Ben. When she saw the painting, she cried, as flashbulbs burst in her eyes. It was of a past she would never live again, a part of her life that haunted her. How she missed her quaint little hometown. How she missed her parents. How she missed the carefree feeling of sailing and swimming in the ocean. She had made her choices, though, and she was happy with them. She had a wonderful husband and a beautiful baby. She had a lovely home. She had it all. Everyone told her so.

Ted, of course, was pleased with himself for being able to give her a gift that meant a lot to her. In reality, he had no idea of the miasma of emotions and swirling thoughts the painting evoked. He thought she simply loved the painting. She was thrilled with the painting, not only because it was beautiful and thoughtful, but also because it meant that wherever they lived, she could take a part of her cherished past with her. She hugged Ted tightly, telling him that it was wonderful, and she would always hang it in a place where she could see it every day.

Now, all these years later, as she sat on the Omnia leather couch in the family room of her multimillion-dollar home in Greenwich, Connecticut, she gazed at the simple painting and let her memory step into it, taken back again to the simple dock and the shimmering cove....

Chapter Four

It was a sunny day, and the breeze blew the scents of lobster, seaweed, low-tide mud, and salt water her way. Tourists filled the streets and shops, but here, behind the shops, she could sit in solitude on the dock and gaze out over the little cove and around the bend out to the bay. With only a few days left of summer vacation, she was sitting with Stephen King's *Carrie*. Her boyfriend, Bill, who was heading off to the University of Maine in Portland in a few days, had given it to her, telling her, "It's a great book, and he's a Maine author. You have to read it." She didn't usually read horror books, but today she was really enjoying it.

She sat on the raft below the dock, listening to the sounds from above of an active little town, most of the boats out for the day. Occasionally a dog or cat would scamper out onto the dock, but other than that, she was by herself, sitting low in her beach chair, her tanned legs stretched out, just watching the birds in the sky. She would be heading off to college in just a week. She wondered for a moment why she had chosen a school that was away from the water. Being in Northampton, Massachusetts, she would never be able to get to the ocean. Well, it was a small sacrifice to pay for a good education. She had dreamed of attending Smith College for a few years now, ever since the new English teacher had told her about it. Her plan was to graduate from Smith and get a job at a small Maine publishing house. She and Bill would be married and live happily ever after. She would become a famous author and publisher, and he would defend the downtrodden of coastal Maine after he graduated from the University of Maine School of Law.

Sometimes Susan wandered down on the rocks to read, especially at low tide, and sometimes she would walk to the beach. But the beach was too crowded on this end-of-summer day, and she found her solitude here on the dock, away from the activity. The sounds and smells of the water gave her comfort, and she could scramble up the ramp to the general store to grab snacks and drinks whenever she wanted them.

After a while, her reading was interrupted by footsteps on the planks above and as she glanced up, she saw Bill and his mother rushing toward her, his shoulders slumped forward, a strained expression on her face. Oblivious to the body language, Susan's face lit up when she saw him, and she ran up the ramp to meet him, throwing her arms around his neck as they reached each other.

"I was hoping you'd be heah," he drawled in that wonderful Maine accent of his as he hugged her long and hard. Sometimes she was sorry that she had consciously obliterated her Maine accent.

"What are you doing here? I thought you had to work at your folks' lobster pound today," she exclaimed. "Did you get the afternoon off?" she asked, excited at the prospect of spending the afternoon with him. Then she noticed the cloudy look in his eyes, and a shiver ran through her despite the sunny day.

"No. I just left. I've got some bad news—some really bad news." As she looked into his eyes, she could see that he wasn't kidding.

"You're scaring me," she whispered. "What's wrong?"

"My mother came into work a little while ago and told me there'd been an accident on Dad's boat. It was bad." As the words came out of his mouth, a group of men came rushing down the dock toward them. One of them was carrying a stretcher, and the sounds of sirens could be heard in the distance. Bill's mother just stood stoically at the edge of the float, looking out to sea.

"No!" she screamed silently. And then audibly added, "It isn't your father. He's okay, right?" But her heart knew the answer.

As Susie held Bill, she heard the boat lumbering into the harbor, an eerie sound for the middle of the day. Lobster boats didn't generally come in at this time, and when one did, it wasn't good. People were gathering on the dock as word spread, but she still didn't know what had happened. Bill broke free to run to the edge of the dock float.

When the boat pulled up, there was his father, lying on the deck of the boat, the gulls circling overhead.

"Dad!" Bill screamed, but he was restrained. The volunteer firefighters effortlessly jumped onto the boat and gently lifted the injured man, placing him on the stretcher. She saw Mr. Deering turn his head and look up at Bill, and as they carried him up the ramp to the dock and to the waiting ambulance beyond, he quietly spoke to Bill between gasps of breath and winces of pain. Susie couldn't tell what was said but if she had, she would have had the key to her life's future mystery.

"Bill, if I don't make it, you've got to promise me one thing. Promise me, Bill." Agitated, Mr. Deering struggled to sit up on the stretcher.

"Dad, lie down. You need to let them get you to Maine Med where the doctors can make you all better. There's a helicopter waiting to take you. Whatever you want, Dad, I promise. But don't talk now."

"No, Bill, you have to promise me that you'll take care of your mutha and your sistahs if I don't make it. The boat will be yours, and the men will stay on. Promise me, Bill."

Seeing how agitated his father was, Bill quietly but sincerely answered, "I promise, Dad. But nothing's going to happen to you. You're strong. You'll be up and about in no time. You'll see. Maybe I can defer going to college for a semester until you're well enough to go back out on the boat."

The next thing Susie remembered was the sadness of Bill's father's funeral, held on the day Bill was supposed to be starting college. It was not only the end of a great man's life, someone the entire town loved and respected, but it was the end of Bill's life as he'd hoped it would be. There would be no going away to college now. He had to take his father's boat out each day before daybreak and return, tired and beaten. He was determined to fulfill the promise he had made to his father the last time he saw him alive.

By the time the helicopter had arrived in Portland, the EMTs had already pronounced his father dead. His injuries had been severe, and his heart just couldn't go on. Bill knew at that moment that his life would never be the same. He loved his invincible dad. It was hard to imagine him succumbing at just forty-two. Bill knew that he would now take care of his mother and sisters, and his plans for college classes and parties, for law school and becoming a small-town lawyer and helping everyone out of their troubles were nothing more than a dream. He also knew he would have to give up his dream of marrying the prettiest girl in town.

It was at his father's funeral—after it, actually—that Bill took Susie aside and told her that he didn't love her anymore. He was uncharacteristically brusque. Standing apart from her, his face averted to hide his glistening eyes, he told her that, with his father's dying, he had outgrown her. He said that she was just a silly schoolgirl, and he was now a man responsible for taking care of a family, that he didn't have any time in his life for her anymore.

Shocked and hurt, she cried and pleaded with him not to make this decision now. She said he was in pain at his sudden change of life's plan. In time, he would realize that they could make it work. They had loved each other for years, had weathered minor storms before and would, in time, weather this major one. But nothing she could say would change his mind. He steadfastly maintained that he didn't want her around him any longer. Finally, he exploded, yelling, "Susie, I just don't love you anymore! I didn't want to hurt you, but there it is."

Of course, what he didn't tell her was how he loved her with all his heart. He didn't tell her how he had lain awake nights planning how he could save her from a life with him. Now that his life had changed so dramatically overnight, he couldn't ask her to give up all her plans for him. She was too special. She was the smartest girl he knew, and the prettiest. She was going to go to college and make something of herself. She was the first person from this little town to be accepted by a Seven Sisters school. He couldn't ask her to stay and simply be a lobsterman's wife. What could he offer her now? No, he wouldn't do that to her. He loved her too much to hold her back. This was how it had to be. She had to think that he had changed, that he'd become cold and heartless. If she thought that, then she would leave and move on. He would rather have her hate him than subject her to a life that was less than she deserved.

Chapter Five

The next year was a tough one for Susie. A few days after Bill's father's funeral, she left for college. Her parents packed her trunks into the back of their Subaru wagon and drove the five hours to Northampton. They deposited her in her dorm, gave her last words of wisdom and advice, told her how proud they were of her, and off they went. She was alone—totally, completely, and utterly alone. Sure, there were people all around. There were classes to attend, books to buy, meals to eat, activities to sign up for, games to attend, a campus to explore, and parties to enjoy. But when all was said and done, she was alone. She didn't know anyone for hundreds of miles.

Shortly after her parents left, Susie's roommate arrived. Katherine Alexander was a force of light as she breezed into the room she would share with Susie Ward, the small-town girl. Dressed in her Upper East Side designer clothes, which she wore as casually as Susie wore her new L.L. Bean ones, she beamed and addressed her new roommate. "Hi! You must be Susie. I'm Katie. How long have you been here? What do you know about this house? Have you met anyone yet? I love your bedspread. Why'd you leave the best side of the room for me? I love this window over my bed. Oh! You have one too!"

Katie talked and talked, asked questions, and rarely waited for answers. Susie was somewhat overwhelmed by her energy and exuberance.

"Do you mind if I play some music while we unpack?"

Susie said she didn't mind. Katie plugged in a radio, and music filled the room. Slowly, Susie's somber mood became brighter. She realized she was going to have a hard time staying sad around this girl. She even smiled as she put away her clothes and set up her desk, Katie prattling away about life in New York City and asking Susie about life in a small Maine town.

Susie settled into college life and studied hard. She didn't have much heart for parties or dating, even though Katie tried to get her out of the room frequently. Susie unfairly soon gained a reputation for being standoffish, snobby, studious—not much fun. She thought about Bill all the time, but he had asked her not to call or write to him. He said that it would be easier for her to forget him if she made a clean break. Well, that's what it felt like to her. It felt like she had been broken in half. Half of her was in college and the other half was yearning to be with Bill.

Sometimes Susie felt as if she could run to him, he would tell her that it had been a big mistake, take her in his arms, and love her forever. Other times, like when she visited her folks during Thanksgiving or Christmas, she would see him, and he would glance at her and look away, a practiced ambivalence in his eyes. He appeared broken to her, but he wouldn't let her fix him. That whole freshman year, she just existed.

If it hadn't been for Katie from New York City, she would have been miserable. By second semester, Katie thought Susie was wasting a great opportunity at Smith to meet independent women who would be friends for life. Whenever Susie would say that she had work to do on a Saturday night, Katie would drag her out to a party, lecture, or concert. Even though Susie didn't act much like her former carefree self, Katie could see the real Susie underneath her sorrow. She would tell Susie that no man is worth moping over. She would make suggestions of things to do and tell Susie, "Nothing ventured, nothing gained. Give it a shot. You never know. You might just have fun in spite of yourself." Then she would laugh, give Susie a big hug, pout, and say, "Come on Susie!" Susie couldn't resist joining her.

Soon the year was over. She had survived her freshman year. When it was time to head back to Oceanside for the summer, Susie was nervous. She still desperately wanted to see Bill, but part of her was angry with him and never wanted to see him again. In fact, the anger was increasingly replacing the sadness. Summer passed slowly. She stayed away from the cove, not sitting on the dock or the rocks for fear that she would see Bill. She didn't know what she might say or do if she saw him. It was easier just to steer clear of him entirely. She spent a lot of time reading in the backyard under the big oak and elm trees. Her parents suggested that she get a job, so she began working in their jewelry shop in town. She knew he would never go in there.

Susie avoided her old high school friends all summer. Jeannie, her best friend, was the only one she saw. Jeannie was sad and lonely, too, missing Doug, who was stationed in Texas, and when Susie and Jeannie got together, it was downright pitiful. They moped and commiserated. Jeannie complained that she should have married Doug before he left and gone with him. Susie whined that Bill was being a jerk and didn't know what he was missing by sending her away.

Jeannie tried not to say anything about Bill, but she was, after all, his friend too, and the two of them were the ones who had stayed in Oceanside. She knew that he had decided to be a martyr and that he was suffering, missing Susie every day. She knew that he was planning to go to U Maine in the fall, commuting to Portland a couple of days a week. Bill had asked her not to talk about him with Susie and, although it was hard not to explain his actions to her best friend, she knew that stubborn Bill would never change his mind, and if she told Susie it would just hurt her. She decided, then, that unless Susie asked her about him, she would keep quiet—and Susie never asked.

Summer ended, and Susie headed back to Northampton. She and her friend Katie shared a double in a nice house on campus, but she interacted with as few people as possible. She just went to classes and returned to her solitude. After a month of this pattern, her roommate decided that Susie needed a kick in the pants. A bunch of girls were driving to Boston for the Harvard–Columbia game. Susie let herself be convinced to join them and that a road trip would be fun. They all piled into the car and headed to Boston. Oh, how Susie wished they could just keep driving up the coast to her little seaside village, back to the life and the people she knew, back to the man she loved. But she smiled and laughed and outwardly had a good time on the ride. She was beginning to adopt the attitude of "fake it till you make it," and it was actually working.

The Smith contingent arrived at the game and found seats in the stands. While Katie and her friends began to prowl for "Hahvahd men" Susie sat alone trying to keep a stiff upper lip. After a while, a young man sat down beside her. He was there with his friends. As the game progressed, they began to talk, and she noticed kindness in his face. When the game was over, he asked if he could call her.

"Sure," she said, and gave him her number, not thinking that she would ever really hear from him again.

As the days passed, she thought about the conversation often, wishing that Ted would call her. It had been a long time since she had wished a boy would call. It felt good. He was tall and handsome, funny and clever. He had made her laugh and forget her troubles for a while. After a couple of weeks had passed, she figured that she'd never hear from him again. She tried to forget him but found herself reliving their conversation at the game as she sat staring out the window in her room. By the second Friday after their meeting, she was planning to spend the weekend studying when she received a call on the house phone.

"Susie, you've got a call! It's someone named Ted. Isn't that the guy from Harvard?" Susie ran down the hall to grab the phone. She shushed her roommate, who had followed close behind, told her to get lost, and answered the phone.

"Um. Hi. Is this Susan Ward?" he asked tentatively.

"Yes. Hi, Ted."

"Well, I wanted to apologize for not calling sooner. School has been pretty hectic. I was wondering if you were going to be in Boston anytime soon."

Susie's heart sank a little. She had let herself get excited, but now he was suggesting that she go to him. "No, Ted. I have no way to get to Boston." It was only a white lie. She could take a bus from Northampton to Boston. She just decided in the moment that she didn't want to. He was a nice guy, but she wanted him to come to her.

"Oh, okay. Well, then, maybe I can borrow a car and come see you there. Would that be okay?"

"Sure. That would be nice." Susie smiled. She had always been good at chess.

"Well, let me see what I can do," Ted said. "Maybe I'll see you soon."

"Oh, okay," she stammered.

The next thing she heard was a click, and Ted was gone.

As the days and weeks passed, Susie realized that she was not going to hear from Ted again. *Well, good riddance,* she thought. *I don't ever want to be with anyone who doesn't want to be with me.* She put him out of her mind, fully comprehending the irony in her thought since she wanted desperately to be with Bill, and he didn't want to be with her. She got on with her life.

Chapter Six

Sophomore and junior years flew by, a blur of classes, studying, friends, the occasional date, summers spent in Maine working in her father's jewelry store, and missing Bill less and less. By the end of her junior year, Susie realized she needed to figure out what she was going to do with her life.

Katie and Susie got a great number in the room lottery, and Susie knew immediately where she wanted to live for her last year at Smith—Lawrence House. Sylvia Plath had lived there when she was a student at Smith, and Susie hoped that some of her writing talent might be in the house. Katie liked the house because it was near the gym and Paradise Pond. They just had to decide whether they would try for singles or share a room. Katie was fine either way, but Susie had always had her own room, and sharing a room for her first three years had been a new experience. But, on the other hand, sharing with Katie was always an adventure. Left to her own devices, Susie would spend most of her time in her room studying or reading. Katie pulled her out of her solitude. They decided that they had enjoyed sharing a room for the past three years. Why stop now?

For three years, whenever Susie mentioned to Katie that someone had asked her to do something she had never done before, Katie told her, "Nothing ventured, nothing gained." She said it all the time, and Susie understood why Katie had done so many things in her life and had so many interesting experiences. It was because of her philosophy of trying everything she could.

One summer, Katie volunteered as a Big Sister in Manhattan and enjoyed the experience so much that she became a Big Sister at school too. She now had two young protégés she counseled and entertained as often as possible. She even invited her New York Little Sister to Smith for a weekend, and Susie had enjoyed seeing how maternal Katie was toward the girl. Party girl Katie spent the entire weekend taking her Little Sister on a tour of the campus, the town, and the area. She even took her to admissions so that she could meet an admissions officer to talk about expectations if she wanted to attend a school like Smith.

When Katie wasn't doing community service, she traveled with family and friends. She spent summer and spring breaks in exotic places like England, Cancun, India, Alaska, and the Hamptons. Susie had never been outside of New England. She reveled in hearing about Katie's stories of her travels and decided that traveling was something she wanted to do someday.

As the two friends discussed their post-graduation plans, Katie shared that she planned to spend the summer after graduation backpacking alone around Europe. She said she had lots of friends in various parts of the continent and would probably get together with them for different periods of time. With no plans and no place to stay, she felt comfortable just taking off. Her parents appealed to her, suggesting family friends with whom she could stay. Part of the appeal, however, was that her parents were appalled that their daughter was going to backpack around Europe. Susie envied her friend's ability to be carefree and courageous, whereas Susie liked to have everything planned. She would want hotels booked and transportation scheduled in advance. She would know which sights she was going to see and with whom. And she could never travel alone. That would be terrifying.

Katie, on the other hand, relied on her two mantras: "If not now, then when?" and "Nothing ventured, nothing gained." They formed her philosophy of life. She planned to travel around Europe for the summer, laying the groundwork for the next year when she would write a travel blog for twenty-somethings. Katie had been a social media maven for years, and this seemed like a natural thing for her to do. Susie envied her free spirit and realized why the two of them had become such good friends. Katie forced Susie out of her comfort zone, and Susie grounded Katie.

When Katie would return from her year of traveling, she had a two-bedroom rent-subsidized apartment lined up on the Upper East

Side of Manhattan. Her aunt, a fellow free spirit, had decided to embark upon her own *Eat, Pray, Love* adventure and was going to let Katie stay in her apartment for two years. Katie just had to pay the rent. She tried to persuade Susie to join her in New York, and the more Susie thought about it, the more she liked the idea. She saw how open-minded and worldly her friend was and thought that she should be a little more like Katie. Did she really want to spend her entire life in a little coastal town? Attending Smith had been the first step in what she now knew was her path away from Maine. She wanted to have different experiences and meet different people. She wanted to swim in a bigger pond. Susie, always a planner, spent the winter thinking about the possibility of moving to New York City with Katie. She made lists of the pros and cons, researched places she could apply for a job, interviewed with on-campus recruiters. Of course, the apartment wasn't available for another year. Susie would have to figure out what she was going to do with the year following graduation.

One day, Susie bounded into their room, hoping that Katie would be there. One look and Katie could tell that something had changed. Susie looked genuinely happy. Susie told her that she was thinking of getting her MFA degree in Creative Writing from Boston University and then joining Katie in New York City if the offer still stood. Katie yelped, "Woo-hoo!" jumped off her bed, where she had been sitting cross-legged listening to music, and began jabbering about all of the fun they would have.

Boston University accepted Susie into their one-year MFA program. Since it was one of the oldest and most prestigious creative writing programs in the country, she was proud of herself. Only ten students were accepted each year, and she was one of them. She knew it would be rigorous, offering the degree in a single year instead of the two years most programs took. This acceleration included a summer of study. When she told her parents about it, she made sure to tell them that *The Atlantic* magazine had ranked the program among the top 5 percent of all creative writing programs for the distinction of its faculty and alumni and had ranked it among the top ten programs overall.

Since every student receives full tuition as well as a stipend, Susie didn't have to worry about how she was going to pay for it. Though she was terrified at the prospect of teaching, she would have to teach an Introduction to Creative Writing course to BU undergraduates as part of her course load.

When word spread that Susie would be attending Boston University for the next year, a classmate approached her and asked if she would like to share an apartment. It wasn't far from the BU campus and if they split the rent, the cost wouldn't be too bad. Susie checked her stipend and realized it would pay for her share of the apartment with some left over. She enthusiastically, if uncharacteristically, agreed, thinking, *Nothing ventured, nothing gained.*

Chapter Seven

Susie went home for one last summer before embarking on her career path. One day in late June, as she sat on her front porch swing reading, she saw her old friend Jeannie walking up the road toward her house with a very handsome, tall man with close-cropped hair. Her first thought was that Jeannie was cheating on Doug, and she was about to reprimand her friend when she heard, "Why Susie Ward. Long time no see!"

Susie hadn't seen Doug for four years, and when he walked up the driveway, she couldn't believe the man she saw before her. He had always been kind of goofy, tall and lanky, but the Army had built muscles, and he had grown into his height. Susie jumped up and ran to meet them. As he hugged Susie hello, she could feel his strong, hard muscles.

"Hey, you two!" called Jeannie. "You're *my* man, remember? And you're my best friend in the whole world and always will be no matter what." She looked at Susie.

Susie was embarrassed to find herself thinking about Doug's body, especially right in front of Jeannie. She teased, "Well, I haven't seen this lug for four years. I figure if we would have hugged each other every time we saw each other, I have a *long* hug coming. She grabbed hold of him again, much to Doug's embarrassment.

"Well, enough is enough," said Jeannie, stepping between them. "We have wedding plans to talk about. Doug, go away and play. We women need to talk." Doug saluted her, turned smartly on his heel, and marched down the driveway, leaving the women on the front porch.

"We just started making plans, but they're coming together pretty easy. So here goes. It's now the last week of June. We're gonna get married the last Saturday in August. You'll be my maid of honor, of course, and Bill will be Doug's best man. I hope that's not gonna be too weird, but you're my best friend and Bill is Doug's. We can't get married without both of you. We're gonna have a wicked small wedding. Our families all live right around here anyway, so it'll be easy. We'll get married at the Congregational Church in town and have the reception at the Odd Fellows Hall. My dad is a member and can get it for us. My mom will make the wedding cake, and we'll ask the family to make some food. I want to wear my mother's dress, and she's gonna fix it up for me." Jeannie paused, a grin spreading across her face. "And, Susie, there's more." Jeannie glowed at Susie.

"I'm pregnant!"

Susie stared, her mouth open, not knowing what to say.

"Um, congratulations? Are you happy?"

"We are ecstatic! It seems that if Doug looks at me, we have to do it." Jeannie laughed. "Seriously, when he got home a couple weeks ago, we couldn't keep our hands off each other. Knowing that finally we were gonna be able to start our life together, we did it like rabbits."

Susie was somewhat shocked by Jeannie's bluntness, but happy for her friend.

"We figure we'll be married soon anyway. We both want to start a family right away.

By the time we get married, I'll be twelve weeks along, and the dress might need to be let out a little. I don't think I'll really be showing yet, though, so no one needs to know. Of course, when little Jason or Ashley arrives three months early, I guess everyone will know, but it's not like it's never happened before around here, and by that time we'll be married anyhow."

"Wow! You've done a lot of planning in a short time," Susie said. "I'm really happy for you, Jeannie. You're getting the life you always wanted. What can I do? If I'm your maid of honor, there must be something I'm supposed to do."

"Well, my mother said that you should plan a wedding shower and help us with invitations. She remembered that you know how to do calligraphy, so now she wants you to address all the invitations. She figured that would add some fancy to our wedding, make it special.

Don't worry, though. There won't be that many. I don't want more than fifty people there."

Figuring that most people would come in couples, Susie figured that there wouldn't be more than a couple dozen invitations. She could do that easily.

The wheels began turning in Susie's brain. "You know how much my mother loves to bake. I bet she'll want to make desserts for the wedding. I know she'll make all of the desserts for the shower." Warming to the idea that her best friend was really getting married, Susie added, "Jeannie, this is exciting! Married! A mother? Wow!" She then decided to tease her old friend just a little. "Are you sure you're pregnant?" she asked with a glimmer in her eye. "I remember the last time and the Dollar General test."

Jeannie laughed and told Susie that she was sure, that she had been to the doctor and everything. The two old friends then laughed and continued their planning.

The summer was a wedding blur. Susie and Bill were each excited for their friends, but being together in the same room was awkward. They tried to stay away from each other. Susie was still angry with Bill and had a hard time covering that anger up. After four years of taking online college classes, commuting to USM in Portland, working on his dad's lobster boat, doing the accounting for his mother's lobster pound, and making sure that his younger sisters' needs were met, Bill was weary. He still believed he had done the right thing by sending Susie away, especially after he saw what a poised woman she had become in the past four years. Somehow the two of them weathered the summer, and before they knew it, the week of the wedding was upon them.

Susie planned a shower for the ladies to be held in her backyard. She and her mother strung white Christmas lights in the trees, and her father brought out some sawhorses and sheets of plywood for tables. They borrowed folding chairs from the church and white tablecloths from friends. Susie drove to Brunswick to a party store and picked up white paper bells and other decorations. Her mom planned a menu, and the ladies cooked and baked for a week. In a small town, a wedding becomes a public affair. Everyone wanted to help if they could.

When the day came, all of Jeannie's friends and aunts and cousins gathered under the trees in Susie's backyard at dusk while an old radio played music in the background. When everything was ready, Susie went to pick up Jeannie, her mother, and her grandmother. The party wasn't a surprise, but Jeannie had no idea what it would be like. When she walked around the side of the Wards' house and saw the twinkling fairyland with all her girlfriends, aunts, and cousins dressed up just for her, she began crying. She walked from person to person, thanking them for coming and grateful that so many thought enough of her to attend. She glanced over toward the back porch and saw a large table laden with wrapped gifts—gifts for her—and her eyes welled up yet again.

The meal was served, desserts devoured, and Jeannie opened her presents, oohing and aahing over each one. She couldn't believe her good fortune or the generosity of these women. After she took off each ribbon and bow, she handed it to Susie who, after cutting a hole in the center of a paper plate, pushed the ribbon through, leaving the larger bow on the top of the plate and the rest of the ribbon dangling below. For good luck, Jeannie would use this ribbon plate as her practice bouquet during the wedding rehearsal. It was an old custom, one Jeannie's mother thought would be fun.

The next week was the rehearsal at the church, and Jeannie dutifully carried her "bouquet," surprising Doug when he saw it. He and Bill laughed out loud, much to Jeannie and Susie's chagrin, but one look at the women's faces put a stop to the merriment. The rehearsal went perfectly, and once everyone knew their roles for the next day, they all went downstairs to the church hall for a bite to eat. The church ladies had put out quite a spread, as they did every time a young couple was about to get married. At the end of the evening, Jeannie and Doug kissed goodnight and went their separate ways, since Doug was not allowed to see his bride again until she walked down the aisle in her wedding dress.

The wedding day dawned sunny and hot—a typical August day. The wedding was planned for four o'clock so the fishermen, lobstermen, and farmers could finish their work and get home in time to clean up and dress for the wedding. Susie had spent the night at Jeannie's house, and in the morning they excitedly did each other's hair and makeup and helped each other get dressed. Soon it was three thirty and time for them to go to the church.

The wedding was simple but beautiful. Jeannie looked lovely in her mother's dress, and Doug was handsome in his rented tuxedo. Bill was resplendent in his, thought Susie, and when she walked down the aisle in her long pink dress, carrying pink and white carnations, her shoulders peeking out of the neckline, Bill thought she had never looked more beautiful. He was sad that she would be leaving soon for her MFA program in Boston but determined to somehow enjoy the little time they had here in Oceanside, sorry that he had wasted the entire summer trying to stay away from her. They even had a dance at the reception, all eyes on them to see if any sparks remained.

After the wedding and reception, Doug and Jeannie climbed into Doug's pickup. As they left for a honeymoon in a hotel in Portland, cans rattled on the road behind them and soap on the rear window proclaimed them JUST MARRIED! They were excited to be Mr. and Mrs. Douglas Henry Bates, and drove off amid cheers and howls and laughter from their family and friends—off to begin their new life. They would return to Oceanside in a few days with stories to tell. Doug's parents were fixing up a double-wide trailer on a lot they owned about a mile from their house. It was twenty-seven feet long and forty-two feet wide, providing nearly a thousand square feet of living space including two bedrooms and two bathrooms. There was an eat-in kitchen and big windows for natural light and views. Its cottage-style exterior made it a home for Doug and Jeannie to begin their new life together, and they couldn't have been happier.

Chapter Eight

The last few days in Maine were bittersweet for Susie. She enjoyed being with her parents and her friends, but she also knew that her life would never be like this again. She had chosen to move away into an unknown future. While she was certain she had made the right decision, she was sad to leave the familiar behind. Bill had been friendly after the wedding, and she had enjoyed spending time with him, even going for a sail for old time's sake. The sparks were still there, but she told herself that he was in her past. She had to look to the future.

September came, and Susie enjoyed the Labor Day celebrations that defined the end of summer. She joined everyone on the green in the center of town for a picnic, sat back on a blanket with her parents to watch the fireworks display, and returned home to her bed for the last time. Her suitcases stood guard at the front door, waiting for her to move them to Boston.

For the next full year, Susie immersed herself in her studies. She was in her element—writing, learning about writing from authors, and surrounding herself with other writers. Everyone she met was passionate about writing, and many had already been published. Susie felt as though she was already falling behind, and she was only twenty-two years old.

She had been hesitant about her competency to teach an undergraduate writing class, but when she discovered that she also had the option to teach at the Boston Arts Academy, a pilot public school, she jumped at the opportunity. She loved teaching there. In fact, she repeatedly told her students that she was learning as much from them as they were from her—and she meant it. Seeing the young faces eagerly absorbing whatever knowledge she had to dispense and reading their stories was exhilarating for her.

The Smith graduate with whom she shared a two-bedroom apartment was pleasant but often not there, spending more of her time with a boyfriend in Back Bay. This left the apartment to Susie most of the time. Her parents came every couple of months to visit and were able to stay with her for the weekend. In the spring, they came down for a baseball weekend. The three of them walked over to Fenway Park and enjoyed a day at the ballpark together before her parents had to return to Maine. Susie wondered why she had agreed to go to New York instead of staying in Boston. Here she had a connection to her family. She knew that once she moved to New York, she would rarely see them.

Since all admitted students qualified for a global fellowship upon completion of their degree requirements, one that allowed them to travel for two or three months anywhere outside of the United States, Susie had to decide where she wanted to go. She would receive her degree at the end of the summer after spending the next two months in London. Following Katie's travel blogs for the past year, she knew that she would go to London. Since she had never been outside of the United States, she wanted to go somewhere where English was spoken. She did not have an affinity for the study of languages, had limped through French at Smith, and decided that she did not need a language barrier on top of her fear of foreign travel.

Once there, though, all her fears fell away. Susie had never been on an airplane before, and even checking in at Logan was an adventure for her. When her flight was called and she walked onto the plane, she was in awe of its size. Following the overhead numbers, she found her seat easily, stowed her carry-on bag overhead as Katie had told her she would do, and tucked her brand-new leather hobo bag under the seat in front of her. She buckled her seatbelt, relieved to see that it operated just like the ones in cars, and sat back to watch the people board. When the plane took off, she gripped the arms of the seat but was more exhilarated than fearful, and when the plane flew out over the Atlantic and she could no longer see land, she knew she was on her way to a new life.

At Heathrow, Susie simply followed the crowd and she got through customs with no problem. Outside the doors, officially on English soil, she was surprised to see a handsome young man standing with a sign that said "Susan Ward." She tentatively approached him, and he told her that his name was Richard and he was a good friend of Katie's who had asked him to pick Susie up at the airport and take her to her flat. Susie said a silent prayer of thanks to Katie, smiled, and walked with Richard to the short-stay parking. When she saw his little car, she chuckled softly, wondering if two people and two suitcases would even fit in it, but Richard made the bags fit, and he and she sat cozily in their seats. There was a black car parked to the right of his Mini Cooper, and the men inside seemed quite interested in her and Richard. New to travel and always on her guard, Susie commented that the men were watching them pretty closely, but Richard told her not to be concerned.

On the way into the city, he chattered about how much she was going to love his London, told her about places she had to see, and by the time they arrived at Susie's new place, she was already in love with the city. He gallantly helped her carry her bags up to her third floor flat, commenting that she certainly traveled differently from Katie.

"When she was here, she arrived with a backpack." Richard laughed at the memory. "She said that if she needed anything else, there were stores in London." Susie laughed, picturing Katie saying that.

"Yeah," Richard continued. "She was here the last time for two weeks and made do with the clothes in her backpack. Of course, our maid cleaned and pressed everything for her, commenting that there wasn't much fabric to be cleaned. You know how Katie dresses." Susie laughed again, thinking of Katie's strappy mini dresses, shorts, and tiny tops. As a size zero, she could fit a lot of clothes in a backpack.

Once the luggage was in the apartment, Richard took a look around, walking from living room to bedroom to bathroom to kitchen. "Well, it isn't much but I guess it will do for two months, eh?" Susie, meanwhile, was looking out the windows and feeling very cosmopolitan, like a world traveler. Looking at Richard, she realized that he wasn't being critical. He was just stating a fact. It was a tiny apartment but would be fine for her.

"So are you too tired after traveling or would you like to join the gang tonight at our favorite club?" he asked her. Susie definitely wasn't too tired, but she wasn't exactly the clubbing type. Taking a page out of Katie's book, though, she said, "When in Rome...."

With a puzzled look on his face, Richard informed her that she was in London, not Rome, but if she would like to go to Rome, he could take her the following weekend. Susie just laughed.

"No, that's okay. It's just an American expression, "When in Rome, do as the Romans do." It means one should acclimate to his or her surroundings."

"Oh," said Richard with a laugh. "Well, the offer for a weekend to Rome is still on the table. Just let me know." He started for the door. With an appraising look at Susie, he added, "I'll pick you up at ten. Wear your LBD. I know every girl has one." With that, he was out the door and Susie was alone in London.

Susie unpacked, took a little nap, and woke at nine with just enough time to get ready. She took out her little black dress, a pair of red heels, and some jewelry. Pleased with her choices, she fussed with her long, wavy hair, taming it into a high, bouncy ponytail, which she secured with a stretchy rhinestone band. After applying more makeup than she normally would, she looked at herself in the full-length mirror and was pleased with the sophisticated young woman who looked back at her.

Richard arrived five minutes early and was surprised that she was ready. "Off we go then, Yankee!" Susie laughed, and the name stuck. For the entire time she was in London, Richard and his friends all called her Yankee. The evening at the club was bright and loud and crowded, and Susie was surprised to discover that Richard had his own table in a corner. Susie was beginning to see that he was well connected and knew people everywhere they went. While they were dancing, a young woman wrapped her arms around him, telling him that she loved him. He simply smiled, peeled her off, and told her he loved her too. Susie tried repeatedly to ask him what he did for a living, but between the music and the constant talking, she couldn't, so she watched in amazement. Bottles of champagne arrived courtesy of one group or another. When he mentioned that he was hungry, the table was suddenly loaded with food. It seemed that what Richard wanted, Richard got. This public persona was quite different from her first impression.

Susie had a good time, and when she announced that she was tired and had to get started in the morning on her real reason for being there, he pouted but snapped his fingers in the air and a man arrived instantly. Richard told him that she needed to be taken home. "Right away, sir," was the reply. Susie really wanted to know Richard's story, but she kissed him on the cheek, thanked him for an amazing first day in London, and followed the gentleman to a waiting limousine. Susie had never been in a limo before and couldn't believe the luxury. She gave the driver her address and sat back thinking that she must be dreaming. She texted Katie, "Thank you for Richard. What an incredible first day in London town!" Instantly, her phone rang.

"So you like Richard, huh?" Katie asked, her voice smiling. "I thought you might. Everyone does."

"What's his story?" Susie blurted out. "He picked me up in a tiny little car, friendly and down to earth. Then we went to a club, and a whole different person emerged. Everyone seemed to know him, and they kept giving him things and telling him they loved him. Who is he, anyway?"

Katie was aghast. "You really don't know?!"

Now Susie was getting annoyed. "Why all the mystery?"

"Susie, Prince Richard is third in line for the British crown."

"What?! He's what?! But he picked me up at the airport in a Mini Cooper. He carried my bags up three flights of stairs. Oh my God! A prince carried my luggage." Susie was embarrassed, amazed, and surprised. Katie laughed.

"Richard is a regular guy. He's the sweetest, most considerate guy I know. In fact, I almost stayed in London just to be with him."

"You and Richard? You never told me."

"I never told anyone. I didn't want to jinx it. We had a great time traveling around Europe, and I really thought he might be 'the one.' Susie, I fell hard. I thought he did too. Then he told me that he was to marry a princess from Denmark. He crushed me. I packed up and left the next day and haven't answered any of his texts or calls—except when I asked him to pick you up at the airport. I figured he'd send someone. I'm as surprised as you are that he went himself."

"That explains why everyone was watching us and taking pictures as we walked through the airport. And, now that I think of it, there was a black car parked next to his with two men in it who pulled out right after us. Up till now, I just thought it was a coincidence."

"Nope. He has security. Even if we went out on his yacht, we always had security with us. They were discreet, but they were there."

Susie laughed, remembering her "when in Rome" comment. "He asked me to go to a club tonight and I told him, 'When in Rome...' and he asked me if I wanted him to take me to Rome. He was serious?" Katie laughed, but Susie could hear an edge in it.

"Susie, I'm in Rome," and Katie's breath caught.

Susie quickly added, "I told him 'Thanks but no thanks.' Katie, just so we're clear, I am *not* interested in Richard—especially now that I know you love him."

"I don't love him anymore," Katie blurted out. "In fact, I hate him...." After a pause, she quietly added, "But I wonder if he knows I'm here."

Susie knew better. Her friend was hurting. Her friend was in love.

After insisting that Katie come to London to visit her, Susie changed the subject, and the rest of the conversation steered away from Richard.

Susie quickly fell in love with the pace of the city. She knew other Smith graduates who were living in London, which made her feel less alone. Katie had told many of her London friends to help Susie out when she arrived. Initially afraid that she would be alone for two months, she found she barely had time to do her work. Richard called her several times, and she went out with his crowd. Every time she was with him, though, she sang Katie's praises, and every time she mentioned Katie's name, she saw a melancholy in his eyes that told her that he cared very much for her friend.

During the days, Susie roamed the city, taking in its sights and sounds and smells. She intended to use these two months gathering material for a novel about a young American's first trip abroad. She stopped periodically at sidewalk cafés to sit and take notes. She visited museums and government centers, parks and pubs. She was there to get material for her novel, and material she got. She popped in and out of antique bookstores and galleries. She talked with people in all walks of life. She walked and took taxis. She rode atop double-decker buses and in the Tube. She hired a horse in Hyde Park and rode with an escort all around the park, observing the locals picnicking, playing games, strolling, and rushing to work. She fell in love with her horse's sweet disposition, and when she was told his name was Ben, she laughed because that was a name she always had thought she would give a son.

After a few weeks, Katie decided to visit. It was easy enough for her to pop over to London for a few days. Susie didn't tell Richard that Katie was coming, and when he came to pick her up one night, there was Katie. Susie knew in an instant that the two were in love, even though they tried to remain aloof. Richard pecked Katie on the cheek, and Katie barely hugged him hello. But, as Susie watched them during the evening, the cues were there. Furtive glances, wrinkled brows, smiles, finishing each other's sentences, anticipating each other's wishes—all told Katie that she needed to help these two be together. For the next few days, she did her best to make sure they always sat next to each other, had opportunities to dance and quiet time to talk at the end of an evening after Susie claimed to be too tired to stay up another minute, leaving Katie and Richard sitting in her living room alone.

Before she was ready, it was time for Susie to return to America. With notebooks full of material, new clothes, and souvenirs packed into her suitcases, she went out for one last night on the town with her London crew. She invited some Smith friends to come along, and they crashed Richard's table. She had just been referring to her friend Richard, and when her fellow Smith alums saw that her Richard was Prince Richard they were astounded. The Susie they had known at Smith had to be practically dragged out for a night of fun, and here she was, hobnobbing with a prince! They held her in new regard.

When her last night in London was winding down in the wee hours of the morning, she grabbed Richard's hand and pulled him after her out of the club onto the sidewalk where it was quieter. She faced him and said, "Richard, I know that you love Katie, and I know Katie loves you. The entire time I've been here, I've not seen you look at anyone the way you look at her. You've not even met this so-called princess you told Katie you have to marry. Richard, think of your heart. Think of your future happiness. You're only third in line. No one would really care if you married a commoner." Richard winced but remained silent. "I don't mean to offend you, but you and Katie belong together. I know she would drop her life in the States and move here in a heartbeat if you gave her any encouragement. Just think about it." Susie rose on tiptoes and kissed Richard on the cheeks. "Thank you for a wonderful time in London. If you're ever in New York, please let me know. I'm going to miss you." She hugged him and was surprised by the length and strength of the hug he gave in return. He then cleared his throat and harrumphed a command to a driver at the curb to give this young lady a ride home. As she got into the car, she looked back and saw him wipe his eyes before going back into the club to join his friends. She hoped that he and Katie would have a chance to talk.

Chapter Nine

Susie flew from Heathrow to Logan, and by the time she arrived in the United States, she felt like a woman ready to take on the world. As she exited customs at Logan, she was shocked to see her parents standing outside the gate. With balloons and flowers picked from the garden, they had driven all the way to Boston to welcome her home. They could hardly believe that she had lived in another country for two months, but they were happy and proud that she wanted to spread her wings and fly.

Riding in the backseat of her parents' car, Susie instantly morphed from a woman of the world into a little girl. She would have to remember this feeling when she wrote her book. All it took was the drive up the coast to make her feel small again. After spending a few days with her parents in Oceanside, she was sad to realize that the town seemed provincial to her. There were no lights at night, no clubs with music and dancing, unless you wanted to go to the Elks Club on Saturday night and dance to a trio of seventy-year-old musicians. When she ran into her old friends Jeannie and Doug, they stared in wide-eyed amazement as she answered their questions about London. When she told them that Prince Richard had picked her up at the airport and that she had been a part of his crowd while she was there, Jeannie almost fainted.

"Oh my gawd! I've seen his pictures in *People!* He is so handsome. You actually know him?" Susie showed Jeannie pictures on her phone of Richard and his gang, many of whom Jeannie recognized from her addictive reading of the tabloids.

After a week in Maine, Susie was ready to leave. She knew she would miss her parents. She would miss her friends. She would miss her ocean. But, she was ready to move on. She headed to New York

City to live with Katie in the two-bedroom apartment on the Upper East Side. Getting there was an ordeal.

Her parents drove her to the bus station where she picked up a bus to Portland. In Portland, there was a brief stop while they loaded more people on the bus and then drove to South Station in Boston. At South Station, she had to collect her bags and schlepp to the train station where she caught a train to New York's Penn Station. Once she collected her bags again, she had to find a porter to take them outside to the taxi stand for her where the bags were loaded in a taxi and she went to the apartment. By the time she had arrived, the doorman had helped her in with her bags, and she had said hello to Katie, she was exhausted.

Katie showed her around the apartment, and Susie was shocked at how large it was. She had known that Katie came from a wealthy family, but she hadn't dreamed of anything like this. In the four years they had known each other, Katie had never bragged about her circumstances or even described her home in New York. Susie could not believe her good luck.

Katie's parents were so happy that she seemed to be settling down in the City that they gladly paid her rent. During Katie's time in Europe, they had been convinced that she would fall in love with some playboy and never come home. Katie had even found the perfect job, as a social media content creator for a travel company. The travel blog she had written for the past year proved to have been more than just fun. It was great experience to lead her to this job she loved. Her job did require a lot of travel, so Susie often had the apartment to herself.

Susie was tempted to take advantage of the fact that Katie's parents were paying for the apartment and not get a job—just write. She then realized that she had not been brought up to mooch off others and quickly landed a job as an editorial assistant at a major publishing house. She figured that by seeing others' writing submissions, she would learn a lot about what to do and what not to do when she wrote her novel.

She soon learned that, while writing was easy for her, and her ideas were flowing from her mind in ways she couldn't even explain, she was writing vignettes rather than a novel. Working in the industry taught her that she could not pitch her story until it was finished, but she didn't seem able to finish it. After a few weeks of struggling to tie all her notes together in an interesting way, and getting distracted by another thought or another adventure, she decided to write short stories and essays. Even getting those accepted was harder than she thought. She did get a few pieces of short fiction published, pieces she wrote about her experiences in London, growing up in a small coastal town in Maine, and being a twenty-something in today's world. The few hundred dollars she received for all her work, though, wasn't enough to sustain her interest in writing. She threw herself into her job and partying with Katie in the city that never sleeps.

After living in New York for about a year, she attended a Jazz at Lincoln Center performance one rainy night, a concert that would change her life forever.

Chapter Ten

Susie loved jazz, indoctrinated and coached by her father her entire life. Living in New York, she discovered the Jazz at Lincoln Center series and went as often as she could. Sometimes she could persuade a friend to attend with her, but one rainy night she decided to go alone because she knew no one who shared her love for Michael Feinstein except her mother, and she was hours away. When Susie suggested to Katie that she might like it, Katie simply replied, "No thanks" and went back to the movie she was watching until it was time for her to get dressed to go out on the town. Feinstein was in the City performing a tribute to Duke Ellington, and Susie wanted to see him so much that she bought a single ticket and went alone.

Because of the design of the performance space, the Appel Room has one of New York City's most dramatic and breathtaking backdrops: a fifty-by-eighty-three-foot wall of glass overlooking Central Park, Columbus Circle, and the Manhattan skyline. On this night, it was raining, and the colors of the park and the lights of Columbus Circle became a magical watercolor complement to the music. Susie was mesmerized.

When the concert was over, the rain didn't hold the same appeal. Susie raised her umbrella and raced to the taxi stand. Seeing a long line of people waiting, she decided to hurry a couple of blocks up Central Park West. Her plan was to grab a cab on its way to the line at Lincoln Center. As the yellow car approached her outstretched arm, she hopped across a puddle to open the door. Her umbrella crashed into another as someone else rushed to open the door of the waiting car. Both potential passengers then found themselves standing under water cascading off the two umbrellas. Faced with a rainstorm at eleven o'clock outside Lincoln Center as dozens of people vied for cabs, she had thought she was being clever by going a couple of blocks away to catch one before it made its way to Columbus Circle. Apparently, this rude man had thought the same thing and now they were vying for the same cab.

"Where are you heading?" he had shouted.

"Upper East Side," she had answered before she had time to think about telling a complete stranger where she lived.

"Me too. Want to share? Who knows when we'll get another cab in this weather."

Before she knew what she was doing, she was climbing into the back of the cab next to a rather handsome man, both of them dripping on the upholstery.

"Thanks for sharing," he began, a million-dollar smile aimed her way. "I'm Ted. Ted Goldman. And you are?"

"Um…Susan. Susan Ward." She tried to smile at him, but her reflection in the window told her that smiling only made her mascara-streaked face look gruesome. She quickly dug in her purse for a tissue to wipe her face but couldn't find one. Without hesitation, a white handkerchief appeared before her face.

"It's the least I can do, Susan Ward."

She took the handkerchief and wiped her rain-soaked face. When she tried to hand the handkerchief back to him with a thank you, he laughed.

"I think that one is yours forever now," he said, pointing to the black mascara, tan makeup, and red lipstick stains on it.

Embarrassed, Susie apologized for ruining his handkerchief, while wondering who carries handkerchiefs in this day and age. She stuffed it in her purse and turned to him.

"I'm really sorry. I just saw my reflection and it was pretty scary," she said earnestly, though she attempted a smile. "I didn't want you to think you were in the car with a crazy lady. I'm really not. In fact, I'm a respectable, intelligent woman."

Ted laughed, instantly taken with her. "Oh, I have no doubt," he said, a slight tease in his voice. "It was, of course, intelligent to escape the madhouse of Lincoln Center to get a cab. And you do appear to be quite respectable."

"You're making fun of me." Susie pouted.

"Not at all. In fact, while I was waiting in that long queue at the taxi stand, I spotted you trotting away up the street, and as soon as you were a block away you started to try to hail a cab. I thought to myself, *That's a really good idea. Why didn't I think of that?* And I followed you."

"So now you're a stalker too?" Susie quipped, but she was beginning to like the sound of his voice. Looking at him wasn't too hard, either. Even with water droplets still on his face and his dark brown hair matted down, she could tell he was quite handsome. And he certainly was a gentleman. There weren't too many of them left in the world—especially in New York.

"A stalker?" He laughed again. "Not quite. In fact, I'm an attorney. I catch stalkers for a living. You're safe with me, ma'am." At that, he produced a business card which he handed to her. "You see? I have the big boy business card and everything. I'm legit."

Susie took the card, glanced at it, and recognized the name of the company as a financial services firm.

"Wait a minute. This isn't a law firm, and this company certainly doesn't catch stalkers."

"You caught me," he confessed with a twinkle in his eye that Susie found most appealing. I'm actually in-house counsel, and my job is probably the most boring one on the planet. Speaking of jobs, what do you do?"

That's always the first question anyone asks in this city, Susie thought. *Everyone should just wear badges with their job titles on them. It would save a lot of time at parties.*

She dutifully smiled and gave her pat answer. "Oh, I'm an editorial assistant at a publishing house. I moved to New York about a year ago to be a writer."

While she was talking, Ted was trying to figure out how old she was. He was twenty-seven, and she looked a little younger. He decided to find out cleverly.

"Where did you work before you moved to New York?" he asked

"Actually, I finished my MFA almost a year ago and this is my first real job."

"I know that's a master of fine arts, but what does that mean? Are you a musician? Was it a tough course of study? Did it take you a long time? I'm so glad to be finished with school. I thought law school would kill me."

Susie liked his self-deprecating manner. "Actually, I found it a lot easier than college. I went to Smith and thought that was tougher than my MFA program at BU. And, no, I am not a musician. My degree is in creative writing. I hope to be a writer. Mom told me that the program was easy for me because I was doing what I loved. When we do what we love doing, it never feels like work."

This statement hit Ted square between the eyes. He thought about what she just said. *If we do what we love doing, it never feels like work. Wow! My job sure feels like work. A lot of work. Hard work. Boring work. Mind-numbing work.*

"Is it something I said?" he heard her asking him.

"Um, no. I was just thinking." He quickly switched gears. "So I'm just going to ask. How old are you anyway? If I keep trying to be clever about figuring it out, I probably never will," and he flashed those perfect teeth again.

"Well, didn't your mother ever tell you not to ask a lady her age?" Ted looked ashamed, worried that he had offended her, so she quickly added, "I'm twenty-five. I graduated from Smith when I was twenty-two, spent a summer helping my folks out with their jewelry store and planning my best friend's wedding, and then spent a year completing my MFA at BU. I spent a couple of months in London on a post-graduate fellowship, and I've been working in New York since last September. That makes me twenty-five now. How old are you?" As she asked this, she looked directly into his eyes.

"Um, I'm twenty-seven. I graduated from Harvard when I was twenty-one, spent three years at Harvard Law, and have been working in the City for the past three years." Ted just looked at her for a couple of minutes and added, "This is going to really sound strange, but I think we've met before. You look really familiar to me."

"Great line, sir," Susie answered quickly. She then looked more carefully at him and began laughing. "You know, I think we have met.

You said you went to Harvard Law? I think you were my knight in shining armor at a Harvard game one cold autumn day."

The proverbial lightbulb went on over Ted's head. "Yes!" he exclaimed. You were the damsel in distress then, too." He chuckled but Susie wasn't so sure she liked being called a damsel in distress, and the thought that both times she had met this guy she was perceived as such did not sit well with her.

"Well, I don't know about 'damsel in distress,'" she answered, not trying to hide her annoyance at the term.

"Lady, this is you!" the cabbie called out.

Surprised that they had arrived so quickly, Susie searched in her purse for her wallet, only to have Ted tell her not to worry about it. He'd take care of it. As she was thanking him and getting out of the cab, he called out,

"You have my card! Give me a call some time, Susan Ward. We can grab dinner or a drink—your choice." With that, the taxi sped off to Ted's home, which was on the Upper West Side. In fact, he lived just a few blocks from Lincoln Center and if it hadn't been raining, he would simply have walked home. "I love the rain in New York!" he said to no one in particular, and got a questioning look from the taxi driver.

All week, Susie looked at the business card she had put on her refrigerator with one of the little lobster magnets her mom had given her. Her mother thought that the lobsters would remind her of home, and she was right. Every morning when Susie opened the fridge to get her coffee creamer, she thought of her cozy shingled home in the little town on the coast of Maine. She thought of her mom and dad and her friends. During the past few days, though, she had thought of Ted each morning when she got the creamer for her coffee and every night when she came home and put her take-out leftovers in the fridge. She thought of Ted, wondering if she should call him.

Who is this Ted Goldman, Susie thought. *I'm going to google him. After all, if I decide to go out with him, I should know who he is. He did stand me up once, though. That doesn't bode well.*

Susie googled Ted Goldman and up popped a picture of Ted standing next to a beautiful young woman. He was in a tuxedo and she wore a deep red gown, her blond hair pulled back away from her face with diamond combs and falling in perfectly curled tresses down her back.

Hmm. If that's your type, then why are you interested in going out with me?

Susie read the copy of the article. It had appeared in *The Greenwich Sentinel* last year. Apparently, it was a fundraiser gala for Make-A-Wish. The woman's name was Ashley Wentworth, and the gala had been held at Mr. Goldman's alma mater, Greenwich Country Day School.

Well, la-di-da, Mr. Goldman. Doesn't that sound fancy?

Curious, she googled Greenwich Country Day School next. She discovered that it is a K-through-twelve private school with approximately twelve hundred students and a student-teacher ratio of six to one.

Must have been nice to have such personal attention. My classes were never under twenty, and in high school they were even bigger.

Susie then noticed the tuition for the school.

Holy crap! I never even knew anyone who made forty-seven thousand a year! His parents shelled that out every year just for school for him? And then they sent him to Harvard? And then to Harvard Law?

Once she had gotten over the sticker shock of the tuition, Susie began reading about the school. It sounded idyllic. What an amazing childhood he must have had. One of the things the school's website featured was a 160-foot giant elm tree. Of all the things they could brag about, they liked their tree. Apparently, it was the oldest tree in the state of Connecticut. She read on. The school was founded in 1926—almost seventy-five years ago. They had their own farm with sheep, chickens, and peacocks. *Peacocks!* They had vegetable and herb gardens. They had botanical gardens and something called "collections." Susie was intrigued so she dove deeper. The farm, known as French Farm, was a four-acre historic farm and was the first Greenwich property listed on the National Register of Historic Places in 1975. In addition to the main house, the outbuildings included the farm's original chicken coop, milking barn, silo, and greenhouse.

Well, doesn't that sound nice, Mr. Goldman?

Susie then found a bio for Ted. He was born Theodore Michael Goldman. He was the son of Thomas and Rebecca Goldman. His father was a senior partner in Goldman, Cohen, & Abelson, a Park Avenue corporate law firm. His mother, apparently, was quite active in the Junior League of Greenwich, having been one of its first Jewish members, as well as a number of other volunteer organizations. Ted attended Harvard University and then Harvard Law School and was currently employed by Smith & Jones Development Corporation, NYC.

Sleuthing further and beginning to feel a bit like a stalker, Susie found Ted's Facebook page. The profile picture was one in which his hair was windblown, and Susie could see water in the background. Maybe he was on a boat of some kind. The cover photo was the iconic Chatham Lighthouse in Chatham, Massachusetts.

Well, apparently, we both like the water.

Susie snooped a little more, checking out the pictures posted on his page, mostly groups of friends, and then she lost her appetite for investigating him. It just seemed creepy.

I'll find out more about him the old-fashioned way—by asking him questions and listening to his answers.

Susie decided to give Ted a call. She didn't know very many people in the city, and another friend would be nice. He seemed like a good guy. Rehearsing what she would say when he picked up his phone, she dialed the cell number on the card. When she heard Ted's voice on the other end, though, she froze.

"Hello? Hello? This is Ted Goldman."

Susie found her voice and said, "Hi Ted. We met in a taxi last weekend and you gave me your card."

"So you decided to call me, huh?" Ted knew he shouldn't tease her, but he couldn't help himself.

"Well, I wondered if you would like to get together for a drink tomorrow night," Susie said haltingly.

"Thank you but I don't think so," Ted said, to her surprise. "I've been thinking about you all week," he quickly added, "and, Susan, I would love to go out to dinner so we would have more time to talk."

Not planning on going to dinner with this stranger, but relieved that he hadn't refused her invitation outright, she agreed. "Um, okay.

That would be nice. Since we both live on the Upper East Side, why don't we go somewhere local?"

Ted laughed in that way again that made her wonder if she amused him or if she had said something stupid.

"I have a small confession to make," he began. "Before we take this any further, I have to tell you that I lied to you."

Susie's antennae went up, sirens blared, and she was about to revoke her invitation. She didn't want to get involved with a liar.

"You see, when we got into the cab the other night, and I saw how beautiful you were, I figured I'd say I lived wherever you did so that we could spend a few minutes together. Then, when I recognized you as the girl I really enjoyed spending time with at the game and then totally flaked out on, I really wanted another chance to prove to you that I truly am a nice guy. Actually, I live on the Upper West Side."

Susie was the one to laugh now. "That's the big lie?" she asked. "I think I can live with that one. Actually, it's pretty flattering."

"Well, okay then," Ted replied as he let out the breath he didn't realize he had been holding. "How about I pick you up at seven tomorrow night? I have a great place in mind."

"Sounds good." Susie gave him her address and hung up the phone smiling. Sure, he had told her a little white lie, but it was because he wanted to spend time with her. That was kind of nice.

At five the next night, Susie was nervously trying on clothes. He hadn't said where they were going. She didn't want to get all dressed up and then go someplace casual. But, she didn't want to wear jeans and then be embarrassed when he took her someplace nice. For the next two hours, she debated. She put her hair in a ponytail and then took it down. She put on makeup and then washed it off. She finally decided on a nice pair of wool slacks, a somewhat dressy sweater, and a blazer. He rang her bell and she buzzed him in. When she opened her door, there stood a very handsome man in a tuxedo, bowtie and all. She looked up at his face and realized that it was Ted. She started laughing.

"Well, I'm glad you're picking me up here. I can go change. I think I'm a little underdressed."

"Yeah, well, I guess I forgot to tell you we're having dinner at the Rainbow Room. I thought a nice dinner and some soothing music and dancing might cheer you up. You had a sadness about you in Cambridge. Plus," he added after hesitating for a minute, "I have some big-time apologizing to do to you. I was lousy to you. I told you I'd call, and then I never did. Actually, I got involved with someone shortly after I said I'd try to get a car and drive to Smith."

Susie was impressed that he had both noticed and remembered that she had been sad back then, but that had been five years ago. Did he think she was still sad? Back then she certainly was, although she had thought she was hiding it from everyone. For months after she got to Smith, she had hidden her sadness and loneliness from everyone but Katie, and here this boy had talked with her for a couple of hours and had picked up on it. But did he also think that she'd been pining away for him all this time? That's a pretty big ego. Wow!

All of this she thought in an instant, but aloud she just said, "The Rainbow Room? Do they even allow people our age there?" She was only half joking. She thought of it as a place for wealthy seniors. "I guess I'd better go change." With that, she ran into her bedroom, leaving Ted standing in the living room with her roommate.

"So, Ted," Katie began, "what are your intentions with Susie?" She smiled as she asked the question, but the edge in her eyes made Ted unsure if she was being nosy, protective, or both.

He decided that she was just a good friend and told her, "I have no idea, honestly. I liked talking with her and thought it would be nice to spend an evening together. We seemed to hit it off briefly years ago, and it seemed like fate brought us together again. Who am I to tempt fate?"

"Why are you trying so hard to impress her? A monkey suit on a first date is pretty strange."

This girl didn't mince words, thought Ted. He liked her immediately. She was a loyal friend.

"Well, I asked myself what I could do that would make an impression. You see, I don't want to just grab a burger and have her forget all about me. When I saw her again after all these years, I said to myself,

65

'nothing ventured, nothing gained.' This will leave a lasting impression, don't you think?"

Katie chuckled at her own mantra being sent back at her. "Good answer! Now, if you'll excuse me, I need to meet some friends," and off went a satisfied Katie out the door.

Fifteen minutes later, Susie emerged in a long white gown that showed off her tanned shoulders. Susie always liked wearing white after the summer. She tanned easily and knew that white brought out her tan even more. While she was looking through her clothes, she thought she wanted to select something that would make an impression on Ted. She didn't want him to forget her like he had the last time they met. There was no time to do anything fancy with her hair, so it was flowing loosely down her back, held in place by a single rhinestone comb.

"Wow!" Ted exclaimed. "Susan, you take my breath away!" He stood staring at her, thinking that she was far more beautiful that the debutantes and society women his mother kept finding for him. Even after she reached his side, he continued to stare, and Susie giggled, telling him that maybe they had better get going. She liked that he had called her Susan. It sounded more grown up and sophisticated than her childhood "Susie." From now on, she decided, she would introduce herself as Susan.

On the cab ride to Rockefeller Center, Ted and Susan rode quietly, but when they arrived at their destination, they talked and laughed and talked some more. Susan had never been to the Top of the Rock and was in awe of the view. Everywhere she looked, lights twinkled from buildings and cars far below. They had a wonderful dinner and, though they had known that they both loved jazz, they now discovered that they both loved dancing the old dances. Susan never wanted the evening to end—and she never once thought of Bill.

"Are you Prince Charming, and at any minute I'm going to turn back into Cinderella?" she crooned to him as he held her close for one last dance.

Ted turned her face up to his and whispered, "If I have anything to say about it, you are going to live happily ever after, Cinderella."

Susan felt dizzy. She wasn't sure if it was from the champagne, the music, or the way Ted made her feel safe and contented.

On the ride back to her apartment that night, they sat holding hands, and even though he hadn't even kissed her yet, Susan knew that she had just spent the evening with the man she was going to marry. She said demurely, after he had walked her to her door, "Goodnight, Ted."

He responded, "Goodnight, Cinderella," and he kissed her on her cheek. She turned and disappeared into her building.

Standing on the stoop looking at the closed door, Ted said aloud, "I'll wait till you're ready, but we will be married someday."

Chapter Eleven

Susan and Ted dated exclusively for the next several months, though they didn't have as much free time as they would have liked. They both were working hard at their jobs, Ted hating his and Susan loving hers. He spoiled her as often as he could, taking her to Broadway plays, expensive dinners in fine restaurants, even front row center seats for the Ice Capades at Madison Square Garden. They spent a summer weekend in East Hampton at a house owned by friends of Ted's, and they had their share of picnics in Central Park. They texted frequently throughout the days.

In midsummer, Susan asked him if he would like to go to Maine with her for a weekend. She was planning to visit her folks and would love it if he came along. Much to her surprise, he readily agreed. She had asked him to go but never dreamed he would say yes.

Susan called her folks and told them she had met a man who was wonderful and successful and treated her well. She had mentioned him in passing during the past few months, but never indicated the seriousness of their relationship. Now, though, she asked her parents if it would be okay if he came to Maine with her the following weekend. Her mother was disappointed because she had been looking forward to some one-on-one time with her daughter. Now that she had decided to live in the big city, she hardly ever came back home, and her parents missed her. To Susan, though, her mother said, cheerfully, "Why, Susie, we would love to meet your new beau. Tell me about him."

As Susan gushed about Ted, tiny furrows formed in her mother's forehead. "Well, he sounds lovely. We're looking forward to meeting him. What time should we pick you up at the station?" Whenever Susan visited, she always took the bus or train from New York to

Boston and then the bus from Boston to as close as she could get to Oceanside. Her parents picked her up there.

"Well, actually, Mom, we're going to be driving up. Ted has the car his parents gave him for graduation from law school, and it will be so much easier to just drive." Sensing that her mother probably thought a car was a pretty extravagant gift, she quickly added, "Just think, we'll have that much more time to spend together. If we leave right after work on Friday, we can be there by midnight. That will give us all day Saturday and half of Sunday together."

"That sounds lovely, dear. We'll wait up for you." As Mary hung up the phone, she thought, *Here we go.*

On Friday afternoon, Ted and Susan both left work a little early, and he picked her up in front of her apartment. On the drive, she told him all about her home state and her hometown. She told him about the farmhouse she grew up in across from a tidal inlet from the cove. She explained the differences among bays and coves and inlets: "The bay is along the coast, and you can get to the Atlantic Ocean from it, but it's protected from the ocean by lots of islands. The cove is the almost round body of water you get to when you are coming back in from the bay. If you looked at it from the sky, it would look like there was a funnel from the bay into it. Lots of boats are moored in the cove because it's very well protected from the open ocean. The inlet that runs from the cove up past my house is narrow and runs from the cove, under a little wooden bridge that crosses Main Street, and ends about a mile inland. Our house sits along the inlet, but across the road from it."

Ted was amused by her descriptions. "I spent every summer of my life on the Cape and no one ever explained the differences as well as you just did. You should be a tour guide or something."

Susan blushed and continued, "Well, when you grow up on the coast of Maine, it's kind of in your blood." Seeing that Ted approved of what she was saying, she continued, "When we pass from New Hampshire into Maine, we're going to cross over the Piscataqua River Bridge." She no sooner had said it when the lights of the green spans came into view in the dark. "The Piscataqua River divides Maine and New Hampshire. My father would always put his arm on the windshield and announce that he got into Maine first." Susan chuckled at the memory. "And my mother would stretch her leg in the passenger seat as far as she could and claim that her foot was farther ahead than his hand. They would jokingly debate for miles who got back to Maine first." Ted liked the softness in Susan's face when she spoke of her parents and evoked an obviously pleasant memory.

As they approached the middle of the bridge, he saw her stretch her foot as far forward as possible, so he reached up and touched the windshield, claiming that he got to Maine first. She laughed and said, "Close but no cigar, mister. My foot got there first." The debate continued for several miles, and Susan knew that a family tradition would be carried on.

As they drove up the Maine Turnpike, Susan told him about the places they were passing, making them come alive for him—places with interesting names like Ogunquit and Kennebunkport. She told him about the old Ogunquit Playhouse and its storied history, starting in 1933 when, during the country's "Little Theatre Movement," a Broadway showman and his wife arrived in town to open a summer theater. He had connections to both Broadway and Hollywood and was able to entice theater legends to the beautiful seaside town to perform during the summer. On opening night, the Ogunquit Playhouse was a state-of-the-art building that rivaled many New York theaters. During the 1950s, summer stock theater became one of the most popular forms of entertainment in the United States, and it continued for four decades.

Ogunquit was a leader among these summer theaters, providing first-class entertainment to those who might not be able to see the plays performed on Broadway. In the 1980s, summer stock theater began to lose some of its popularity. Ogunquit succeeded where other theaters failed by beginning to produce its own shows. By the turn of the century, a new artistic director had changed the format to all musicals, extended the season into the fall, and added a holiday show produced for The Music Hall in Portsmouth, New Hampshire. Annual attendance has climbed from 40,000 to over 100,000 each season, with most shows sold out. Theatergoers are treated each season to beloved returning stars like Sally Struthers, Carson Kressley, Valerie Harper, and Stefanie Powers. It's now one of the largest nonprofit arts organizations in New England.

Ted was impressed that she knew so much about the theater and asked her why she knew its history. She told him that every summer she and her mother, and sometimes her best friend, Jeannie, would drive all the way to Ogunquit from Oceanside for a play. They would go to a restaurant for lunch followed by a matinee, making it an all-day adventure. It was something she looked forward to every year.

As they approached Kennebunkport, Ted asked if that was where President Bush had his place. She laughed and put on a tour guide voice. "At the Kennebunkport exit from the Maine Turnpike, you follow signs for Kennebunkport. When you reach the quaint New England town, follow Shore Road to Walker's Point where first the forty-first and now the forty-third president of the United States summers with his family at the Bush compound, Walker's Point Estate. As you drive by, you will note the understated but ever-present security for the promontory. The estate consists of a guardhouse at the entrance, a large weathered shingled main house consisting of nine bedrooms, four sitting rooms, an office, a den, a library, a dining room, kitchen, porches, and decks. Next to the main house is a four-car garage, pool, tennis court, dock, boathouse, and guesthouse. The house is surrounded by spacious lawns, including a small sports field for family scrimmages. When a president is in residence, the presidential flag is flown beneath the nation's flag, signifying to locals that the president is there." Amy returned to her own voice and Ted laughed, marveling at her knowledge of her state.

By the time they got to the exits for Portland, Susan was asleep. Ted would have liked her tour guide impressions of the seaside city, but when he looked over at her and saw the way she had snuggled into the seat with her head leaning on the door, he didn't have the heart to wake her up just to satisfy his desire to learn more about Portland.

Susan woke when they exited the turnpike and began traveling north on US Route 1. Ted noticed a tiny furrow in her brow and made a joke about being the only car on the road. Ted could tell that she was eager to see her parents, but the cute way she was biting her lower lip made him think she was nervous about him meeting them. Pulling into town a little before midnight, all was quiet. There were no streetlights, neon shop signs, or traffic lights to illuminate the scene. Ted drove slowly, and Susan spoke only to tell him where to turn. As they approached her house, the porch lights were on, as were most of the lights inside the house. Each window beckoned cheerily into the night. Susan smiled, thinking that her mother must have had to hold her own for all those lights to be burning. Her dad was the type who insisted on a light being turned off if you weren't using it.

Hearing the car coming down the road, her mother woke her father, who was snoozing in his recliner in the living room, and they hurried out to the front porch. Her mom was fussing with her hair and her blouse, smoothing out the wrinkles. Her father just stood sleepily watching the car approach.

The car had barely stopped before Susan jumped out and ran to the porch, arms outstretched. Ted got out slowly, watching the touching reunion, popped the trunk to get their bags, and took his time walking to the house so that the small family could have their private moment. Susan's dad noticed Ted first and said, "Well, young man, we don't want you to think that we have no manners up here in Maine. The small lines by his eyes crinkled as he gave Ted a welcoming smile, hand outstretched. I'm George Ward, Amy's father, and this here is Mary, her mother. You can call us George and Mary if you like."

Ted appreciated the welcome but became uncharacteristically nervous sensing that he was being judged. He hoped, for both his sake and Susan's, that he passed. Being a pretty good judge of character himself, he decided in the moment not to try to impress these people. He would just be himself and hope that was enough.

"It's very nice to meet you, sir," he said, shaking George's hand. Mary broke free of Susan and welcomed him with a hug, saying, "I'm a hugger, Ted. If you plan to be around for a while, you may as well get used to it now." Her laugh was the same as Susan's as she hugged him, smelling of cookies and lavender perfume. Ted felt at peace with these people. If he was honest with himself, he felt calmer in their presence than with his own parents. That was an unsettling thought, one that Ted decided he would have to unpack later.

"Well, Susan can tell you. I'm a hugger too, so bring it on," Ted challenged with a smile. Mary liked him immediately. She just hoped that he wasn't a city slicker type who could morph into whatever character he chose to play. She had read about city people who knew how to do that. They put everyone at ease because they just mimicked what they saw the other person doing. She'd have to pay attention. If he was faking it, she'd know.

"Well, I don't know about you young folks, but I am mighty tired," ventured George. "Let's all go get some shuteye and reconvene in the kitchen in the morning. Goodnight all!" He turned and headed into the house and directly up the stairs. Mary took her daughter's hand, whispered how nice it was to have her back home, and led her into the house, with Ted following, carrying the bags.

They trooped upstairs where she announced, "Ted, this is Susan Elizabeth's room." Pointing across the hall, she continued, pointedly, "And this is yours." She gave a patented mom look that told them she expected them to stay in their own rooms while in her house. Hearing her middle name used, Susan shyly went into her room, and Ted placed her bag on her bed and then quickly went into his room, Mary watching the entire time. After Mary and George's door had closed, Susan called Ted. "I forgot to tell you that there is no hanky-panky in the Ward house." Ted groaned, "Set your alarm for 7:00 a.m. If we don't get to the kitchen before seven thirty, my mother will probably come get us, and that would be embarrassing—for you." Ted told her that he loved her, said goodnight, and each drifted off into their thoughts and to sleep.

Saturday morning came, and Susan and Ted enjoyed a scrumptious New England breakfast with her folks. Sizzling bacon, scrambled eggs filled with cheddar cheese, baked beans sweetened with molasses and brown sugar, and freshly baked blueberry muffins greeted them when they arrived in the kitchen. Cups of strong, hot coffee sat on the table. After everyone related how they had slept, George excused himself and headed into town to open his shop. Susan and Ted spent an hour or so chatting with Mary about New York, their jobs, and their friends. Mary asked Ted about his family, and he downplayed their wealth, merely telling her that they lived in Connecticut and that his father was a lawyer and his mother a stay-at-home mom. Even though Susan knew there was more to them than his basic description, she decided that it was best to defer to his choice to make them seem ordinary.

After helping her mother clean up the breakfast dishes, she asked if it would be okay for her to show Ted the town. She wanted to walk and told her mother that they would grab a bite of lunch in town and be back by midafternoon. Even though Mary was disappointed that they were choosing to spend a good part of the day away from her, she smiled and readily agreed.

The young couple strolled hand in hand down the road toward town. Susan was a little apprehensive about the possibility of running into Bill, but since it was midmorning, she figured the odds were slim. He was probably out on his boat. As they walked, she pointed out friends' houses and answered Ted's questions about the inlet, the trees, and the birds.

Before long, they were in town. "What an amazing place to grow up," he commented as they strolled along Main Street, past the little shops where one could buy all sorts of products made in Maine. They stopped first in Mrs. Ayers's jam shop. She had the best collection of jams and jellies, including one Susan decided Ted had to taste since it was her favorite and something you couldn't buy in New York. Mrs. Ayers made a crabapple jelly to die for. Susan remembered being afraid to eat it for years when she was little, after she had learned that the seeds contain cyanogenic glycoside, which your body metabolizes into cyanide. Whenever her mother would put a dish of crabapple jelly on the table, little Susie would look at it in horror. When her parents would eat it, she was sure they were going to die. It was only as she got older and realized that the fruit of the crabapple is fine that she began enjoying its sweet but tart taste on her toast. She now told Ted about the seeds of the crabapple and he, too, was hesitant to try it. She finally persuaded him, and he pronounced it the best jelly he'd ever had.

"I guess it's like eating fugu," he said, and Susan returned a blank stare. Ted explained, "Fugu is a Japanese delicacy. It's a blowfish, and if you make the smallest mistake when preparing it, it can kill you. If you prepare it correctly, it's delicious."

Susan answered that she had overcome her fear of crabapple jelly. She figured she would stay away from this fugu stuff and stick with lobster and haddock and scallops.

As they walked along Main Street, popping in and out of the shops, Ted felt like he was on vacation. In fact, he said aloud, "This is the kind of place everyone goes for vacation, and you lived here. Was it weird seeing so many tourists in your town every summer?" He was in awe.

"Not really. It was just the way it was. I didn't know anything different." They had made their way to her father's jewelry shop. As they stepped inside, a tiny silver bell tinkled overhead and her father came out of the back room.

"I was hoping that you two would find your way here today," he smiled. "I'm only going to keep the shop open until noon, but this way I get to see you for a few minutes."

George hugged his daughter and shook Ted's hand in greeting. Looking around the shop, Ted was amazed at the quality of the jewelry. Mostly silver and native Maine stones, he saw tourmaline and quartz, topaz and garnet. Delicate pieces were mixed with bolder ones. Now he knew where Susan got the unique jewelry she wore. Discovering that her father had crafted all of the pieces, a twenty-minute conversation ensued on the art of jewelry-making. Ted was genuinely interested, and she was proud of her father's unique talent as he explained the processes to Ted.

After they explored the town, neither of them was hungry, so they decided to surprise her mother and return home. They walked back up the road beside the inlet to the homestead, and as they approached the porch, Susan called out, "Ma, we're home!" She could almost feel the smile she knew was on her mother's face somewhere in the house. Her mother came through the screen door wiping her hands on a towel.

"I thought you two were going to have lunch in town," she said, obviously pleased that they had decided not to do that. "Are you hungry? I could whip up some sandwiches."

Susan groaned and said, "Mom, after that breakfast, I don't think we'll ever be hungry again." She laughed and turned to Ted to make sure he agreed.

"I'm still stuffed," Ted said. "Most of the time I grab a bagel and coffee and don't take time for more than a salad at lunch. I think we ate more for breakfast than I would eat in a day." He then quickly added, "But it was delicious!" He turned to Susan, his eyes twinkling mischievously, and asked, "Do you know how to cook like that?"

Susan assured him that while she did know how, they were not going to be eating that way every day. To her mother, that sounded like a long-term plan, but she just kept smiling and wondering. She had to admit that she did like the easy banter between these two. She liked the way they nonverbally checked with each other often to make sure that they were on the same page.

Susan then motioned to Ted to sit with her on the porch swing.

"Wow!" he exclaimed. "I've seen these in movies, but I've never known anyone who actually had one." Susan found that odd. Just about every house in Oceanside had a porch swing. Ted sat beside her and wrapped his arm around her shoulders—even in front of her mother. His longer legs easily found the porch and pushed them slowly back and forth as Susan curled her legs up on the swing.

"This is nice," Ted murmured. "It's relaxing and calm and really pretty. I just love your quaint little world here, Susan. Seeing you in your element in New York, I never would have guessed that you came from here."

Ted meant it as a compliment, but something about his description made Susan angry. Even though she knew he meant it as a compliment, it sounded more like an insult. Was he belittling her background? Her parents? Her home? Her town? Her way of life? He was smiling, and she decided to let it go. She would think more about it later. For now, she just wanted to enjoy being here in Ted's arms.

Before long, her father's pickup truck came lumbering down the road. He pulled into the gravel driveway and called out, "A little help? Ted, you want to give me a hand?"

As Mary and Susan went into the house to start preparing for a Maine shore dinner, Ted jogged to the truck to help. Together, he and George carried baskets of lobsters and clams, seaweed, and corn on the cob to the backyard where her mother got a fire started in the firepit.

Knowing that the fire was going to have to burn for a couple of hours before it was ready and that the potatoes would take a long time to cook once they were wrapped in foil and buried in the coals, Susan asked Ted if he would like to see her secret reading spot. She took his hand and led him back around the house and up the road a bit. They clambered down over the rocks to a granite shelf situated on the banks of the inlet. It looked like a couch straight out of *The Flintstones* to Ted, and he said so to Susan. This made her laugh, a sound Ted never wanted to stop hearing.

"Whenever I wanted to go someplace private to read where no one would find me, I would come here," she explained. They sat on the rock, and Ted expected it to be uncomfortable and hard. He wondered why she would choose to sit on rocks. Once seated, though, he realized that the slant of the rock behind him formed a supportive back to his seat and was surprisingly comfortable. They kicked off their sneakers and socks and just sat there. Susan told him to look around. From this spot, they were hidden from the road. There were no houses within view across the inlet. The water was shallow at this end of the inlet so no boats would be venturing this far up.

"Wow! This really is a secret hideaway," he said. Then he shot her a lascivious look. "You know. Being this private but outdoors in the sunlight makes this a pretty tempting spot to ravish you."

"Mr. Goldman, that is not why I brought you here," Susan said demurely.

"Really?" Ted wasn't so sure. He reached over and pulled her closer to him, his arm wrapped around her shoulders.

She pulled away slightly, and the two of them sat next to each other, appreciating the natural beauty, the privacy, and each other. Ted reached over and undid the snap on her jeans. She let out a quiet moan which he took as assent and he continued, pulling her zipper down and carefully removing her jeans, leaving her silk panties between her and the stone. He then pulled her sweater up over her head, his breath hitching when he saw that she wore nothing underneath. In seconds, she lay on the warm rock, basking in the sun and in his eyes, nothing but a bit of silk keeping her from total vulnerability. She wasn't even embarrassed. He didn't touch her. He just looked appreciatively and lovingly at her. Ted simply wanted to drink in her toned body.

"I see that you wore a bikini last summer, Miss Ward," he whispered as he traced the outline of her bikini top and bottom with his finger.

With her eyes closed, Susan could feel his gaze. Then he began to lightly trace her shape as he continued to marvel at her beauty. He started at her hairline and traced her face, lightly following his finger with his lips. Then he moved down to her shoulders and traced their outline, allowing a bit of his tongue to follow his fingertips. As he traced her breasts, he lingered, tracing circles round and round until she thought she would explode. *What joy! What pure, simple joy!* He refused the temptation to lower his mouth to her breasts, continuing his journey down her body. He positioned himself slightly differently then, lying at a forty-five-degree angle to her and gently traced her stomach and her hips. As she anticipated the next stop on his trip, she moaned and rose to meet his touch. As she rose, he slid his sweater under her hips, and when she lowered her hips, they came to rest on soft, warm cotton. *This man thinks of everything.*

"Ted," she began tentatively.

But he hushed her. "Shhhhh. Don't say a word, Susan. I want to remember every inch of your body. I'm concentrating." And she quieted.

As Ted resumed his trek, his fingers barely touched her but they took with them the wisps of silk in their way. Now using the silk to tease her, he pulled it down her thighs, gently moving them apart ever so slowly as the silk worked its way to her ankles. When he had them separated, and the silk was lying at her feet, he leaned back and looked at her face. She seemed content and happy. He was sure she really wanted to make love with him. It would finally happen. As though sensing his gaze, she again nodded, her eyes still closed, and her Mona Lisa smile told him everything he needed to know.

Ted turned and hovered above her on his hands and knees. He deftly removed his jeans while balancing on alternating hand and foot then slowly lowered his face to hers to kiss her passionately. They explored each other frenetically with their hands and their mouths as the spring sun baked the rock, and the gentle breeze tickled their skin. Finally, when she didn't think she could stand another minute of this, and he thought he would burst, they joined as one, body and soul.

Lying on the warm rock, the sun toasting their skin, Ted and Susan simply lay still. No words were spoken. They just held each other and breathed in the salty air and each other's scents. Suddenly, in the distance, they heard a cowbell ring. The spell was broken. Susan giggled guiltily.

"Oh, my God! That's my signal to come for supper. When I was little and out playing, my mother would ring that old cowbell, and I would know that wherever I was and whatever I was doing, it was time to go home."

Ted laughed loudly into the sky. "Well, there's nothing like a girl's mother ringing a cowbell to spoil a mood." This made Susie giggle even more. "Please tell me that she never surprised you on this rock doing what we just did." Susan smiled and reassured him that this was the first time her secret reading spot had been used for anything but reading.

The two conspirators got dressed and headed back to the house at a jog.

"Well, it looks like you are about to be treated to an authentic Maine clambake," Susan said, laughing as they jogged into the backyard, flushed and slightly out of breath. "Ma, I was showing Ted my secret reading spot up the road, and we heard your bell and came running. I feel like I'm eight again."

"Well, it's good to know that it still works," Mary replied, cocking her head to one side as she looked first at Susan and then at Ted. *Hmm,* she thought. *I think I caught those two in some hanky-panky.*

Everyone pitched in, and soon the meal was ready. Sitting at a big red picnic table in the backyard, under the shade of the old elm and oak trees, they piled their plates high with lobster and clams and corn. Her mother dug some potatoes out of the coals and placed them on the table.

"We might not be fancy," her father said, "but you will never go away hungry from this house."

This was a real treat for Ted because the only time he ever had lobster was when his folks would spend a few weeks in the summer on the Cape. He had no idea that it was just another meal for some folks.

Susan's mother fussed around making sure everyone had everything they needed. Did they have enough melted butter? Did they need another bucket for shells? Who wanted lemonade and who wanted beer? As she fussed, both she and George watched silently for cues to this relationship. They knew that their daughter's heart had been broken before, and they didn't want it to happen again. This young man seemed to be in love with their daughter. He seemed to want to make her happy. He also seemed to be ambitious and wealthy. Susie was absolutely glowing. She was definitely in love. Their little Susie had changed a lot since going out into the world, and maybe this was the type of man she now needed. Mary hoped his ambition wouldn't eventually blind him to her daughter's emotional needs.

The four of them stayed up late playing Scrabble, talking, and laughing. Ted was treated to stories about Susan's childhood, all of which tactfully left out Bill. When Ted asked about any high school boyfriends, Susan would jump in and tell him that he already knew about her first love, Bill. They had dated in high school and then gone their separate ways since he wanted to stay in town and she wanted to see the world. A look passed between George and Mary at that oversimplification that did not go unnoticed by Ted.

The next morning, after another hearty breakfast, Jeannie and Doug arrived with a toddler and a baby in tow. Jeannie knocked on the door and walked in like she always had, and she was face-to-face with Ted. Blushing, she stumbled over the words but introduced herself and then Doug and asked where Susie was. Ted, ever steady, told them that he was glad to meet them and that Susan was in the kitchen with her mother and father. He turned and led the way. As he entered the kitchen, he exclaimed, "Look who I found breaking into your house."

"Jeannie! Doug! Oh my God!" Susan jumped up and ran to them, embracing them in turn. The baby started crying since he was crushed in the hug. Without skipping a beat, Ted reached in and took the baby, snuggling it onto his shoulder and walking a few steps away to leave the threesome to their reunion. The toddler was happily eating a cookie by now, provided instantly by Mary, who was pleased to see the ease with which Ted had intervened to care for the baby. Not many men would have done that.

Soon, the adults were seated around the table. The toddler was sitting on the floor playing with Tupperware and wooden spoons. The baby was nestled against Jeannie, sound asleep.

"When we heard you were in town, we couldn't let you leave without comin' to say hi," said Doug. "I think if I hadn't drove Jeannie over, she would've walked."

Everyone laughed, but Jeannie defended herself. "Well, Susie is just my best friend in the whole world and, besides, it's not that far anyways."

For a second, it seemed odd for Jeannie to still think of her as her best friend. If Susan was honest with herself, Katie had replaced Jeannie in that spot. She would never tell Jeannie that, though. The beaming smile on Jeannie's small-town face made Susan want to protect her feelings to her dying day.

After everyone caught each other up, with the parents listening in, happy to have the young people in their house again, enjoying the laughter, it was time for Susan and Ted to head back to the City.

"I really hate to be the one to say this, but we have a seven-hour drive in front of us—and that's if we don't hit any traffic. We really do need to get going." Ted hated that he had to break up the obviously good time these old friends were having. "I'll tell you what. I'll go load the car, and that will give you a little more time." Ted got up from the table, as did George, and the two men went upstairs to grab the bags and take them to the car.

George wanted a chance to talk with Ted alone, anyway, so he was pleased. When they were outside, the bags all loaded in the trunk, George suggested that they sit on the porch and give the kids a few more minutes. Both men lowered themselves into Adirondack chairs. Ted sensed a conversation coming.

"Ted, it has been nice to meet you. You seem like an upstanding young man. Of course, no one is ever good enough for a man's daughter, but when I see the way she looks at you and, more importantly, the way you look at her, it warms the cockles of my heart. I've been watching you this weekend. In my mind, a man's measure is in the little things he does, not what he says. I've seen you wait for her before going through a door, pull her chair out for her and not sit until she has. I've seen you touch her arm lovingly when you thought no one was looking. I've seen the glimmer in your eyes when she related a happy memory as though you want her to always be happy. I saw you grab that crying baby just so she could hug her friends. I saw you run to help me with the food. I just wanted to take this opportunity, man to man, to let you know that you are A-OK in my book."

Ted was pleased but surprised too. Her father mentioned some things he didn't even know he had done. He did love Susan. He did plan to ask her to marry him someday soon. He did want to have a family and a life with her. He hadn't planned to broach those subjects yet, though. As he thought for a minute, he realized that there was no time like the present. He said, "Mr. Ward, I do love your daughter with all my heart. I had one chance with her years ago, and I blew it. I know she told you about that. I now have a second chance, and I am not going to mess it up. I want to have a life and a family with her." He paused to let that sink in, and then he continued, "I'm hoping to take her to meet my parents next weekend in Connecticut and not wait too long to ask her to marry me…if I have your blessing." Ted expected to see shock on her father's face, but instead George smiled.

"Ted, you do have my blessing. But, if you hurt her or make me regret this decision in any way, I will hunt you down and make you feel pain." His eyes did not match his words, for his eyes were smiling the whole time. "One other thing: my daughter is an independent, modern woman. If you ever tell her that you asked me for her hand in marriage, she will probably refuse your proposal." With that, George slapped Ted on the knee and got up, going into the house, letting Ted think about that by himself.

On the drive back to New York, Ted gushed about what a great weekend it had been. He told Susan that he felt like he had been on vacation. For her part, Susan was feeling a little put out. She decided to confront him.

"Ted, you are acting like you've been to an amusement park or a circus. That is my life, my family. I find it a little insulting that you think we're all so 'different' and 'interesting' and 'amusing.'" She sat back in her seat and looked out the window.

"Wow! You've got me all wrong, Susan. I really loved it. When something is different from what you know, you tend to look at it differently, don't you? Your world that you consider your everyday life was what I always considered my vacation time. Every summer we would go to the Cape and spend a few weeks living the life that you knew as just plain life. If the truth be known, I'm envious. Wait until you meet my folks. You'll see why."

Ted had not mentioned taking her to meet his parents before. Now that he had, she was a little apprehensive, though the elephant was out in the room now. Ted decided that he would like to take her to Greenwich to meet his parents. After some negotiating on dates and times, they decided to drive out to Greenwich the following weekend.

Chapter Twelve

As they passed along the tree-lined drive, Susie's breath caught when she saw the stately brick colonial in front of them.

"This is your house?" she gasped.

"Yeah, this is home," he replied nonchalantly. "It's just a building, Susan. Don't be judgy. You'll like my parents, I promise. And they will love you."

Susan tried to smile, nervously checked her makeup, and wished she had dressed better for this meeting. Ted had shown up wearing jeans and a sweater, so she had followed suit. Now, in her nicest jeans and blazer, L.L. Bean Back Cove slip-ons on her feet, she felt severely underdressed. She wanted to make a good first impression and wasn't sure that these were the clothes to do that.

"Come on," Ted said quietly as he opened her door for her. He took her hand as they approached the big double doors. Just as he reached for the door, it opened, seemingly on its own, and there stood his parents. Susan almost laughed. Both of them were wearing designer jeans, his mother in a lovely green-and-white-striped Ralph Lauren shirt and navy linen blazer, and his father in a navy three-quarter zip cotton sweater with a light blue polo shirt underneath, collar popped. The whole picture had the feeling of a previously choreographed scene.

Putting her at ease, Ted's mother reached out and gave her a small hug, followed by air kisses on each cheek. "It's about time we got to meet you, young lady," she said, admonishing Ted with her tone. His father stepped forward, put his hand out for a shake, and told her it was wonderful that they could come for lunch. He mentioned that Ted talked about her every time they were together, and he had been wanting to meet her for a long time. Susan could see the appraisal being made as he said this, and she wondered how she was stacking up.

The afternoon that followed was somewhat stilted but pleasant. Susan told Ted's parents her life story, in brief, and her plans for the future. His mother asked her why she had chosen Smith College, something neither parent could understand, since he was a Harvard man and she a Radcliffe woman. Susan had met Radcliffe graduates before, and, even though Smith was as much a Seven Sisters school as Radcliffe, graduates of the latter always felt superior. Susan easily defended her choice by joking that several of her favorite books had been written by Smith graduates and, since she wanted a career in publishing, it felt like a good fit. She began listing them: Margaret Mitchell '22, author of *Gone With the Wind*; Madeleine L'Engle '41, award-winning author of *A Wrinkle in Time*; Betty Friedan '42, author of *The Feminine Mystique*; Sylvia Plath '55, poet and author of *The Bell Jar* and *Ariel*; Margaret Edson '83, teacher and author of the Pulitzer Prize-winning play *Wit*.

"Now, do you see what you've done, Rebecca?" commented Ted's father. "You Radcliffe women just think that there is no better school." He winked at Susan, and she liked him immediately.

"I did not say that. In fact, I didn't say anything. I merely asked this lovely young woman why she had chosen Smith. There was no implication. Smith is a fine school. In fact," she aimed her comment conspiratorially to Susan, "you and I are sisters, right, Susan? We both attended Seven Sisters schools, which gives us a bond for life."

"Okay, Mom, that's taking it a bit far, don't you think?" Ted interjected. "We can all agree that we all attended fine schools. Now, let's move on." Susan flashed him an appreciative smile.

"I'm sorry. You know I love my alma mater," Ted's mother answered meekly. "I'm sorry, Susan, if I put you on the spot. I sometimes get carried away."

"Sometimes?" Ted said with a laugh. "Susan, just ignore her. I'm proud of you going to Smith."

"Well, growing up in a town where I'm the first resident to ever go to a top-tier school, I certainly have never had to defend the choice before." Susan smiled but was sad that Ted's parents didn't think she had made a good decision to go to Smith. She could have chosen

Radcliffe. She really had picked Smith because of its amazing comparative literature department and its illustrious graduates. She also had liked the idea that it was in a small town rather than a big city. She realized that she should have led with that argument.

Luckily, a maid appeared from the kitchen to announce that lunch was being served. Susan was a bit shocked to see that they actually had a maid who announced lunch, but she tried to keep her surprise to herself.

Lunch was more formal than Susan was used to, but she could see by the ease with which Ted dug in that it was normal for him. Forks and spoons and knives for every purpose rested on white linen napkins beside the china plates. There was no food spread out on an oilcloth in the backyard here, no cowbell to call them to the table. Plates were deftly served and removed, and new plates arrived with food artfully displayed. She simply followed Ted's lead, and soon lunch was over.

Susan was used to clearing the table and helping to do dishes, but in this house, she was expected to simply walk away from the table and let others attend to those chores. The four of them retired to a bright sunroom on the rear of the house that overlooked gardens in bloom and a sparkling pool. Off to the side, behind a hedge, Susan could see the upper screens of a tennis court. She remarked on the beauty of the home and was rewarded with an approving glance by Ted's parents. His father proudly announced that someday this would all be Ted's.

For the afternoon, the four of them talked about their work, their hobbies, and plans for the future. Ted surprised her by telling his parents that he hoped to buy a place in Connecticut in a year or two. He was waiting until just the right time. As he said that, he looked at Susan and winked.

Driving back to New York after spending the afternoon with Ted's parents, Susan nervously asked him if he thought his parents liked her.

"You couldn't tell?" Ted was shocked. "They loved you. My mom never would have given you such a hard time about Smith if she hadn't liked you. And my dad never would have stopped her. In fact, just before we left, my mother took me aside and told me that they one hundred percent approve of you. I was shocked."

"You were shocked that they approve of me?" Susan asked incredulously.

"No, no," Ted laughed. "I was shocked that my mother thought that *anyone* was good enough for me. She can be pretty protective."

"Oh," responded Susan simply.

Chapter Thirteen

Susan and Ted returned to New York and to their hectic lives. He worked long hours and often there was no time left at the end of the day for getting together. Susan ate lunch at her desk most days and hoped for a promotion to Assistant Editor someday soon. She took on increasingly more responsibility than her job title would suggest, showing what she could do for the company.

Meanwhile, Ted plugged along at his job, becoming more dissatisfied with it every day. He increasingly wondered why he had rejected his father's offer to join his law firm after graduation. Back then, he had wanted to succeed on his own, to prove that he didn't need his father or his influence. Now, though, with a few years of experience in the real world, Ted understood that his father had made the offer because he knew his son better than Ted knew himself. He knew that working in a successful law firm would offer the panache, the perks, and the monetary rewards that Ted didn't yet know he wanted.

After a few months of this schedule, and Ted's dissatisfaction with his job, Susan asked him how they could change their lives so that they could spend more time together. She missed him, only seeing him on the weekends and an occasional quick dinner. It was as though they had a long-distance relationship, even though they lived in the same city.

Ted decided then and there to take his father up on his offer to join the firm. When he had graduated from Harvard, he had wanted to make it on his own and rejected his father's invitation. Instead, he had taken a job with an investment company as an associate corporate counsel. All he did all day every day was advise team leaders on legal matters related to the company's compliance with securities, real property and other relevant laws, and assess key legal risk areas pertaining to real estate investments and structuring. The work was mind-numbingly dull. Maybe it was exciting for others, but he just couldn't do it any longer. What had Susan said? If you love what you're doing, it doesn't seem like work? Well, his job felt like work. It was time he grew up and admitted he should take advantage of his father's offer, if it were still out there, and join his firm. He knew he would be starting at the bottom of the ladder, but that was okay. Listening to his father talk over the years about the corporate cases he was trying had always been exciting to Ted. He was a quick learner, and it wouldn't take long for him to make a name for himself. After all, he knew all the partners, had socialized with them. Grinning, he picked up his phone and called his father.

"Dad, are you and Mom going to be at home this weekend? I have something important I'd like to talk over with you." His father tried to persuade him to tell him what this conversation was about, but Ted insisted that he wanted to talk in person. After assuring his father that he wasn't in any trouble and didn't need any money, he hung up, satisfied that he had taken the first step on the ladder to success. He saw the kind of life his parents afforded on his father's income and felt that if he was going to get serious with Susan, he should be able to provide her a good life.

The weekend came quickly, and Ted was driving up to Connecticut, rehearsing what he was going to say to his father. When he arrived, his mother was in the garden and his father was sitting in his office going over some files.

"Ted, my boy," his father greeted him and rose to give him a handshake and a hug. "I have been trying to figure out what you wanted to talk about that couldn't be discussed on the telephone and I'm afraid I have come up blank."

Hmm. Getting right to the point, Dad, thought Ted.

"Well, here it is," began Ted. "I have been thinking about my decision to turn down your offer to work at the firm. The more I think about it, the more I realize it was immature and ill-advised." His father held back a smile that was trying hard to emerge. "If the offer still stands, I would like very much to leave my current position and join you." There, he'd said it and not minced words.

His father sat in his chair behind his big mahogany desk and gave Ted no hint of what he was thinking. He just sat quietly for a couple of minutes. Then he said, "And what, may I ask, precipitated this change of heart?" He felt pretty sure that it had something to do with that attractive young lady who had visited with them. He wanted to hear Ted say it, though.

"Well, I just think that when I graduated, I wanted to be independent and make my own way without any nepotism. I landed a decent job and have been working at it for the past few years. Now that Susan and I are getting more serious, and I am thinking about my future, I guess my mindset has changed." He sat back in thought for a minute, deciding whether or not to say anything else. His father, experienced in negotiating, sat still and waited.

Ted's rehearsed speech didn't seem to be enough for his father, so he decided to lay it out in plain English. "Oh, heck, Dad. I was immature and not thinking about my future when I refused your help. Now that I see how the world works and who gets ahead and how they do it, I realize that a little nepotism is a good thing. Not to mention the fact that I hope to ask Susan to marry me someday soon, and I want to provide her with the life I enjoyed, the life you were able to provide for Mom and me. Let's face it. I'm not going to do that working in the place I am now on salary."

His father smiled then, pleased that his son was growing up, becoming a man, and he said so. They spent the next hour discussing the details of what would happen next, and the hoops Ted would have to jump through to join the firm. Even though his father was the senior partner, there were other partners' opinions to take into consideration. When they had reached an agreement and each knew his next steps, there was a light rap on the door. It seemed as though his mother had been listening and waiting for the conversation to conclude.

Ted stayed for an hour or so, visiting with his parents, and then he headed back to the City to tell Susan his good news.

Ted gave his notice the following day and began working at the law firm two weeks later. Susan noticed a change in him immediately. Even though he still worked long hours, he was happier. He seemed to enjoy the work. He enjoyed the benefits of the job as well as the clients with whom he was dealing. He liked seeing his father around the office. He liked being closer to where Susan worked so that they could grab lunch sometimes.

Katie and Susan's two-year sublet was coming to an end. Katie only had the apartment for another few months before her aunt returned. At that time, Susan would have to find another place to live. Would it be with Katie or with Ted? Her problem was solved when Ted arrived one night before Susan got home and found Katie alone.

"Okay, Ted, here's the scoop," Katie began. "You and Susie are obviously crazy about each other. You know that you're heading toward proposing to her. We have this apartment for another few months. If you propose to her now, that leaves just about enough time for her to plan a wedding and for the two of you to figure out where you're going to live. How long can it take to plan a wedding in Maine? It's not like she has to book the Plaza two years in advance." Katie stood staring at Ted who was grinning. "Well, Dimples, what are you going to do?" Ted laughed out loud. Katie had been calling him Dimples since shortly after he and Susan had begun dating. It made him laugh every time he heard it. He just adored this girl. She was the best friend to Susan and had become his friend too.

"Well, Katherine," he began, and she winced at hearing her full name. "As a matter of fact, your timing is, as always, impeccable. Can you keep a secret?" He knew that she could. She nodded. Ted pulled a light blue box out of his jacket pocket and handed it to Katie.

"Oh, you shouldn't have," she quipped. She opened it and there rested an ice cube attached to a platinum band. She gasped. "Ted, this is gorgeous! I love all the tiny diamonds surrounding the big one. Ooo, and there are more diamonds on the band. Nice job. Susie is going to love this," she gushed.

"Well, let's put it away and you forget you ever saw it. This Saturday night, we're going back to the Rainbow Room where we had our first date, and I'm going to propose there."

Katie wanted to swoon. "Oh. My. God. That is so romantic. It's like something out of one of those Hallmark movies Susie loves. 'And they lived happily ever after," she intoned in an announcer's voice.

"Well, you're actually on the right track. When we were there on our first date, Susan said that she felt like Cinderella, and I told her that if I had anything to say about it she was going to live happily ever after. That's why I want to propose there."

"Well, if she says no, I'm available, you dashing, romantic man."

Just then the door opened, and Susan walked in. She saw Ted and Katie standing in the foyer looking like Cheshire Cats.

"What are you two up to?"

They just continued to grin.

"Come on. What are you up to? You're obviously up to something."

Putting on her best Sergeant Schulz voice, Katie said, "I know nothing. I see nothing." She turned and went into her bedroom.

"What was that all about?" Susie was confused and suspicious.

"That was Katie being her dramatic self." Charlie laughed, kissed Susan long and passionately, and changed the subject. "So where do you want to go for dinner tonight?"

Chapter Fourteen

The following Thursday, Ted called Susan at work.

"Hey Susan! Would you like to go out for some dinner and dancing Saturday night?"

"Dinner and dancing? Where can we do that?" Susan stopped short. The only place she knew of where you could have dinner and dance was the Rainbow Room. The only reason she could think of that they would go there was if Ted was going to propose. Katie had been acting suspiciously since Susan found them Monday night. All of these thoughts flashed through her mind in quick succession, and she said to Ted,

"That sounds wonderful. I'd love it."

"Then it's a date," Ted replied. "I need to work on Saturday, but I'll pick you up at seven. And, Susan," he teased. "No slacks and blazer, okay?"

She laughed along with him and agreed that she would be ready at seven on Saturday night.

Saturday night came fast, but the time dragged at the same time. Susan got a manicure and pedicure. She had her hair done in cascading waves and splurged for a professional makeup job Saturday afternoon. When Ted arrived, she greeted him in the same white gown she had worn the last time they went to the Rainbow Room.

"You take my breath away, Susan Elizabeth Ward," Ted gushed. Susan could tell that he was not just saying it to please her.

"You're a vision yourself, James Bond," she retorted. "Why can't men wear tuxedos all the time? If you guys knew what you did to women when you wore those, you would wear them every day. My knees are buckling."

In his best James Bond accent and tone, Ted said, "Well, ma'am. I'm at your majesty's secret service. Goldman. Ted Goldman." Crooking his arm for her to hold, the two left for their magical evening.

Riding up in the elevator to the sixty-fifth floor, hand in hand with the man she loved, Susan felt like she was starring in her very own Hallmark movie. When they were led to a table next to a window looking downtown, she knew that Ted had something special planned. She smiled demurely and exclaimed that the view of the Empire State Building took her breath away. Ted simply smiled, happy that she appreciated his insistence that they be given a table on this side of the room.

After ordering before-dinner drinks, he stood and asked Susan to dance. As they walked to the dance floor, Susan felt that all eyes were on them. Few people were dancing this early in the evening, and she and Ted had plenty of room to waltz around the dance floor, each lost in love for the other. When the orchestra finished the song, the leader asked everyone to please take their seats. Surprised, dancers returned to their tables—all except Ted who dropped to a knee right there on the dance floor. Even though Susan had suspected a proposal was afoot, she had thought it would be a quiet proposal at the table following dinner. This show of public affection took her totally by surprise. Ted took her hands in his and said, loud enough for many to hear, "Susan Ward, I suspected that you were a keeper years ago when you were the damsel in distress who made me feel like your white knight when I was able to take your sadness away for a short time. Years later, fate brought us together again on a rainy evening and I left our next meeting up to you. You called me, and our first date was right here. At the end of the evening when you closed your front door I said to the universe, "I will wait until she is ready, but I am going to marry that girl someday." Well, I'm hoping that someday will be soon. Cinderella, would you do me the honor of becoming my wife and living happily ever after?"

Susan beamed, shook her curls and said, "Of course I will, Prince Charming." Ted placed the ring on her finger, the room erupted in applause, and the orchestra began playing again as Ted and Susan swayed around the floor, joined by well-wishers.

Chapter Fifteen

Summer was a blur of driving back and forth between New York and Oceanside. Often, Susie's mother met her in Portland or Boston to make it easier. When they met in Boston, Susan could take the Acela Express from Penn Station in New York, and three-and-a-half hours later would meet her mother in Back Bay. More often, though, she would borrow Ted's car and drive to Oceanside where she and her mother could settle down in the living room or at the kitchen table or even on the front porch and make plans.

Susan wanted a small wedding, but Ted's parents insisted that there were business associates and friends they just had to invite. Soon, the numbers were totally out of control. Her parents couldn't afford to host two hundred people, nor did Susan want to have so many people attending her wedding, people she didn't even know. She decided that she had to talk with Ted about it.

One afternoon, while sitting on a park bench, taking a break from their walk in Central Park, she broached the subject.

"Ted, whose wedding is this going to be?"

Ted looked confused. "Um, ours?" he asked.

"Right. Ours. Yours and mine. So, when you think of your wedding, what do you picture? Not what you think I want or what your parents want. What do *you* picture as your wedding?"

"Do you really want me to be honest?"

"Yes."

"Well, I guess I'd be happy if we invited our friends and our parents and went to this nice restaurant on the Cape that we've been going to for years. We could get married out on the porch overlooking the water and then have the reception dinner in the restaurant."

"Seriously?!" Susie exclaimed. "That's really what you would like?"

Ted was sure that he was in trouble now. After all, for months, they had been planning a huge wedding.

"Oh, Ted, I do love you," Susan cooed, and hugged him tightly. "Big question. Do you have the guts to tell your parents that? I really don't want a big wedding and I really don't want all these people I don't even know to be there. I know they'll give us nice gifts, but that's not what a wedding is about. It's about two people who love each other standing in front of the people they love and promising to be together forever, to take care of each other, and to be there in sickness and health."

"So you don't want the big circus either? But my parents will be furious."

Susan knew that Ted's parents' wedding had over three hundred people in attendance. She asked Ted now to simply tell his parents that they'd had the big wedding that they wanted. Now it was time for him to have the small one he wanted. Ted agreed, even though he knew that all hell was about to break loose in Greenwich, Connecticut.

The following weekend, Ted drove out to Connecticut to see his folks. Susan had thought it would be better for him to go alone. In reality, she didn't want to be any part of the conversation she knew would be uncomfortable and challenging. When he returned to New York, he stopped at her apartment. Her roommate, Katie was there, waiting with Susan for moral support. Before Susan had a chance to ask, Katie jumped in, "So? What did they say? I don't see any bruises." She laughed. Then she added, "Oh, I forgot. Rich people don't hit with sticks. They hit with words. Did they lay a guilt trip on you?"

Before she could go on, Susan interrupted and asked her if she could go out for a while so that they could make plans. Reluctantly, Katie stormed off, not at all happy to be excluded from this moment and promising to be back soon, arguing that she was the maid of honor and deserved to be in on the details.

"She's really something, isn't she?" Ted asked.

"She's a good friend, has been since college. She knows what I've been through and she really cares. We're more like sisters than friends. So what did your folks say?"

Ted related the conversations that had taken place with each parent, as well as with both of them together, the raised voices and the quiet guilt. He had stayed strong, though, and in the end his parents had agreed to invite only family and close friends. They had said that they were going to blame him and Susan one hundred percent if anyone was upset about not being invited. Ted had told them that was fine with him. This wedding was going to be what he and Susan wanted.

When Susan called her mother later that night, after Ted had gone home, she could hear the relief in her voice.

"Susie, we were going to try to make it work, but I had no idea how that was going to be. This is much more manageable." The wedding list had been cut almost in half. Her mother was surprised when Susie then asked her to cut some of the people she wanted to invite too.

"Mom, we do not have to invite the entire town. If Ted's parents were nice enough to cut out people they wanted to invite, we need to do the same. We'll invite family and close friends, but we'll cut townspeople who aren't close friends, okay?" Her mother reluctantly agreed, and soon the list was down to seventy-five, a number Susan and Ted were comfortable with. It could now be the small-town wedding Susan had always wanted. Her vision began to take shape more easily.

Not forgetting the description Ted had given her of his idea of a perfect wedding, Susan suggested that they hold the ceremony in the town gazebo on the edge of the cove. The setting was lovely, and if townspeople happened to peek in from the edges, so be it. They then could have the reception in a favorite restaurant of Susan's (and now Ted's) in the next town over. It had a large banquet room with a deck that ran around the outside and overlooked the marina. It wasn't fancy, but it was more in keeping with their vision. They would plan the wedding for high tide so that the boats would be afloat, and they would smell the ocean and not the mud. As Susan said the latter, she chuckled at the things that seemed normal to her but strange and different to Ted. She was pretty sure this would be one of them.

Jeannie declared that theirs was going to be a wedding to be remembered, and city girl Katie fell in love with the charm of the place when she visited to get her mind off the news that was in all the papers: Prince Richard was marrying Princess Alexandra. Katie wouldn't admit it to anyone, not even her best friend, but her heart was broken. She and Richard had seen each other whenever she was in England or he was in New York over the past couple of years, always enjoying each other's company and skirting their attraction to each other. Katie knew that he was destined to marry Princess Alexandra, but she held out hope that he would choose love over duty until she saw in the news the plans being made for the royal wedding. She knew she had to get away, and what better place to go than to Maine to be with her bestie.

When Katie arrived in Oceanside, Susan knew immediately that she was heartbroken. She apologized for Katie having to go through all of the wedding plans and be at her wedding at this time. Katie pushed her feelings aside, though, and put a smile on her face. She was determined not to let her own heart ruin her friend's special time.

Finally, the weekend before the wedding arrived. It was a warm August Friday, and Susan rested in the porch swing, reading a magazine and waiting for Ted to arrive from New York. She heard a car coming down the road. Knowing it was too early for Ted to be arriving, and wondering who it might be, she looked up to see a brand-new, bright red F-150 pickup truck. She didn't know anyone who drove one of those. The door opened, and Bill jumped out of the driver's side and ambled up to the porch.

"Hi, Suz," he said, as though no time had passed since their last time together.

"Hi, yourself," she responded, a little put out that he should pick this particular time to happen by. She hadn't seen or spoken to him by design since Jeannie and Doug's wedding, and here he stood in front of her, silhouetted by the sun behind him, his strong, tanned lobsterman's arms glistening in the heat of a late summer's day, and his dark hair falling in his eyes the way she so fondly remembered it.

"I just figured I'd stop by and give you my blessing. I hear you're getting married to some wicked rich city guy, and I wanted you to know that I'm real happy for you. It looks like you're gonna get all you ever wanted out of life. Good luck, Suz. Be happy."

Before she had a chance to say anything, he turned on his heel, hurried back to his truck, revved the engine, and drove down the road. Susan sat bewildered, staring at the dust that lingered after he left.

"What the hell just happened?!" she yelled out loud. Her mother came racing out of the house, scolding her for her language. Taking one look at her, she asked what was wrong.

"What the hell was Bill doing coming here today? I haven't seen or heard from him for three years, and the week of my wedding he decides to come here and tell me that I have his blessing? His *blessing*? *I'll* give him *blessing*! Who the *hell* does he think he is?" With that, she stormed inside, letting the screen door slam behind her and leaving her perplexed mother standing on the porch, watching the dust settle on the road behind Bill's retreating truck.

"That girl doesn't have that boy out of her system yet," she muttered, as a scowl wrinkled her forehead. She decided to go after her daughter.

"Susan Elizabeth Ward, come down here right now," she called up the stairs.

"Not right now, Mom," Susan answered, and her mother could tell she was crying but trying to hide it.

"Right now, young lady."

Susan wiped her eyes, blew her nose, opened her bedroom door, and slowly descended toward her mother who waited at the bottom of the stairs with open arms. Susan hurried down the last few steps and crumpled into those arms.

"Oh, Mom," she sniffled. "Bill ruined everything. I hate him so much."

"I know, I know," her mother purred, still holding her daughter close.

"Why did he push me away, stay away, and then decide to come here today of all days? And what did he mean by saying he gave me his blessing? I don't need his blessing. Who does he think he is?" Susan was getting mad again and pulled away from her mother's embrace. She paced around the living room while she raged.

"Seven years ago, I thought I had my whole life planned. I was going to Smith and Bill was going to USM. We were going to see each other whenever we could during school and spend our summers back here, me working in your store, and him helping his dad out on the boat or working with his mom at the Lobster Shack. Then we'd graduate, and he was going to set up a website for the Shack and market lobsters all over the world and bring tourists here to see the operation. I was going to get a job at a publishing house here. We'd build or buy a little house and get married and have a family and…" her voice faded to a whisper, "he ruined it all."

"Susan, have you talked with Bill about why he did that?" her mother asked quietly.

"No. He never would talk to me. He just told me he didn't love me anymore, that he had to become a man and take care of his mother and his sisters and keep the business going. He didn't want to be with me anymore."

Even as she said the words, seven years of maturity suddenly told Susan the rest of the story.

"He didn't want to stop me from going away to school, did he? He was afraid of holding me back. He did still love me. He lied to me. He wanted to protect me. He didn't think he was good enough as just a lobsterman." These last few sentences came in fits and starts as Susan's tears began again. "Oh, Mom, he might still love me. But I love Ted now. I'm marrying Ted a week from today. I *am* marrying Ted a week from today. Why did he have to come by? Now he's ruined everything." Susan slumped down into a wingback chair, exhausted.

"Susan," her mother began quietly, standing behind her and stroking her daughter's hair. "He hasn't ruined anything. If Bill is your past, Ted is your future. By coming here today, Bill is allowing you to put him in your past. You made a decision to marry Ted, and I've seen how happy you are with him. He makes you laugh. He makes you crazy sometimes. You have similar hopes for your life. When you left here seven years ago, you were a small-town girl. You aren't now. Being in the City has changed you. It's given you a view of the big, beautiful world out there, and you wouldn't be happy in this little town now. I noticed the change when you came back from London, even before you moved to New York. With Ted, you'll have adventure and excitement. He will give you the life you now dream of. We all look back and wonder what might have been. We all think about our first love with fondness, but remember that you are not the girl you were in high school. You're a young woman who enjoys visiting here for a taste of home, but you belong in Ted's world now. Think about it."

Mary kissed her daughter on her head, gave her shoulder a little pat, and went into the kitchen to prepare lunch.

Susan sat quietly thinking about what her mother had said. If she were honest with herself, her mother was right. She did love to visit here but really couldn't imagine living here again. Everyone knew everyone's business. Conversations were always the same. Nothing new happened. If someone drove to Portland to go to a play or dinner, it became the talk of the town. Even the little publishing house in the next town over that had seemed like such a glamorous dream had no appeal for her now. She could become an editor at a big Manhattan publishing house if she and Ted were married. She could write her novel and be a published author.

Seeing Bill was a sucker punch to her gut because she still had feelings for him. She didn't love him. He was her past, her wonderful, carefree past. Ted was her future, her adventurous, exciting future. Her mother was right. She needed to pull herself together and put Bill out of her mind for good. He could live this small-town life if he wanted to. She was moving on up to the East Side, as the song went, to a deluxe apartment in the sky. She even smiled. Then she couldn't get *The Jeffersons'* theme song out of her head. She walked into the kitchen, giggling and singing, "I'm movin' on up to the East Side to a de-luxe apartment in the skyyyyy...." Mary, somewhat shocked at the quick emotional turnaround, wondered for a minute if her daughter was making this decision to marry Ted for the right reasons, brushed that thought aside, and was just happy that her daughter was happy again.

After grabbing half a sandwich from the kitchen counter with her mother scolding her that they were for lunch and lunch would be in a few minutes, Susan ran upstairs as she munched it. She washed her face, put on some makeup, brushed her hair, and went back down to the porch to wait for Ted. She had no sooner sat down on the porch swing when she heard the low roar of Ted's Porsche. She jumped up from the swing and ran to the car to greet him. Almost before he had stopped, she was leaning into his open window and kissing him.

"Wow! I need to stay away more often if this is the greeting I get when I return," Ted said as he quickly got out of the car.

"You, sir, will get this greeting every time you come home for the rest of your life," Susan told him. "If you are gone for a week or a day or just to the store, I will greet you like this when you get home." And she planted a long, loving kiss on him while holding him tightly.

"Well, if you'll excuse me, I'm going to drive to the end of the road and come back," Ted joked as he pretended to get back into his car.

"Oh no you don't. My mom has lunch ready and Daddy is coming home to eat with us." As she said this, she heard her father's old pickup truck approaching. "See? Here he is now!"

Her father pulled up next to Ted's car and shook Ted's hand, gave his daughter a peck on the cheek, and whistled at Ted's car. "Woo-ee, that's a beauty. I think I like it more every time I see it. We don't see many of them around here." Ted thanked him, and the three of them headed into the house for lunch.

The rest of the weekend was spent going over all the details for the upcoming wedding, taking long walks, swinging on the porch swing dreaming of their future together, and sneaking in the occasional walk to her secret reading spot.

Chapter Sixteen

Monday of wedding week arrived. Susan became *The Bride.* Everything revolved around her. Her best friend from home, Jeannie, spent every minute she could with her. It was a little hard for Jeannie, though, because she and Doug had been married in an old-fashioned church wedding and started their family immediately, their honeymoon a weekend in Portland. She already had two little ones at home. It was exciting for her, though, to spend time with her old friend who had left town and now had such an exciting life. Katie arrived midweek in a shiny red sports car, and Jeannie declared that the New Yorkers were invading.

Even though Jeannie was a country mom and Katie a cosmopolitan woman, they got along great, much to Susan's relief. The three of them had long talks, went for final fittings of their dresses in Portland, and talked about Ted. Jeannie didn't know him very well and felt like she was being unfaithful to her friend Bill whenever they talked about Ted, but she had to admit he was a hunk. He looked like something straight out of that *GQ* magazine that she saw on the Hannaford rack when she was checking out. And he was rich. Wow-ee, was he rich! Jeannie just stared at him sometimes, admiring his clothes and his way of talking, the places he'd been. In fact, Doug asked her one day if she was getting gussied up to go see her boyfriend, Ted. She blushed and told him not to be silly, but she really did take extra care when she was going to be seeing him. She wasn't jealous of her best friend or anything, but Ted sure wasn't like any man she had ever met. She didn't want to embarrass her old friend by looking like a hick. She could see why Susie loved him.

One day while the three women sat on the porch, enjoying a few moments of solitude away from wedding plans, Katie told Susan that her aunt was coming back to New York, having eaten, prayed, and loved her way through Asia, and that Katie had to vacate the apartment. Katie had found a smaller place on the Lower West Side, much to her parents' horror. Katie giggled at the thought of their faces when she had told them that she was moving to "the other side of town." Susan, having met Katie's folks on numerous occasions over the years, laughed as well, but poor Jeannie didn't have a clue what they were talking about.

Katie explained that her parents were Upper East Side snobs who didn't think there was any reason to go west of Fifth Avenue except to go to the theater or a concert, or maybe a restaurant. On those occasions, it was only acceptable to take a hired car door-to-door. Jeannie still didn't understand but she nodded politely and smiled, wondering why. She had never been to New York City, and her only exposure to it was from her secret obsession with the television show *Sex and the City*. Those women went all over the City and seemed to have a good time.

At any rate, Katie was glad that her friend had made arrangements for all her things to be moved to Ted's apartment while they were on their honeymoon. Ted had a one-bedroom, one bath with den in an upscale Upper East Side high-rise in the eighties. Susan had arranged with the doorman before she left New York to let the movers in. This conversation was alien to Jeannie, but she listened in awe of a world she knew nothing about. She had a fleeting thought that maybe someday, she and Doug could go to New York City to visit Susie and Ted.

The wedding day arrived, and Jeannie and Katie helped the bride get ready, with Susan's mother flitting around attending to details—a brush of Jeannie's hair, a tuck of a tag into Katie's neckline, a smoothing of the long veil on Susan's back. Soon it was time for the three women to leave to go to the town square. Susan and her father would follow in precisely fifteen minutes.

After the three had left, Susan opened a drawer in her dresser and pulled out a plastic bag. She took out its contents and tucked them deep into her bouquet. *There's my something old,* she thought. *The night I got it I always knew that it would someday be my something old.* She picked up the bouquet and looked at it carefully to see if anyone would be able to see the smudged handkerchief in the center. Satisfied that it was hidden, she grinned and descended regally down the staircase she had run, jumped, hopped, and slid down her entire life. She was elegant in her designer dress, her one concession to New York style. Standing at the bottom of the stairs was her father. She had never seen him dressed in anything more formal than a blue suit on a few occasions, but now he wore a black tuxedo, a white rose in his lapel. His tanned, lined face gazed upward at his little girl as she glided toward him down the stairs.

"Susan Elizabeth," he choked out, "you are a beautiful bride. You look just like your mother did at your age. When I saw you walking down those stairs, I saw your mother for an instant."

"Thanks, Dad. Are you ready? We have a wedding to attend." Susan saw the emotion in her father's eyes and wanted to lighten the mood. "Come on, slowpoke. Do I have to wait all day for you?" She stuck out her tongue at him and breezed past and out the front door.

As Susan and her father arrived at the town square, she noticed the New York and Connecticut limousines and Porsches, BMWs, and Mercedes lined up alongside the pickup trucks, station wagons, Jeeps, and Subarus of coastal Maine. For a minute, she almost lost control of herself. She knew if she started laughing, she wouldn't be able to stop, but all she could think of were the Hatfields and McCoys. She told herself to look at the pretty sunshine, the blue sky, the baskets of flowers lining her walk from the road to the gazebo where Ted stood, looking like he had on their first date, only this time in a bespoke tuxedo made for the occasion.

Before she had time to think, her father was proudly walking her down an aisle lined with baskets of flowers on the freshly mowed lawn, and people were standing in front of their white folding chairs, smiling and whispering how lovely she was. She saw designer on the right and homespun on the left, but everyone was smiling at her. She looked up toward the freshly painted gazebo, and there stood Ted, beaming and mouthing, "You're beautiful. I love you," and she was propelled forward on her father's arm. She saw Katie and Jeannie grinning at her in their matching pink dresses, and almost started laughing again remembering Katie's comment when she had been told she would be wearing pink for the wedding. Katie had opened her mouth and her eyes as wide as she could and simply said, "You have got to be kidding." When Susan assured her that she wasn't, Katie had said that the photographer would have to take lots of pictures that day because it would be the one and only time in her life she would wear pink—and only for Susie. Susie had told her that she could change the color, not wanting to offend her friend, but Katie had assured her that it was Susie's wedding and her word was the law of the land. She warned Susie, though, with twinkling eyes, that if she ever got married, she was going to make Susie wear black.

Susie remembered all of that as she walked toward the gazebo. In a slow-motion blur, Ted had said, "I do" and she had said, "I do," and they were practically running back up the aisle and into a waiting limousine with people racing after them, tossing birdseed at them and the car.

As they pulled away from the town square on their way to the reception, she glanced out the window to take a look at her beloved cove and there, leaning against a telephone pole, stood Bill. He quickly turned away and headed down the ramp, but before he did, Susie saw his face, tears streaming down his weathered cheeks. It was a sight that would haunt her for years.

What have you done? What have I done? Damn you, Bill. How could you tell me that you didn't love me and then cry when I get married? What was I supposed to do? Wait for you forever to change your mind? Well, no, sirree. I am going to live a wonderful life with Ted. He loves me, and we are going to have it all.

Chapter Seventeen

Susan and Ted returned to New York after their fourteen-day Seabourn Jewels of Western Europe honeymoon cruise and realized that living in Ted's apartment was not going to work. Movers had filled every room with Susan's boxes and the few pieces of furniture she had acquired during her time with Katie. Ted opened the door, swept Susan up into his arms to carry her over the threshold, and almost toppled both of them onto the floor as he tripped over a box.

"Well, that was an ignominious entrance, Mr. Goldman," Susan teased, as she righted herself, leaning against another box.

Ted wanted to move a few boxes and try it again, but Susan said that he only had one chance to carry his bride over the threshold, and this was the one they would remember for the rest of their lives.

"Well, okay then, Mrs. Goldman. If you say so."

"I do."

"You already said that at the wedding, remember?"

Susan grinned and said "I do" again. They both tumbled onto Ted's couch laughing.

"What are we going to do with all of this stuff?" Susan asked Ted.

"I don't suppose you'd consider getting rid of it and just staying naked and at home all the time?" Ted teased.

"Um, that definitely is not the solution to this problem," Susan sternly replied.

"Well, you can't blame a guy for trying. In that case, I suggest that we get a good night's sleep, and tomorrow morning head to Connecticut and find ourselves a home."

Susan gasped. "Are you serious?"

Not wanting to tell her his secret, but moved by her excitement at the idea, Ted told her that he had already been working with a realtor in three different towns and had identified several homes for them to see. They actually had appointments for the following day.

"Well, aren't you full of surprises?" Susan leaned over and kissed him long and tenderly, the kind of kiss that would lead to more.

I guess she likes the idea, thought Ted as they rose, still kissing, and headed for the bedroom. *Phew. I didn't know if I was overstepping by taking the lead on this without telling her. Tomorrow we begin the next chapter.*

Chapter Eighteen

Once the movers had set their furniture in place and had dropped boxes in the appropriate rooms, Ted and Susan walked around their new house. Susan could hardly believe that they could afford such a lovely home. From the gleaming hardwood floors to the crown molding, the chair rail in the formal dining room, and the fireplace in the family room, she was in love with the house. The kitchen was her dream. Double ovens stood ready for her to prepare Thanksgiving dinners, and a large granite island waited to be loaded with seasonal goodies. She had never seen a Sub-Zero refrigerator before and was amazed that its doors looked just like the white cabinets of the kitchen—her kitchen. She had to pinch herself to believe that it was true. As she stood at the farmer's sink looking out into the backyard, she imagined barbecues on the brick patio, children swimming in the pool, and swings hanging from the old maple trees.

Ted snuck up and wrapped his arms around her, whispering in her ear, "Are you seeing our children playing out there?"

"Mmm," she murmured, enjoying his nibbles on her neck.

"How about we get started on making that dream come true? The beds are all set up."

Susan spun around. "Ted! Look around at this place! How can you even think of sex when we have so much to do?"

Ted just smiled and said, "Susan, there will always be stuff to do. I want you."

Her lips wouldn't pay attention to her commands, and before she knew it, she was smiling and agreeing. They ran off to the bedroom, to their new king-size bed holding court in the center of the room, attended by bedside tables and a low sofa in the bay window.

"Ted, there aren't even any sheets on the bed yet!"

"Where does it say in the marriage manual that there have to be sheets on a bed for two newly married people to enjoy each other? I contend that there is no such language written anywhere demanding sheets on a bed."

"Well, counselor, I demand sheets on a bed—at least!" Susan exclaimed, and found the box marked LINENS, cut it open, pulled out a fitted sheet, and asked Ted to help her put it on the bed. Knowing that he had lost the battle but was about to win the war, he agreed, and two people never put a sheet on a bed so quickly.

Then, the war was won.

Chapter Nineteen

For several months, Susan and Ted commuted into the City each day for work. He worked longer hours than she did, so she usually made the commute alone. He took an earlier train in and a later train out. By the time he got home each night, Susan had decompressed, but he was tired from work. Sometimes she would cook dinner, only to have him tell her he had grabbed a bite at Grand Central while he was waiting for the train. Sometimes, he was just too tired to eat and would go straight to bed. They couldn't seem to get on the same page, but even when they couldn't talk about their days or have a nice dinner together, when Susan slipped between the sheets, whether he had been awake or not, Ted migrated to her side of the bed. They were newly-weds, after all, and Ted couldn't get enough of her. He also wanted a family and believed that the more they tried, the greater their chances of starting a family. Susan knew that having a child would change everything. It might mean the end of her working in the City, and she loved her job and the atmosphere of the publishing world. She became less interested in trying.

After only a few months in the new house, Susan thought that she might be pregnant. She wasn't sure how she felt about it. She wasn't sure what this would mean for her job or for her marriage or for her relationship with Ted. She saw him working sixty or more hours every week, bringing work home to do over the weekends, and rarely having time for fun. Adding a child to this mix seemed, on the one hand, to be company for Susan. On the other hand, she would have to share the little time she had with Ted.

She saw a doctor during her lunch hour one day and her pregnancy was confirmed. She was surprised that once she knew for certain, she realized that she wanted this baby very much. She knew that her life would change in big and little ways, but that was okay. She was actually excited to see where life would take her next. She spent the afternoon planning how to tell Ted. She left work early and, after making a stop to buy an adorable newborn onesie, headed home where she set the table with their wedding china, crystal, and a vase of fresh flowers she had picked up on her way through Grand Central. She tossed a salad, using baby peas, baby corn, and baby spinach, giggling at her idea. Then she prepared the petite sirloins with baby asparagus and hollandaise sauce, roasted tiny potatoes with Italian spices, and waited for Ted. She had asked him to come home earlier than normal since she needed to talk with him about something important. He had promised that he would be home by seven at the latest. At six thirty, she had his drink mixed and waiting for him. She'd add ice when she heard him come in. At seven, she put the steaks under the broiler and began steaming the asparagus.

Seven came and went. Seven thirty came and went. Eight came and went. At eight thirty, Ted rushed through the door, apologizing for keeping Susan waiting. When she didn't greet him at the door with the usual kiss and hug, he knew he was in trouble. He walked through the kitchen, calling to her but getting no response. Glancing into the dining room, he saw the burned candles and the cut flowers, a wilted salad, and dried out steaks on the plates next to wrinkled asparagus coated in congealed hollandaise sauce. He walked into the family room and there, lying on the couch on a tear-stained pillow, he found Susan sleeping. In her hand, tucked up under her chin was what looked like a baby's undershirt.

Ted fell into the leather chair by the couch. He stared at his sleeping wife and realized that she had planned to tell him that they were going to have a baby. This was probably the biggest night of their lives, except for their wedding, and he had spoiled it by taking one more call at the office after hours. That meant he'd missed the train he had planned to take and, looking at the Cartier watch his parents had given him for Hanukkah, he was ninety minutes late. She had given up on him. She had, obviously, cried herself to sleep. How was he ever going to make this up to her? The answer came quicker than he would have liked. He wasn't. There was no way he could get a redo on this moment, any more than she would let him have a redo on carrying her over the threshold when they returned to the apartment from their honeymoon.

Ted sat and let the news he hadn't heard sink in. He was going to be a father. He had another human being's life in his hands, responsibility for keeping it safe and fed and clothed and educated. He then began to wonder if Susan was going to want to keep working, in which case they would need to hire a nanny. If she wanted to stay at home, his would be the only salary. Until he made partner, he would make a good income but needed to do some planning and discussing with his financial adviser to see if they could maintain their lifestyle on just his salary.

As Ted was musing about their financial well-being, Susan became aware that he was in the room. She was angry and hurt, but mostly disappointed that her surprise had been ruined. She opened her eyes just enough to see through the slits and surreptitiously watched Ted. Seeing his brow furrowed deep in thought, she worried that he had guessed her news and was not happy about it. That was confusing, since he was the one who had been pushing her to start a family. She watched him run his fingers through his hair, purse his lips, and look at the ceiling. This did not look like a man who had just found out he was going to be a father. Her anger subsided, replaced with concern. She opened her eyes and sat up. "Well, I guess you figured out my surprise," she pouted, holding up the onesie for him to see.

Ted, realizing that she was now awake, jumped from his chair and knelt at her feet, his hands on her thighs. "Susan, I am so sorry that I wasn't here for dinner. I had a call that I shouldn't have taken, and the blowhard went on so long that I missed the train and had to wait for the next one. I should have at least called you. I really don't know what I was thinking." Taking the onesie in his fingers, he asked, "Does this mean what I think it means?"

Susan nodded and couldn't keep from smiling. Ted pulled her down on the floor with him, hugging her tightly, and whispered in her ear, "Susan, you have made me the happiest man in the world. We're going to have a little boy or a little girl?"

"Well, those are the only two options so far as I know," Susan replied.

Ted kissed her, and soon they were making up in front of the fireplace. When they were spent, Susan lay on Ted's shoulder and jibed, "You do realize that I'm already pregnant. That doesn't make us have two?" They laughed and all was forgiven—but not forgotten.

Chapter Twenty

The months passed quickly. Susan worked until her ninth month, when taking the train into the City each day became too much for her. Rather than quit her job, she took a leave of absence, giving her a little more time to figure out what she was going to do. During that last month, staying at home all alone, time seemed to stop. She called the office several times a day, waddled up and down the street, and watched movies on television. She puttered in the baby's room, folding blankets, hanging up clothes, and storing diapers in the changing table. She wished that she and Ted had found out whether they were having a boy or a girl because she was a traditionalist and would have painted the room pink or blue. As it was, they had chosen a pale yellow that was pretty, but too gender-neutral for her taste. Several times, she was tempted to call the doctor and ask if her baby was a boy or a girl, but she and Ted had agreed that they wanted to be surprised, and she couldn't weaken now.

One afternoon, about a week before her due date, Susan awoke from an afternoon nap with a pain in her back. Thinking that she may have slept in a strange position, she tried to walk off the pain. Soon, though, she realized that she was having sustained pain every so often. Never having been in labor before, she wasn't sure if this was it or not. She certainly didn't want to be a hysterical female who ran to the hospital with false labor over and over again. Her due date was still a week away. She told herself to wait a while and see what happened. When Ted came home, they could figure it out together.

Just as Susan had decided to wait for Ted to come home, she had a pain that made her double over. Scared that she might be in labor and was alone in the house, she called a neighbor who had been friendly since Ted and Susan moved in. Raye was a little older, had four children, and Susan figured that she would know what to do. The neighbor came over, took one look at Susan who was in the midst of a pain, and called 911.

"There's no reason to call 911," Susan said when she could catch her breath. "I'm probably having Braxton-Hicks and they'll stop soon."

Hearing the siren nearing the house, Raye kindly but firmly informed Susan that this was not Braxton-Hicks. She was in hard labor and might even have the baby in the ambulance. Susan was shocked and scared. Now the sound of the siren approaching was comforting. When the next pain subsided, she called Ted and told him that she was in labor and he should probably come home. Well, actually he should not come home, but get to the hospital where she was going now. She explained that the neighbor had called the ambulance and they were pulling into the driveway.

Ted calmly assured her that EMTs deliver babies all the time and if she didn't make it to the hospital, she would still be fine. He asked her to put the neighbor on the phone. As the EMTs came in, put Susan on a stretcher, and took her out to the waiting ambulance, the neighbor filled Ted in and told him to hurry.

Only because the hospital was just a few miles from Susan's house did she not deliver in the ambulance. They no sooner had her in a bed in the maternity ward when her OBGYN rushed in, telling her to relax. Susan had a pain that she didn't think she could endure. She let out a cry and the doctor checked and saw a little brown-haired head trying to make its way into the world all on its own. With just a single big push, Susan delivered her son.

Susan's labor progressed so quickly that she didn't have time to call her parents to tell them that she was having the baby. After he was born and she had been settled into her bed, she called. Her mother picked up on the first ring.

"Oh, Susan, is it time? I have our bag all packed. You say the word and we're on the road."

"Mom, your grandson's name is Benjamin Ward Goldman, and he is seven pounds four ounces and twenty-one inches long. He has dark hair like his daddy and is waiting to meet you."

"Oh, Susan! You had the baby already!"

Susan went on to explain what had happened, and Mary was sorry that her daughter had to go through that all alone. A mother should be there or a husband. Her poor little girl had to be all alone. She must have been so scared. Thank goodness for the neighbor. To Susan she said, "Your father and I will leave first thing in the morning. It will take us about six hours to get there, so expect us around noon. I just can't wait to see that little bundle. Give him a big kiss from Grammy, okay?"

Susan realized that tears were streaming down her face. Just hearing her mother's caring voice soothed her and released the emotions of the past few hours. She assured her mother that Ted would be there soon and would stay with her until they arrived. He planned to sleep on the couch in her room designed for dads.

"Well, dear, you close your eyes and try to get some rest. Having a baby is exhausting."

By the time Ted arrived at the hospital, their son had been cleaned up, swaddled in a blanket, and was sleeping in a bassinet next to Susan's bed. She had brushed her hair but was wearing a hospital johnny, since in her haste to leave for the hospital, she had forgotten her bag. Ted took one look at mother and son and felt pure joy mixed with sadness. He hadn't been there for Susan when she needed him most. He had missed the birth of his son. He felt like he was failing already, but he felt more love than he thought imaginable. He just stood motionless in the doorway to her room, breathless, carrying a large teddy bear and a huge bouquet of flowers. A nurse arrived and guided him to the chair next to his wife's bed, taking the flowers and the teddy bear from him and placing his son in his arms. Ted whispered to the little bundle that he was going to do better. He was now going to be at home more. And, when he said it, he meant it. He just hoped that it was a promise he could keep.

Ted sat there until Susan woke, just staring at her and at his son. His son. Every time he considered the words, his heart grew. When Susan opened her eyes, he apologized to her. He told her that she was beautiful.

Chapter Twenty-One

T ed's parents arrived a couple of hours after Ted called them. They breezed into the room congratulating Susan and Ted. His father went straight to the bassinet and picked up his grandson. "Well, hello there, little guy. I'm your grandpa. We're going to have great fun together. We'll go to Yankees games and the circus and...." His wife interrupted him and told him he was monopolizing their grandson. She took the baby and told Ted and Susan that he looked just like her Theodore. Not one to show emotion in public, she said that the baby shouldn't be passed around like a football and she placed him in Susan's arms.

Susan's parents arrived the next morning earlier than expected, explaining that they had been too excited to sleep so they had just started driving. They were overwhelmed with joy for their new grandson. "My baby has a baby," Mary mused, and a teardrop landed on his little head.

"Mom, you're getting my son wet," Susan said, and then jokingly reminded her mother that she was in the room too, although she was thrilled that they were so taken by the baby.

Since Ben had been born on a Friday night and came home from the hospital late the next day, Ted was at home with his new family all of Sunday before returning to work. Susan's father left Monday morning too, declaring that he would be back when he could take Ben fishing. Ted brusquely implied that caring for a baby was women's work and that he agreed with George. He said that he would go to work and stay there until the boy could walk and talk and use the potty and feed himself. He laughed, but Susan wondered how much truth there was behind the joke.

Midafternoon on Monday, Katie swished into the house, carrying a baby doll and a blue teddy bear from FAO Schwarz. "Oh, Susie! You look wonderful! You're a mom! I'm an auntie!" She gave Susan a hug and explained, "I'm sorry, I was out of town when he was born. In my hurry to get here today, though, I forgot to ask if the baby was a boy or a girl so I got these." She held out the two gifts and added, "But maybe he'll like having a baby doll. Who knows?"

Mary stayed for two weeks, helping Susan to adjust to caring for her newborn. They bathed the baby and changed his tiny diapers. They dressed him, and Mary offered advice when Susan had trouble nursing him.

Jeannie called a couple of times each day with suggestions and advice. She was sad that she couldn't see him, but was looking forward to the first time the new family visited Oceanside.

Susan's neighbor, her Florence Nightingale, dropped by a few days later to see how mother and son were doing, and Susan gave Raye the enormous gift basket Ted had bought for her to thank her for helping out in the emergency. Susan knew that she had a new friend.

Finally, two weeks had passed, and the new mother felt pretty sure of herself in caring for the baby. It was time for her mother to return to Maine. Susan bundled Ben into his car seat and drove her mother to the bus station. As the bus pulled away, Susan waved Ben's little arm at his Grammy, who was watching them out of the bus window, and Susan saw tears dampen her mother's smile.

"Well, kiddo, it's you and me now. You do your part, and I'll do mine, and we'll make it just fine. And, Ben, get used to me talking to you because you're going to have to listen to my voice for the rest of my life."

Chapter Twenty-Two

Susan, who ultimately quit her job to be at home with her son, spent days alone with the baby and nights alone as Ted came home and fell asleep after a quick bite of dinner and a kiss on Ben's forehead. She decided that this was not going to work, that it was time to make her own new social circle. She couldn't change Ted's habits, but she could change her own. One morning she woke with a brilliant idea. She dressed little Ben in his cutest outfit, put on a nice pair of slacks and a cotton sweater, pulled her hair back into a ponytail—an easier style to maintain with a new baby—put on a little makeup, and took off for the local park. Going old school, she had a notepad and pen tucked into the corner of Ben's carriage, and as she walked she sought other mothers with small babies. If she saw someone who looked nice, she approached and started a conversation about motherhood or the park or even the weather. If the woman was receptive, Susan told her the plan—to collect a group of new moms and meet at the park every morning for a walk and chat. It took several trips to the park that week, but soon Susan had a group of six women who all had babies under three months old. They shared phone numbers and agreed to meet at nine each morning in the park if the weather was good. Susan was elated. She had formed her pack and one for Ben as well. These babies would grow up together.

As the women walked, pushed carriages, and talked each morning, they realized that they had a lot in common. First of all, they had all worked for a living before having their first child. One had been an advertising executive, another a legal assistant. The others were in fashion, insurance, and sales. Each of them had made the decision to take a break from their careers to be at home with their first child and each was going stir-crazy without the stimulation their jobs had provided. As a result, they talked and laughed their way around the park each day, getting exercise for both their minds and their bodies. Susan discovered that she now loved motherhood more than she thought possible.

She no longer felt lonely and sad about being at home. Just two hours a day of conversation was enough to sustain her. She found that she loved her quiet time with her son, who amazed her every day. She watched his eyes as he tracked everything he saw, cooing at the birds and the leaves on the trees blowing in the wind. She was in awe as she read to him, and he looked up into her face with such adoration that she was sure he understood what she said to him.

Within a few weeks, the group of six decided they wanted to go out to lunch. They laughed and joked about how they would do that, logistically, until one of the women stated, "That's not our problem. It's the restaurant's." They agreed on a local place, casual and not usually too crowded. They decided to wait until after the lunch rush and meet at two o'clock. The day arrived, and Susan wished she had been recording the reactions on the faces in the restaurant as six mothers with six babies arrived for lunch. The hostess didn't even blink. She was an older woman and had probably seen it all. She simply ushered them to a table for twelve and instructed a busboy to remove every other chair. Within minutes, they were seated mom-baby-mom-baby around the table. A couple of the babies were old enough to sit in booster seats, while others slept in their strollers (except for Ben who was too busy taking in this new environment). The women had a leisurely lunch and felt like their old selves again. Occasionally one of them would pick a fussy baby up and hold it, not missing a beat in the conversation or the meal. Susan was proud of Ben who simply lay propped up in his carriage so that he could see everything. So long as he could see what was going on around him, he was happy. His little thumb would occasionally find its way to his mouth only to pop out when he saw something that interested him.

Meeting at the park for walks was a daily event and soon going out to lunch once a week became the group's norm. They always got a kick out of the looks on the faces of the other patrons as they broadened their scope of restaurants. Some people were amused, some annoyed, and some just waited for babies to scream and ruin their own lunch. The babies, though, seemed to understand their part in this routine and were beautifully behaved every time. In fact, lunches were such a success that one day, a suggestion was made to go out for drinks. Susan wasn't sure she liked the idea of taking her baby to a bar, but she did miss going out for drinks with coworkers. They each checked with their husbands and, after much discussion, landed on a date when their husbands could all meet them at a local bar that was walking distance from the train station. Babies in tow, the women arrived at the club early in order to stake out enough real estate for their group. They told the host that six men would be joining them soon and were seated in a quiet corner. The corner wasn't quiet for long. It wasn't the babies making the noise, but their parents. The men had been wanting to meet this group of six as well as each other and this was their chance. After a couple of drinks, everyone was sharing stories and the babies appeared so astounded by what they were seeing and hearing that they remained quiet. Susan was enjoying herself but kept watching the door for Ted. Ninety minutes after the time everyone had agreed to meet, Ted came bustling in. Susan could tell that the others were just about ready to leave and was both annoyed and embarrassed, but she kept her cool and simply said, "Well, look what the cat dragged in. Everyone, in case you thought I was making up this husband of mine, here's proof that he does exist." She smiled, but Ted could see the anger behind the smile.

"I'm so sorry, everyone. This dang commuting thing can be a pain sometimes. I missed my train and had to wait for the next one." He then recognized a couple of the other husbands as men who took the same train as he did every morning. The men started up a conversation about work, and the women found themselves back as a group of six, even though their husbands were there.

On the drive home, Ted knew he was in trouble. Susan was silent from the moment she said goodnight to her friends until they got home. He tried several times to apologize for being late, but she just stared straight ahead. When they got home, she took Ben out of his car seat and got him ready for bed. Ted changed and sat in the family room sipping a drink, waiting for her. He knew she would come to find him.

Walking into the room, Susan's anger deflated. She sagged into a chair and just said, quietly, "Ted, I don't work anymore. My friends are my universe. They are important to me, and I was really excited for you to meet them tonight. I was hoping that if you got to know them and their husbands, we might be able to have parties on weekends and enjoy our life. But you couldn't even make a point of getting there on time. I'm beginning to think that Ben and I aren't much of a priority to you."

Ted was shocked. She and Ben were his world, the entire reason he worked as hard as he did. Didn't she know that? By working hard, he could afford to provide her with a nice home in a safe community, the freedom to stay at home with Ben, and ensure that their future would be secure. And she didn't think she and Ben were a priority for him? He didn't know what to say.

Interpreting Ted's silence for agreement, Susan sadly got up and trudged off to bed, leaving a silent, brooding Ted sitting alone with his drink.

For the next year or so, Ted worked sixty or more hours every week. Even when he was at home, he often was tucked away in his office working. She was glad that she had her friends and that Ben had his. Occasionally, she would be able to persuade Ted to attend a group barbecue or party with her, but as often as not he would tell her that he had work to do and that she should go and enjoy herself. He didn't understand how embarrassing it was for her to constantly go places alone when everyone else there had a spouse. She watched the other couples' interaction and saw the little touches and pats of endearment in passing. She saw the offhanded kisses and hugs. She felt lonely. She tried to tell herself that Ted was absolutely loving what he was doing, and that was important. In fact, when he had attributed his decision to go to work for the law firm instead of the investment company to her offhand comment when they first met in the taxi, she was flattered. She remembered telling him that when you love what you're doing it doesn't feel like work. She tried to understand that since she had quit her job, the responsibility for earning a living was solely on his shoulders, and he felt obligated to provide for his family. But still, she was lonely.

Two years later, when Susan found out that she was pregnant again, she wasn't sure how she was going to manage a toddler and a newborn with no help from her husband, but she knew that she would do it somehow. And she did. Ted was rarely there to change a diaper or feed a child. He never gave a bath or dressed a son. If Susan was there, he loved holding his sons and reading to them, tossing them into the air to make them squeal with delight, and cuddling them while he watched a baseball game. But he never spent any time alone with the boys until they could walk and talk and fend for themselves. Susie remembered the joke he had made in the hospital when Ben was born about getting involved when the boy could walk and talk and use the potty and feed himself. She had wondered at the time if it was a joke and, apparently, it wasn't.

Now that David was three and Ben six, Ted was more comfortable being with them alone. She knew that he had never been around children, and his own were the first he had even held, but they were, after all, his sons. She thought that he would have wanted to learn how to care for them, but he seemed happy to relinquish that responsibility to her. He saw himself as the playful dad who made the boys laugh. At least now, if she were lucky, she might be able to run out to go grocery shopping without two children in tow or get her hair cut without having to entertain them in the salon, hoping that they wouldn't get into anything. Ted would stay at home with them for a couple of hours at a time now.

Chapter Twenty-Three

One morning while Ben and David were playing quietly, and Susan was enjoying a good book, she received a phone call from her friend Katie. They had stayed in touch over the years but didn't see each other as often as they would have liked. On this day, however, Katie's voice danced into Susan's ear. "Susie! I don't care what you have planned for today. Cancel it! You are going to have company this afternoon. Put on some decent clothes, apply a little makeup, and get those boys of yours into some nice outfits. We'll be there at two o'clock this afternoon."

Susan was a little put out that Katie would presume to tell her how to dress and invite herself out to Connecticut on such short notice. And that was David's nap time. Hearing the excitement in her voice, though, she just agreed and asked why Katie was coming. She also wanted to know who the "we" were. Katie just laughed, told her that she'd find out soon enough, and hung up. Susan sat staring at her phone. *Katie always adds a little excitement,* she thought. *Why should anything be different now?* She fed the boys their lunch and put them down for their naps. Then she changed out of her jeans and sweatshirt, took off her headband, and pulled her hair up into a respectable ponytail. She applied a little of her seldom-used makeup and thought, *I don't know what you're up to, Katie, but I'm ready for you.*

At 2:02, a limousine pulled into the driveway. Susan looked out her window and saw her old friend Prince Richard hurrying around the back of the car to open Katie's door. Not knowing that Susan was watching them, he pulled Katie up out of the car and into his arms, smiles of love shining on both their faces. *Oh, Katie. This is a new development.*

Susan didn't wait for them to ring the doorbell. She ran to the door, flung it open, and found herself in a three-way embrace, everyone talking at once. After a couple of minutes, she remembered her manners and invited them in.

"Okay, you two. You both look like the cat that swallowed the canary. What's going on?"

Without answering, Katie flung her left hand out and Susan let out a gasp. "What? How?" She then put on her best Desi Arnaz impression, saying, "You two have a lot of 'splaining to do."

Laughing, Richard regained his composure first and told her that he had ioved Katie since he met her years before and, although he felt he had to marry Princess Alexandra, there was no love there. They had tried to believe that a marriage borne of duty was enough, but neither of them felt fulfilled. After a few years, they realized that they could not spend a lifetime in service to the people but with no passion or love in their lives. Richard had started visiting New York more frequently, and Alexandra had begun traveling to Sweden as often as possible. Finally, they had admitted that they each were in love—but not with each other. As difficult as it was, they were granted a divorce and were free to be with the ones they truly loved. Richard leaned over and kissed Katie tenderly.

"Katherine has been the one for me since the day we met. I just didn't want to admit it to myself. It was too complicated. Then you came over to London," pointing his chin at Susan, "and reminded me of what a great girl Katherine was. That made it even harder. Still I went through with the sham marriage. Now, though, Katherine and I are free to live our lives as we see fit."

By now, Susan was beaming with love for her friends, together at last. Before she could congratulate them, Ben and little David came creeping into the living room, David dragging his blanket behind him, sleep still in his eyes. When they saw someone they didn't know in the room, they both stopped and looked at their mother questioningly. Susan jumped up and whisked David into her arms, giving him the happy kisses she had in her heart for her friends. Holding Ben's hand, she then introduced the boys to Richard and reminded them that they knew her friend Katie.

"Do you remember what Daddy and I taught you to do when you meet someone new?" She whispered in David's ear, "Shake hands, remember?" Ben was already walking up to Richard, extending his little hand. Richard got down on one knee and gently shook the little boy's hand, telling him how nice it was to finally meet him.

Ben responded the way his parents had taught him. "It's nice to meet you too." As he said it, he looked back at his mother for approval. She smiled and motioned for him to come to her for a hug.

Putting David down on the floor so that she could give her six-year-old a hug, Susan was surprised to see David walk right over to Richard and put out his little hand to shake Richard's big one. Richard took his tiny hand in his own and told him how nice it was to meet him, too. David smiled, proud of himself, then toddled back to his mother's open arms.

"Well, someday soon we'll have a little one to play with Ben and David," Katie began.

Susan gaped at her friend, her eyes questioning. Katie simply nodded.

"Oh my God, Katie! That's wonderful! So when's the wedding? When are you due? Oh, I have so many questions."

Katie and Richard explained that wedding plans were in motion and since he was divorced, he had been able to obtain approval to be married in the States. "I told my mum that it might be less embarrassing for me to get married quietly in New York, away from the prying eyes of the British press. After much deliberation, she agreed. And furthermore, Katie and I plan to live in New York City."

Susan was ecstatic. She couldn't believe that her best friend was going to be living permanently nearby. She began picturing lunches in the city, their children growing up together, going to plays, to museums.... When she emerged from her daydream, Katie was telling her that the wedding was going to be a small, private affair held at Katie's grandparents' home in the Hamptons in three weeks.

"Three weeks?!" Susan exclaimed. "How did you manage to plan a wedding so quickly?"

"Well," Katie explained, with a mischievous glimmer in her eyes and a wink at Richard, "when I told my mother I was pregnant, she insisted that the wedding take place immediately. She started planning with military precision. In two days' time, she had the venue, caterer, flowers, minister, and music lined up." Katie laughed. "You know my mom. When she sets her mind to something, there's nothing she can't do."

"The apple doesn't fall far from the tree there, does it?" asked Richard. Katie just smiled, planted a sweet kiss on his cheek, and continued.

"My mother had always dreamed of my wearing her dress and since it is a designer, one-of-a-kind dress and I have always loved it, I figured, why not? I was just a trip to the tailor away from having my wedding dress. We could get married tomorrow if we decided to."

"Well, maybe you should leave it at three weeks from now. I need to get Ted's parents to agree to watch my monsters for the weekend, and Rebecca and Thomas have very busy social schedules."

Katie then became more serious. "Susie, there's another reason for our coming here today." She paused and then continued, "I wanted to ask you to be my matron of honor."

Tears welled in Susan's eyes. She jumped up and rushed to Katie, who stood as they embraced. "Of course I will. I'd be honored. I don't have much time to plan a shower, do I?"

Katie assured her that she did not want a shower, nor did she want a bachelorette party. She just wanted to, as she put it, "put the handcuffs on this guy and keep him in my life forever." Richard smiled lasciviously at the image, and Katie punched him in the arm. "You know what I mean," she berated him, smiling all the while.

The next three weeks went by quickly, and soon the wedding weekend was upon them. Susan hadn't asked Ted if he could go to the wedding. She had told him that he would go. Trying to get out of it because of work was not an option. Ted agreed readily, and Susan was looking forward to a grown-up weekend away with him. His parents had jumped at the chance to spend a couple of days with their grandsons, although Rebecca was a little envious of Susan and Ted going to a "royal wedding" as she put it. She made them promise to tell her all about it when they returned.

As Susan and Ted drove up the long hedge-lined driveway of Katie's grandparents' Southampton estate, Susan felt that they were on their second honeymoon. Ted, dressed in his tuxedo, and she in her long-ago-promised black gown, emerged from the car, relinquishing it to the valet, and joined the people who were arriving for the event. Ted headed to a bar while Susan went off to find Katie, who was all dressed and ready to go, even though the wedding wasn't for another hour. Her mother was fluttering around her and nervously hoping that everything was perfect. After all, royalty was in attendance. Katie, meanwhile, was the picture of calm. She was sure of her love for Richard, and her conviction was apparent in her demeanor. Susan stood in the doorway and watched for a minute before announcing her presence.

"Katie, you are ravishing!" she exclaimed. "You're right. That dress is gorgeous. Mrs. Alexander, your dress is magnificent. You must have been a beautiful bride."

Appreciative of the compliment, Katie's mother was quick to point out that Katie was the most beautiful bride ever. Although she had worn the dress first, she was convinced that it was really made for Katherine.

Katie laughed at that and then turned to Susan. "I told you that you would wear black at my wedding," she giggled. You made me wear pink."

Susan laughed out loud and then told Katie that the dress was beautiful and that she thought a black and white theme for the wedding was truly elegant. She added that when she was married, she was younger and still thinking that pastels were all the rage for weddings. Now, she had changed her mind and couldn't think of anything more wonderful than black and white.

"Well, see there, Mother? Susie thinks it's a great idea." Turning to Susan, she added, "My mother didn't think black and white was an appropriate color scheme because women are going to wear white dresses as well as black, and it's gauche to wear white to a wedding. I couldn't care less. I'm the only one in a wedding dress—and I get Richard."

"Well, enough of this chatter, you two," Mrs. Alexander said. "It's time to get this show on the road. Let's go." On cue, they heard a knock on the door, and Katie's father stood there waiting to walk his daughter down the aisle. When he saw her standing in front of him beaming, he remarked that she looked just like her mother had on their wedding day, a single tear finding its way to his cheek. He brushed it away, cleared his throat, and said to his only daughter, "Sweetheart, it's time to marry your prince charming." They joined arms and followed Katie's mother and Susan to the lawn where the guests were seated.

Chapter Twenty-Four

As time passed, and Ted rose to partner in the firm, he could have worked fewer hours and had more time to spend with his growing family. Instead, he came home most nights after the boys were in bed and left most mornings before they got up. He kissed them as they slept and stood over them, knowing that he was missing precious time with them but telling himself that he was doing it for them.

Just when she thought she had this parenting solo gig figured out, when Ben was eight and David was five, when both boys were going to be in school full time, and she had begun thinking about getting back into the publishing world, she discovered that she was pregnant with her third child. She had no idea how that had happened. She had taken precautions. Ted was thrilled. Susan was not. Her hopes of having a career were dashed. In another five years when this baby would be in school, she would have been out of the publishing field for thirteen years—far too long to expect to jump back in. What could she say she had for experience? Reading books to her children?

Susan accepted that she was a full-time and forever-stay-at-home mom. She figured she could now finish writing the novel about her time in London that she had started years earlier. Then the school asked her to be a room mother. She agreed. The PTA asked her to chair a committee. She did. Soon her thoughts of writing slipped away again into the background, and she threw herself into volunteerism. She figured that if she volunteered at her sons' schools, she could still use her abilities and have a connection to them. She would know their teachers and classmates. She could keep tabs on them and pave the way with their teachers. She could prove to herself that she still could do things besides cooking and cleaning and shopping and driving children around.

Her mother-in-law introduced her to the Junior League, and she became involved in their fundraising galas. She enjoyed that work because she could be sure that Ted would attend the events. After all, they were for charity, and it looked good for him to bid on auction items that benefited the charity. He liked that.

She became president of the PTA and used her writing skills to produce an elementary school newspaper filled with information from various classes. She shepherded the yearbook at the middle school, taking it from paperback to hardcover and from forty pages to a hundred. She called her old publishing house and recruited children's literature authors to speak at the school and do book signings. She organized a fashion show, using moms as models and her walking friend who had been in the fashion industry as the procurer of the clothes. Susan kept busy. At times she wondered why she worked so hard at volunteer activities. She never thought too much about it, though. Who had time to think?

Every year, Ted would take exactly one week off from work and would plan a vacation for the family. They were never consulted on where they would like to go, but always had a good time together. One year they went to Disney World and another to a dude ranch in Montana. They were always big, flashy vacations where Ted could have internet access and cell phone reception, and the boys and she could have fun. They did have lots of fun, but he also spent a part of each day working while Susan and the boys went on grand adventures together.

Susan remembered going to Ireland one year, excited because she had always wanted to go there. They stayed in a castle, and Ted worked for a few hours each day while she and the boys explored. One day she suggested taking a bus trip around the Ring of Kerry, and Ted said she and the boys should go. He had work to do. She had a wonderful time, and the boys were mesmerized by the sheepherding exhibition they saw on the way. A border collie ran this way and that on whistle commands, herding the sheep down a hill. When the four of them returned to the castle, they found Ted on the telephone motioning them to be quiet for just a minute. By the time he got off the phone, the boys' excitement had waned, and Susan had to prompt them to tell him about their day.

Occasionally, Susan tried to plan a weekend excursion to Maine to visit her parents. Each time, the prospect was argument inducing. She never could understand why he always had some reason why they couldn't go to Maine to see her folks. They were only a few hours away. If they left at sunrise, they could be there by lunchtime, but Ted always suggested that her folks come to their house instead. They had a comfortable in-law suite over the garage where her parents could settle in and be comfortable, could see the boys in their own environment, and could attend games or shows the boys were in. Susan tried to explain to Ted that her parents ran a store and that her father was an artisan. They couldn't do their work in Connecticut. When the boys were small, once or twice a year Susan would simply load them in the car and drive to Maine for a couple of days without Ted, but it wasn't the same. It embarrassed her to have to explain to her parents why Ted hadn't come, especially since she herself didn't know. Eventually, she stopped going, inviting her folks to Connecticut more often.

When Christmas came around each year, Ted welcomed the grandparents at their home but flatly refused to go to theirs. It didn't matter to his parents since they didn't celebrate Christmas anyway. Ted had agreed that the boys would celebrate all the Jewish and Christian holidays, but hers were never important to him. He didn't realize or didn't care that by inviting her parents for Christmas, they had to shut their shop on Christmas Eve and drive half the night to Connecticut. Susan worried about them on the road on Christmas Eve, especially if it was snowing. Several years they were forced to stay at home and make video calls with the boys on Christmas Day because the roads were too treacherous to make the long drive. They felt left out. Susan was their only child, and Ben, David, and Sam their only grandchildren. Over the years, Susan's resentment grew.

Chapter Twenty-Five

When little Sam was just two years old, Ted's father died suddenly. He had a massive heart attack at the office and didn't even make it to the hospital. Ted was devastated. His mother was lost. Her husband had been her guiding force for thirty-nine years. While Ted was dealing with his own grief, he needed to help his mother put her life back on track. She decided there was no way she could continue to live in their big house all by herself. She and Ted had a long talk, and she told him she wanted to get a condo in Palm Beach. Many of her friends had moved there, and she felt she would be happier if she made a clean break. Ted understood and didn't want to make life harder for her, but he really wanted to ask her to stay close by. Sensing this, she told him that a move for her would be wonderful. They could visit her in Florida and take the boys to Disney World.

After much discussion and explanation, Ted's mother made him an offer he really couldn't refuse. She wanted him to sell his house, and she would sell hers to him for one dollar. He would be able to raise his family in the house in which he had been raised. They would have bigger rooms, a tennis court, a home theater, and a kitchen Susan would love. He told his mother he would discuss the offer with Susan and get back to her the next day.

Ted did discuss the offer with Susan and was surprised to discover that she wasn't sure she wanted to move to Greenwich. It was only a couple of towns away, but it would mean the boys would have to change schools, and she would be farther from her friends. Ted reasoned that Sam was just a toddler. David was only seven years old, and Ben was ten. If they were ever going to move, this was a good time to do it. He reminded her of the gourmet kitchen and the tennis court. He told her how much the boys and he would love the home theater his father had installed a few years ago.

"Can't you see them as teenagers down in the game room playing pool or foosball with their friends, watching a movie, swimming, or playing tennis? They would have so much to do." Besides," Ted added, "it would be awfully nice for the boys to go to my alma mater. The campus is in town and you could drive them all to school each day. It's only a few minutes away."

This wasn't the first time Ted had suggested that he would like the boys to attend the same school he had. Susan did the math and couldn't believe the amount of money it would cost to send all three boys there. Even though Ted assured her that they could easily afford it because they would have no mortgage, Susan was concerned. They would have three children to put through college also. Did Ted plan to start printing money? They argued and debated for days, but in the end, she gave in. Ted told his mother they would happily accept her gracious offer.

The next few weeks were chaotic with maintaining Ben's and David's activities while transitioning them to the idea that they were going to be going to a new school next year—if they were accepted. She and Ted went for interviews, as did Ben and David. She made appointments for them to take the admissions tests and collected their school records for the admissions committee to review. Ted was certain that they would be accepted since he was an alum and since his mother had held many fundraisers for the school over the years. Susan wasn't as sure, and a part of her almost hoped that they weren't. There was absolutely nothing wrong with Greenwich schools. In fact, they were very well rated, among the top five hundred schools in the country with a student to faculty ratio of twelve to one. In only a few days, the letter came informing them that both boys had been accepted. Ted cheered and toasted the boys' success over dinner that night.

Susan was given the job of supervising the move since, in Ted's words, she "didn't work," a phrase that made her blood boil every time she heard it. He may work sixty hours a week but she was on call 168 hours a week, 365 days a year. She took on the responsibility of shepherding the move, though, and made a binder, divided into sections: House Listing; Moving Estimates; Utilities; Medical; School; Mail.... There were lots of sections to the binder, each one with its own distinct purpose, but together they kept her organized. She did not forget to do anything. If the checklist at the front of each section of the binder was fully completed, then she had no doubt that she had remembered everything. She was the creator and keeper of the binder, and though Ted teased her about her excessive organization, she knew he appreciated it.

Just four weeks after Ted's father passed away, Rebecca was ensconced in a two-thousand-square-foot Palm Beach condo with a wraparound terrace that faced the Atlantic Ocean. Her building had its own restaurant, pub, exercise room, and games room. She had a large master bedroom, a guest room, a den, a large gourmet kitchen, and a living room with a water view—all she needed, in her opinion. She was ready to shop, dine out, play mahjong with her friends, and enjoy her senior years in the warmth of Florida.

Susan and Ted sold their home in just two days once they put it on the market and were glad that they didn't have to worry about finding another house. Since Rebecca wanted to start fresh, she took very few pieces of furniture with her. She did take her favorite artwork but left almost everything in the house when she drove away. She didn't think that her northern furniture would fit in her new Florida condo, so she bought all new furniture for it. Susan then had to decide which of her in-laws' pieces to keep and which to sell. The boys wanted their own bedroom furniture, as did she. Ted tried to tell her that his parents' bedroom set was much nicer than the one they had, but Susan could not bring herself to sleep in her in-laws' bed. Ted wisely realized that since he had won the battles of moving to the house and sending the boys to the school of his choosing, he would give in on Susan decorating the house however she wanted.

When they drove up the driveway thirty days later, moving into the house, the boys were quiet. Just before getting out of the car in the three-car garage, David said, "This is going to be weird. This seems like Mimi and Papa's house, not ours."

Susan assured them that in no time at all it would feel like their home, even though she agreed with David. When they all walked in and saw what Susan had done with the house, they felt more at home. She had changed its entire feel, making it warmer, more casual, more welcoming. The boys saw familiar colors, furniture, and artwork, and relaxed a little. Once they made it to their new rooms, they were fine. Susan had recreated their old rooms. Looking out the window onto the backyard, she heard Ben call out to David, "Hey, David! We can play tennis whenever we want without getting Mom to drive us!" She knew the move would be okay.

The family of five fell into a routine in their new home. The boys quickly made friends, and Susan just as quickly was recruited for volunteer positions. Ted continued to work long hours, but as the boys grew, he tried to take part in their lives more, realizing that their child-hoods were rapidly disappearing. If he blinked, they would be gradu-ating and heading off to college, and he would have missed everything.

Much to Susan's surprise, Ted volunteered to be an assistant coach for Ben's baseball team and attended as many of David's and Sam's games as he could. He actually made most of their performances, though he was usually late. She drove and drove and drove, learning her way around town by running everyone's errands, taking the boys to friends' houses, to practices, to games, to rehearsals, and to school each day. When she wasn't driving one of the boys somewhere, taking part in PTA or Junior League meetings, or helping out in classrooms or on field trips, she was cooking meals and shopping for their needs. Occasionally, she was able to meet her old friends for lunch.

When Sam was also accepted by Greenwich Country Day School, Susan thought she would finally be able to write. After all, there were no children at home for five hours each day. Unfortunately, those five hours were easily taken up with her family and community responsibilities.

Chapter Twenty-Six

Susan got the call that every child dreads, no matter how old. When her father phoned her, she was thrilled but wondered why. It was her mother who always called. Then her dad would take the phone and talk for a couple of minutes, handing the phone back to his wife to finish the call. Today, though, it was her father's voice she heard—and it sounded older, sadder, empty. Just the timbre of his voice sent shivers down her spine, and then he said the words she would never forget: "Susie, she's gone. We've lost her."

With no further explanation, Susan knew exactly what he meant. She dropped to the floor in her kitchen, leaning against the cabinets, and asked how. It seems that her mother had been driving home from Portland where she had gone to enjoy a rare weekend away with a friend. It was a girls' weekend and she had looked forward to it for weeks. The night was dark and foggy and her car had gone off the road, flipping until it landed at the bottom of a deep gully. She might have fallen asleep at the wheel or just been confused by the fog, but the ME told George that she would have died instantly. It was sudden and cruel and unnecessary.

Susan listened to the pain in her father's voice and matched it with her own. She told him that she and her family would be there the next day to help him make arrangements, but he told her that wasn't necessary. He knew she was busy in her own life and he would rather take care of it himself. He told her how much he loved her and that he would tell her when the funeral would be, and then he was gone. Susan sat staring at her phone, her tears staining her pants as the drops grew bigger and bigger. She had never imagined a life without her mother, and as she sat on her kitchen floor, she grieved for the time not spent with her mom. She grieved for the Christmases and birthdays and vacations when she did whatever Ted wanted, ignoring her parents' wishes. She grieved for the grandmother who never developed the relationship she had wanted with her grandsons.

Ben was the first to arrive home, having been dropped off by his friend's mom, after having had breakfast at his favorite diner after a sleepover. He found her still sitting on the kitchen floor and had no idea what had happened. He ran across the room and sat down in front of her, asking her what was wrong. Susan noticed him then and reached out, grabbing him into a warm embrace.

"Benjamin, when you get married, please make sure that you still spend time with me and your dad sometimes. Don't get too busy or preoccupied and ignore us. Please?"

Poor Ben was confused, but sensed that his response had to be, "Sure, Mom. Anything you want."

"And, Ben, make sure that even if you don't like your wife's parents, you still let them be a part of her life and a part of your children's lives." Susan looked haunted, scaring Ben into agreeing that he absolutely would do that, even though he wasn't sure what they were talking about.

Susan then realized that she hadn't told Ben what was wrong. She wiped her eyes, blew her nose, stood up, pulling Ben up with her, and said, "Ben, sweetie, I have some terrible news. Nana was in an accident. Her car went off the road in the fog, and she is gone." She then didn't wait for a response, but hugged him tightly.

Just then, Sam burst through the door, excited to tell his mother about the frogs he and his buddy had caught in the pond behind his friend's house. When he saw his mother and Ben hugging, he knew something was wrong but didn't know what or if it involved him.

Seeing her youngest, his face so innocent, big eyes looking fearfully up at her, Susan released Ben and pulled Sam into her arms. "Sammy, Mommy is very sad today because Nana had a bad accident and got hurt and we won't be able to see her anymore."

"You mean she went away?" he asked.

"Yes, sweetheart, she went away to heaven and we will still love her, but we won't be able to visit her, and she won't be able to visit us." Sam still looked confused.

Ben burst out, "Sam, Nana's dead like your pet fish. She isn't alive anymore and they'll have a funeral and bury her in a box like we did for Nemo and Goldy."

Sam's eyes grew wide. He couldn't picture his nana in a box being put into the ground while people who loved her stood there saying nice things about her. While he was trying to figure it out, David came in, wondering what was going on. Everyone looked sad.

"Oh, David," Susan cried out, "I'm glad you're home. I have to tell you something very sad. Ben and Sam know already."

"Did Dad die?" David asked, tears gathering in his eyes.

"Oh, my goodness, David. No!" Susan cooed. "Daddy's fine. I just got a call from Grampy, though, and Nana was in an accident and she didn't make it."

"Nana's dead?" David exclaimed. "Mom, Nana is your mom. Are you okay?"

Susan marveled at her sentimental son. He was always concerned for everyone. She decided to be honest with him, and said quietly, "No, David, I'm not okay, but I will be. I'm very sad, but we'll all be okay." She then realized that she had just dropped a bombshell on her three sons. "Are you guys okay? Do you have any questions?"

Sam was the first to speak—out of the mouths of babes. "Mommy, do we have to see her in a box?"

Susan had a hard time holding herself together at the image that evoked, but she said as calmly as she could, choking back her tears, "Sammy, that's up to you. There will be a funeral and Nana will be in a casket, but if you don't want to see that, you don't have to. Okay, sweetie?" She brushed the hair off his forehead, almost patting him.

"Okay," Sam said, and ran off to play. Susan actually laughed at his quick turnaround, then looked at her two older sons.

"Are you guys okay?"

"Sure," Ben muttered, giving her a quick hug and heading off to think.

"We're okay, Mom," David reassured her. "We really didn't know Nana very much. I'm sad that she died, and I hope it didn't hurt, but it's not as if it was you or Dad."

Susan felt that she had been punched in the gut with her son trying to be brave and make her feel better while, in reality, reminding her how she had neglected her mother. She choked back a sob and told him that she was glad he was okay with it and told him to go to his room and get his homework done. She'd be okay.

Once her three boys had left, Susan realized that she hadn't told Ted yet. She breathed in deeply, bracing herself yet again, and dialed his work number. When she got him on the line, she told him what had happened. He immediately asked if she and the boys were okay and told her how sorry he was. She then heard someone in his office and he was talking to that someone while covering his phone. The words were muffled, but he wasn't talking to Susan. In the middle of the biggest crisis of her life, he had, in effect, put her on hold. Susan hung up the phone without waiting for him to come back to say anything else.

Two minutes later, her phone rang and she saw that it was Ted. She pushed "answer" and said coldly, "Oh, do you have time now for me to tell you my mother is dead?" Ted apologized and told her that they could discuss it when he came home. "Oh, when will that be?" Susan asked, knowing the answer. Ted hesitated and then said that he would be home just as soon as he could get away. She knew that was Tedspeak for "I'll be home when I'm good and ready, when my work for the day is done and I've taken care of everything I want to do here." She sarcastically laughed and thanked him for his consideration, then hung up. He didn't call back.

The funeral was three days later. Susan had the boys dress in their suits and ties, and they left their house before dawn. She was quiet on the drive to Maine, speaking only when spoken to, lost in her memories. The funeral was sad, as she expected it would be, crushing her every time she glimpsed her father's devastated face or glanced at her mother's casket. When her old friends approached her to tell her how sorry they were, she barely held her emotions in check. When Bill walked over, back hunched and a sad empathy on his features, she braced herself.

He simply gave her a brief hug and told her that he would help her father out with whatever he needed.

Susan was about to say that he didn't need to do that because she and her family were there, when Ted approached, telling her that it was time to leave. He ushered her away from Bill and her friends, back to the car. Susan thought they were going to her parents' home, but, instead, she saw that they were heading for the main road out of town. She glared at Ted and asked him why they weren't going to her house. He simply said, "We are," and kept driving toward Connecticut.

Chapter Twenty-Seven

O ne day, when Sam was seven, David was twelve, and Ben was fifteen, Susan found herself sitting in her car in the parking lot of a Little League field trying to decide whether she was going to schlep the team treats to the field or just back her car out and drive away. While she was sitting there, Ted called to tell her that he was sorry, but he wasn't going to be able to make the game after all.

"Ted, you promised Sam you would be here! He's playing short-stop today, and he's excited for you to see him. I don't care what you're doing at work, please drop it and be here for your son."

"Susan, you know I'd like to be there, that I'd rather be there than here in this stuffy office, but I just can't. A big client is coming in and has been delayed. I have to wait until he gets here, and then we need to discuss his case. I'll be lucky to make it home by midnight."

Susan, already near her breaking point, didn't get angry. She quietly asked, "Ted, are you having an affair? I'd rather know than not know."

Ted sputtered, "Susan, how could you ask that? I told you why I'm stuck here. Just explain to Sam that I want to hear all about it in the morning. I'll go in a little late so we can talk at breakfast. How's that? I'm trying here, Susan."

"Yeah, just not trying hard enough," Susan answered almost in a whisper and hung up the phone.

"Well, Sammy boy," she said aloud to the car, "I'm on my way. I'll cheer for you. I always have, and I always will."

She got out of the car, slinging her chair over one shoulder and her purse over the other. She then dragged the cooler filled with Gatorade out of the back, picked up the tray of brownies, and trudged to the field. When she got there, she told the other mothers that she was going to run away from home.

Chapter Twenty-Eight

That night, after driving home from the game, explaining to Sam that his father wanted to be at the game but got stuck at work, Susan thought more about her role in the family. As she was tucking Sam into bed and telling him again what a great job he had done in the game and that his father wanted to hear all about it in the morning, she kept thinking about how easy her husband's life was. He came and went as he pleased. He participated in family life if he chose to but not if it was inconvenient. He took her out to dinner occasionally, but only if he wanted to. Everything in her universe was done on his terms. She was getting rather tired of explaining to the boys why their father wasn't there.

She decided to stay up and wait for Ted to come home and explain to him once and for all that he had to place more of a priority on his family. Unfortunately, he was so late and she was so tired that she fell asleep before he arrived home.

"Honey, wake up. Susan, you fell asleep in front of the television again. I just got home. Come on up to bed." Ted was gently shaking her, trying to wake her.

"No, leave me alone," she growled. I'll just sleep here." Ted shrugged his shoulders, grabbed a bottle of water from the fridge, and stormed toward the stairs.

"Suit yourself," he spat at the dark family room. "Sleep on the couch and get a stiff neck. See if I care." With that, he continued up the stairs, angrily got into their king size bed, and slept another night alone.

Great, thought Susan, lying on the couch. *Now I prefer to sleep on the couch alone than to go to bed with my husband.... What's happening to me? Why am I so dissatisfied? Why does Ted not want to spend time with us? Maybe it's just that I'm turning forty soon. That must be it. Lots of my friends find that they're dissatisfied with their lives when they turn forty.*

Susan's thoughts played devil's advocate with her. *I'm just acting like an ass. I have the perfect life. I have everything I ever hoped to have. I have a husband who loves his children and who works hard to provide for us. I have three sons who are kind and considerate most of the time, who do great in school and don't get into trouble. I have lots of friends and volunteer activities to keep me busy. We go on great vacations and live in a big, beautiful house. We belong to a country club and are respected members of the community.*

Why am I lying here staring at the ceiling night after night? Why doesn't Ted ever hug me or kiss me anymore? Why don't we ever go away for romantic getaways? I know he's had affairs with women at work. Why do I keep forgiving him? Why do I just want to go home to Maine and push the restart button? That's a ridiculous thought. I can't go running home just because the life I thought I wanted isn't the life that makes me happy.

Susan Ward Goldman, you cannot keep thinking these thoughts. You have a wonderful life. You love your boys with all your heart. You never could leave them. They are your world. I know that, but would Ted even miss me? I know there are trade-offs in life. Maybe Ted's not being around as much as I would like is just a trade-off for all of the comfort he provides for us, all of the trappings of a good life. But would he even miss me if I wasn't here? Or would he just miss the way I take care of everything so he doesn't have to? All he has to worry about is his job. Everything else is on my shoulders. And then he has the audacity to keep telling me that I don't work.

Susan began thinking about what Ted might miss if she wasn't there.

Well, who would take the boys to school and their activities and the doctor and the dentist? Who would make sure that everything got done around here? Who would help the boys with their homework and prepare meals and do laundry and clean the house? Who would plan the social at the club and take care of Ted? Who would do the shopping and take the boys to appointments? Who would run the dozens of errands I run every week?

As she lay in the dark, Susan felt her cheeks flush and her hands begin to tremble. Her heart began to race, and the truth of her life hit her. *My God! People could be paid to do almost everything I do around here.*

She tried to admonish herself and tell herself that she couldn't pay someone to be a wife. Then she began wondering if that was exactly what Ted was doing. By providing a beautiful house and expensive car and clothes and jewels and the freedom to shop and charge whatever she wanted, wasn't he paying her to be his wife? Not wanting to accept that this could be true, she told herself there was more to their relationship than what he gave her. When she started thinking about it, though, she thought, *When was the last time Ted and I really laughed? When was the last time we danced around the kitchen just because our song was playing on the radio? When was the last time he hugged me for no reason? When was the last time we put on shorts and walked on the beach? When was the last time we went sailing or hiked in the woods? When was our last picnic?*

After only a moment's honest reflection, Susan realized that they never did any of that. Ted never hugged her any more or kissed her like he used to. They never laughed because they were just being silly. When they were younger, he would walk into a room and grab her to dance with him because he liked the song that was playing on the stereo. He hadn't done that in years. He would rather die than go on a picnic, and they had never walked hand in hand on a beach. She could never get him to go for a walk, let alone a hike in the woods, and even though he had loved sailing as a boy, telling her about his sailing adventures on the Cape with his friends during summers spent there, they had never gone sailing together.

Susan sat up on the couch, staring into the darkness of the night and finally saw the light. *How did I become this person who accepts less from life than I want or deserve? When did stuff become enough? When did I decide that I would simply live the life Ted prescribed for me rather than the life I wanted? Was this ever the life I wanted, or did it just happen to me? Does Ted even love me anymore? Does he even like me? I love him, but I'm not sure I like him.*

With that thought, Susan stood and declared out loud to only herself, "I'm going to run away. I'm going to see if anyone even misses me around here. Maybe if I leave for a while, Ted will remember what we once were and why he chose me in the first place. Maybe I'll remember why I chose him. Maybe I'll remember the kind of person I want to be." She hurried into the kitchen, turned on the light, and sat at the table. She grabbed her laptop and began planning.

Susan wanted to make sure that the boys' needs were taken care of and that they wouldn't have to miss any activities. For the next few days, she researched. She found a laundry and dry cleaner who picked up and delivered. She found caterers who had started a private meal preparation company that would cook a week's meals at a time and deliver them to her home. They would even interview the family members to discover their food preferences and cook meals accordingly. She found drivers to pick up and deliver the boys at their appointed times. She found people to take her place with her various volunteer activities, explaining to each one that she had too much on her plate right now and needed a break. She hired a full-time house-keeper and a college student who wanted some extra money tutoring for two hours each night.

By the end of the week, Susan had hired people to do everything she normally took care of, and no one had any idea what she was up to. She typed out a list of things to be considered, schedules for the next two weeks, love notes to each of her boys, and a lengthy letter to her husband, asking him not to worry about her, but to understand that she needed some time by herself. She reassured him that her feelings for him had not changed (although, in all honesty, she wasn't sure if that was good or bad) and that she would return. She told him that he would have to play a bigger role around the home for the boys while she was away.

When Susan wasn't planning, she spent all her time with her family, running from Sam's baseball game to set building with Ben. She played games with David and took all three boys to a movie they had been wanting to see. She drove them to and from school and to friends' homes. She cooked wonderful meals and lavishly entertained

Ted's partners at a previously scheduled formal dinner at her home. On Sunday, she persuaded Ted and the boys to go for a long walk around the neighborhood. They talked and laughed and tossed a frisbee to each other as they walked. In fact, the day was so pleasant that Susan began to doubt her scheme. But she had planned everything carefully and she had all of the pieces of the puzzle in place, so she decided to stick with her plan. If nothing else, it would be a nice vacation.

On Monday morning, she calmly got out of bed when her alarm rang. She showered, got dressed, and went to wake up her sons. She lovingly jostled each one until they were all awake. She sat calmly on the edge of the bathtub talking with her husband as he shaved and dressed for work. He smiled at her, confused at why she was there but happy that she was. He had always loved it when she kept him company, but she hadn't done that for ages.

As everyone finished getting ready, she ambled down the long, curved staircase and went into her gourmet kitchen to prepare breakfast for everyone. When each member of her family arrived at the table, his favorite breakfast was waiting for him: waffles and strawberries for Ben, blueberry pancakes and hot cocoa for David, cereal and bananas with a glass of strawberry milk for Sam, and a toasted bagel with lox and cream cheese and coffee for Ted. Her sons and husband looked suspiciously at her and Sam asked her if this was a special day. Susan stifled a giggle and replied, "Every day should be special, Sammy. You remember that. Every day should be special." Ted glanced at her over his coffee cup, convinced that she was up to something but enjoying the harmony of the morning too much to ask what it was.

Last week, Susan had asked Ted to take the boys to school on Monday, and he had reluctantly arranged his schedule so that he could. When it was time for everyone to head off, she gave each boy a big hug and a kiss. She told them how much she loved them and that they should always remember that. When it was Ted's turn, she hugged him and cryptically whispered in his ear, "The next time you see me, I am going to be a changed woman."

Ted looked quizzically at her, shrugged, and said, "Just please don't become a redhead. You'd look ridiculous as a redhead."

After they were gone, Susan placed the notes to each of them in the center of the big granite kitchen island. She cleared the table, started the dishwasher, and went to the back hall closet where she took out her packed suitcases and stored them in the back of her SUV. Then she went back in and loaded a cooler with some drinks and snacks. Once that was in the car, she strolled from room to room of her home, remembering happy times spent in each room. After this one last walk around her home, she checked her watch and saw that it was midmorning. When the dishwasher stopped, she put all the dishes away and then went to the garage where she climbed into the SUV, sighed, and attempted to smile at herself in the rearview mirror. She said out loud, "I sure hope you know what you're doing, Susan Ward Goldman." And with that, she drove off down the street, waving gaily to neighbors as she passed by. She couldn't suppress nervous giggles as she thought about the rumors that would fly. These biddies would have a heyday gossiping about the mom who just ran away. Well, let them have their fun. She planned to have hers.

As she drove up I-84, getting farther and farther from her Connecticut life, Susie felt free—and guilty. As she turned off I-84 and onto I-90, the sign read, "Boston-NH-Maine" and she thought *I'm already beginning to feel more like myself. Massachusetts, New Hampshire, and Maine, here I come!*

As Susie crossed the Piscataqua River Bridge and entered Maine, she realized she was hungry. She had been so focused on making everyone his favorite breakfast that she had forgotten to eat. Now that it was lunchtime, she was ravenous. She exited the interstate and merged onto the coastal route in Kittery. She passed touristy shops, outlet stores, and restaurants until she saw Bob's Clam Hut up ahead. Its bright blue facade welcomed her and made her feel like she was home at last. She pulled into the crushed stone parking lot and walked up to the window to order her favorite—clam cakes and sweet potato fries with salt and vinegar. She took her order out back under the trees and sat at a picnic table, savoring the taste of home.

Looking around at the people enjoying their meals, she wondered if their lives were as happy as they seemed to be. *I'm a prime example of not being able to tell what someone's life is really like just by seeing it from the outside. Cheating husbands and unfulfilled lives don't necessarily show on people's faces.* With that thought, she began amusing herself by creating stories for each family she saw. A young couple sitting side by side at a picnic table were, in her mind, eloping. Their parents had forbidden them to see each other, and they were driving out of state to be married. The older couple sitting at the table next to her had just celebrated their sixtieth anniversary, and none of their children had come to visit them. They were sad about that but had each other. The platter of fried clams, scallops, shrimp, and haddock sitting between them was their anniversary meal. The family across the lawn was taking one last family vacation before telling the children that Mommy and Daddy were getting divorced. Both parents were attentive with the children but barely looked at each other.

Susan sat alone, munching on her clam cakes, laughing to herself at her imaginative backstories. *Hmm. Maybe I'll write while I'm in Maine. My imagination seems to be in good form.*

Back on the road, Susan decided to stay on US Route 1 instead of returning to the highway. She passed through small towns just waking up from their long winter's nap. Painters were sprucing up vacant motels. Shop owners were planting flowers. The doors of the majestic Ogunquit Playhouse were wide open, giving the grand lady an airing out after her long snooze and getting her ready for the thousands of people who would flock to be entertained this summer.

In Portland, Susan decided to detour through the city and take a stroll around the Old Port area. Positioned beside the harbor, it was relatively quiet on this springtime Monday, as it too prepared for the coming tourist season. She wandered up and down cobblestone streets, looked in shop windows, and even treated herself to an ice cream cone. Strolling through these familiar streets, licking the black raspberry ice cream from her sugar cone, she felt young again. She didn't have a care in the world. There was no one to pick up. No one was complaining about something she did or didn't do. She wasn't sad to be alone because it was her choice. Being alone when she was at home with Ted was hard, but being alone here by herself felt right. She stood at the end of the Maine State Pier and gazed at the sailboats partying playfully in the harbor, the ferries shuttling passengers to the islands and back to the mainland, and tugboats guiding an oil tanker up to a dock.

Just a couple more hours, she thought. *I'm almost home.* And she found herself getting both nervous and excited about being home again. She found her car and, on her way back to Route 1, she drove up the high hill overlooking Casco Bay, known as the Eastern Promenade. She slowly drove down into Fort Allen Park, holding her breath in anticipation of the scene she knew would unfold before her when she reached the parking area. Slipping her SUV into a parking space, she smiled as she absorbed the beauty of the working harbor with its oil tanker docked on the other side, and a brightly painted yellow, black, and white ferry dutifully making its way out to Peaks Island and beyond. Lobster boats making the rounds of their traps, and sailboats dotting the bay made her smile. Her eyes passed over several of the Calendar Islands, so named because legend says there is an island for every day of the year. (Actually, there are 785 islands, if you count ledges exposed at low tide as islands here in Casco Bay.) Several ocean kayakers were hugging the shoreline, and a flock of tiny white sails identified the sailing school where children were learning to handle the craft. Off to her right, she could see one of the first cruise ships of the season at dock. Merchants would be happy today as hundreds of tourists poured into their shops and restaurants. The ocean's green-blue surface sparkled in the warm sun, and as she opened her window, she breathed in the salty air and was greeted by a couple of greedy seagulls who thought she might be tossing them a treat. They flew right up to her window, startling her. When they realized that she wasn't going to give them anything, off they flew, crying "Mine, Mine." Susan laughed remembering when her father had pointed out to her that gulls' cries sound just like a child crying "mine."

She noticed a flag flying on the six-acre Fort Gorges, a former US military fort on Hog Island Ledge in the middle of the bay. Built from 1858 to 1864, no battles were ever fought there and no troops were stationed there. Advancing military technology, including ironclad ships and long-range guns, made the fort obsolete before it could be used. It still stood proudly guarding the harbor, though, and now had an American flag flying high over it.

Susan decided she had better get going. She continued her drive up Route 1 and could feel her heartbeat pulsing, could hear it in her ears as she drove. Her eyes began to shine every time she caught a glimpse of "her" ocean, more beautiful to her here in coastal Maine than anywhere else. A true smile began to pull up the corners of her mouth and she heard herself sighing over and over again.

As the sun was beginning to set, she approached her hometown. She laughed out loud as Bon Jovi's voice rang out from her radio, seemingly telling her life story:

> *I spent twenty years trying to get out of this place*
> *I was looking for something I couldn't replace*
> *I was running away from the only thing I've ever known*

On the outskirts of town, Susan came across the new Hannaford grocery store that was many times larger than any other shop in town, but as she pulled into the tiny, mostly deserted village she called her childhood home, it was just as she remembered it. Nothing ever changed here. In May, the tourists hadn't arrived yet and driving down Main Street past the Bait and Tackle, past the tourist shops, and over the little wooden bridge that crossed the inlet that ran up past her house, she smiled at the simple beauty. She passed the diner, the Lobster Shack Bill's parents had owned, and her parents' jewelry shop, now closed. She was going to have to figure out what to do with it. At Mr. Gump's general store, she tried to peek behind to where her childhood dock floated. This was the dock represented in the painting her husband had given her. Opening her window, she took in a deep breath and shivered as much from the familiarity of the salty air as from the chilly breeze. She glanced out at the bay and the little cove closer in and the boats bobbing at their moorings. Everything was painted now in reds and yellows by the setting sun, and she saw the *Beautiful Bea* resting for the night at its mooring, its traps stacked and waiting for another day. *So Bill is still here,* she thought and her heart skipped a beat as a flush rose to her cheeks. *Good grief. I can still blush. I haven't done that in a long time. Who would think a high school crush could cause me to blush all these years later?* She looked for *Windfall*, the sailboat she and her friends had rescued, but didn't see it. *Either Doug doesn't have it anymore, or it isn't in the water yet.*

She hadn't been back here since her mother and father had died several months before. Both deaths had been mercifully quick, her father dying of a heart attack that felled him not two months after her mother's accident. *They had both died too young*, Susan thought. She'd always wondered if he had been chopping all that wood alone behind the shed trying to cause a heart attack. Her mother and father had shared a rare love from the time they were kids, and Susan would understand if her father didn't want to live without her. *That's what wedding vows say, but how many people really understand what they mean? Ma and Dad knew what loving each other as long as you both shall live meant, and they fulfilled their promise.* But Susan would never know for sure if her father had intentionally brought on an attack. She just hoped he hadn't suffered. All she knew for sure was that she hadn't been there for him. He'd been all alone.

Bill was the one who had found her dad, ax in hand and a smile on his face. Susan hadn't even been available when the call came. She had left her cell phone at home because she was hosting a ladies' luncheon at her club. She returned home to hear Bill's pained but familiar voice telling her that her father was dead. She remembered sitting on the floor and crying inconsolably for her father, for her parents' love that would make her father lose his will to live without his wife by his side. She cried for her own guilt that she hadn't been there. She cried for the life she missed. She cried from hearing Bill's voice and wanting him to hold her and make it all better. She cried for knowing that, even if she called Ted, he wouldn't come home and hold her.

Susan had cried until the phone rang, unanswered, and she heard Ted's voice leaving her an annoyed message because she had forgotten to pick up the boys from school. Slowly, she had lifted the receiver and said calmly, "Ted, my father's dead," and hung up the phone. Ted had called back several times, but she just didn't want to talk to him right now. She remembered how he had reacted when she had told him of her mother's accident. Finally, his last message said that he was there for her when she was ready to talk. But he didn't come home until much later when his workday was finished.

The next week had been a blur as Ted handled all the arrangements, took care of the boys, and drove them all to Maine for the funeral. Given Susan's emotional state, he had thought it best to whisk her away from Maine as quickly as possible again and they had returned to Connecticut as soon as the funeral was over. They left their home at five in the morning, drove to Maine, attended the funeral, and drove back home, arriving home by nine o'clock that same night. Susan remembered numbly agreeing to do whatever he thought best, but wishing she could spend some time in her home, remembering her days there with her family.

Even her parents' deaths had brought her only briefly to this hamlet. She had dutifully come for the funerals and then, on Ted's advice, had left the details to the lawyer. She had breezed into town, buried each of her parents, and not even stayed to accept the condolences of her childhood friends. When her mother had died, she should have stayed to help her father, but Ted had persuaded her to return home to take care of him and the boys. He told her that her father needed to be alone, to mourn the passing of his wife. Susan wondered if Ted really had just wanted his own needs met.

"Susan," he had said, "this isn't who you are anymore. What can these people possibly have to say that would mean anything to you now?" She had listened to him, knowing all the while that he was wrong. She always listened to him and did whatever he thought was best for her. It was the only way to keep the peace.

Now, though, after running away from home without so much as a discussion or warning, this visit was on her terms. *Not this time,* she thought. *This time I'm going to decide what's best for me. If Ted can't deal with it, then I will have learned something very important.*

Susan pulled into the packed dirt driveway, surprised at how nothing had changed. She got out of the car and stood with her eyes closed listening to the birds in the trees, the water lapping the shore not a hundred yards away, and the sounds of the gulls circling the cove. She breathed in the smells of the ocean and the pine trees and felt contentment wash over her. Opening her eyes, she kicked off her shoes, picked them up out of habit, and neatly placed them on the seat of the car. She walked barefoot through the new spring grass to the front of the house. She noticed the old porch swing still watching over the house and her mother's rocking chair rocking gently in the breeze. The weathered wood seemed to be telling her that her mother was still there with her. As she put her key in the lock, the one she had carried on her keyring her entire life, she half expected her parents to come running to the door to welcome her. She had to remind herself that no one would come. She was alone with her memories.

Susan stepped into the foyer and was young again. This house always made her feel safe, and it was a good feeling—especially now. The sadness she thought she would feel when she reentered her childhood home was, instead, one of tranquility. She felt at peace with the world, as though nothing could hurt her here. There was a lot of love in this house. She felt her parents' love. She felt her love for them and theirs for her. She felt the love of friends who had spent many happy hours here. And, if she were honest with herself, she felt Bill's love here. As she entered, the home's love enveloped her. She wandered through the house, drawing out memories from every room. Making out with Bill in front of the living room fireplace while her parents slept in their bedroom above. Arguing with her father about affairs of the world over the old pine table as her mother filled the kitchen with the smells of home—freshly baked bread, pies, cakes, and cookies. Sitting with assorted relatives and friends at the dining room table for special holidays, eating and laughing and sharing good times. Her parents always had welcomed every stray they knew to join them for Thanksgiving, Christmas, and Easter meals. *That surely is different from our holiday meals now. Ted would never ask anyone to join the five of us. He doesn't want strangers in his house. Heck, he doesn't even want friends or family there for holidays. He really doesn't get the true meaning of generosity and gratitude.* Then the devil on her other shoulder asked her if she had ever insisted or if she had simply agreed to whatever he wanted. She had to admit that she had never put her foot down. She had just assumed that if she agreed with him there would be peace in the home.

Climbing the stairs to the second floor, she was five years old again, going to bed on Christmas Eve, her father telling her that the sooner she was asleep, the sooner Santa Claus would come. At the top of the stairs, she hesitated for a moment. Should she go into her parents' room or should she leave it as it had always been—a private place for just her mother and father? They had always insisted that their room was off limits to her. If there was a raging nor'easter and she was afraid in the night, her mother would go to her and curl up next to her to keep her safe from the storm, or they would trudge downstairs, where her mother would cover her up with an old afghan on the couch and then curl up in the big wing chair by the fireplace to stand guard over her for the night. But she was never allowed to enter her parents' room or crawl into bed with them for comfort. Maybe that was their secret to their many years of happiness. They had a haven that was all theirs.

In the end, as curious as she was about what lay behind the closed doors, Susan decided that she would honor her parents' memory by not entering their private retreat—at least not tonight. She turned toward her childhood room.

When Susan opened the door to her room, she gasped. Her parents had left it exactly the way it was the day she left home all those years ago. Her high school honors hung on the walls. Her pink bedspread still neatly covered her bed, its ruffles somewhat wilted by time. Her stuffed kittens stood guard by her pillows. Her white porcelain cat lamp sat on the bedside table, and her desk still had wedding announcements, notes and cards from friends, and ribbons from her bridal shower hanging from the bulletin board. The now yellowed veil that she wore when she was married hung from the mirror where she had thrown it when she dashed into her room to change for her honeymoon. The only change she could discern was in her closet—the closet stuffed with posters, projects, boxes of schoolwork and report cards, school photos, and love letters from Bill. Her parents must have assumed that someday she would return to clear out her things and tried to make it easier by packing them in here.

Guilt washed over her as she realized that she had not returned long enough to even notice this in the past sixteen years. The dam broke. Tears flowed freely, and she cried for the time she hadn't spent with her parents. She cried for friends left behind. She cried for her "perfect" life with Ted, and she cried for the life she might have had with Bill. She cried until she realized that she was sitting in the dark and hadn't turned on any lights in the house when she arrived. When she thought there were no tears left to be shed, she got up, felt her way to the door, and turned on a light. She then walked back down the stairs and through the house, turning on lights as she went. When she got to the front door, she opened it to get her things from the car and let out a scream that probably brought the bears out of hibernation. There, standing at the door, arm raised as if about to knock, was a twenty-three-year-older Bill.

"Oh my God! I'm so sorry I scared you. I'm Bill Darling, just checking on the…Suz? Is that you? It is!"

"Yes, it's me, and this is my house, and why wouldn't I be here?" she blustered, afraid of the emotion the sight of Bill at her door evoked.

"Well, I was driving by and saw lights going on. I got worried that maybe someone was breaking in and messing things up. The tourists aren't here yet, and no one's out this way at night. I usually drive by just to check on the place. I really liked your folks, and I'd hate to see anything happen to their house. By the time I got to the front door, I heard footsteps. I was about to knock when you opened the door. Sorry if I scared you. I didn't mean to do that."

All of this came burbling out of Bill in one breath. Susan just stood there staring at him. Suddenly, he abruptly changed his tone and yelled, "What the hell do you mean sneaking around here anyway? You haven't been back in all these years, and now all of a sudden you're sneaking around in the dark. Why am I apologizing to you?"

Since Susan had spent the past hour crying, she felt emotionally drained and seeing Bill in this way was not what she had expected. She just stood there dumbly listening to him rant. Then she smiled. She truly smiled. Her face radiated the youth of a teenager as she smiled at him. She looked at the wrinkles around his eyes, his leathered skin drawn about those familiar cheekbones. She noticed his dark hair with its wisps of gray still falling in his eyes.

As Bill barked, "What the hell are you smiling about" she smiled even more. Finally, he got a little worried that maybe something was wrong with her. He calmed down and asked gently, "Are you okay?" When she continued smiling, he asked again, quieter this time, "Suz, are you okay?" She just kept smiling, and now he really was getting worried. He frowned, gently pushed past her, and closed the door behind him. He turned to her and gently took her arm, leading her to the couch where he sat her down and then joined her. Turning to face her, he asked, "Are you okay, Suz? Has something happened?"

As if on cue, Susan snapped out of it, looked up into his eyes, smiled a genuine smile, and said, "Nothing is wrong, Bill. In fact, everything's right. I've got a strange story to tell you if you've got some time." Then she realized she might be overstepping her bounds and added, "That is, if you don't have to get home to your family."

"Suz, I never had a family," Bill said quietly. "I never wanted anyone but you, and even though I tried lots of times over the years, I never could find anyone who measured up to my dream of you. I took care of Ma and my sisters for years, and by then it just didn't seem right to be an old single guy on the prowl. I still live in Ma and Pa's old house out on the point and run Pa's traps. I ended up getting an online degree and somehow got into U. Maine for law school. It was tough but somehow I ran Pa's traps, helped Ma out with the Lobster Shack when I could, saved enough money for the girls to go to school, and graduated. Now I'm kind of the town lawyer. It doesn't pay much, and I have as many people paying me in haddock as in cash, but it's what I always wanted to do. I guess you could say I'm a big fish in a very small pond." He chuckled at his own joke.

Susan just sat quietly taking it all in. So he had helped out his mother, taken care of his sisters, managed to go to college and get a law degree. All this time she thought he had given up his dreams and settled for being a lobsterman—an honorable profession but not his dream.

"That's not what you're used to, I know," he continued. "You're used to the big fish in the big pond. You really did get it all, didn't you? I'm real happy for you, Suz. I knew you'd make it. I have wondered, though, why you're not an editor somewhere. That's what you always wanted. I keep checking on Amazon too. I expected to see a book by now."

Susan wasn't sure what to make of what Bill was saying. She just sat quietly and listened.

"Your folks kept me up to date with your life, and of course Jeannie had to tell me whenever she talked to you. Your folks were always so proud of you. They showed me pictures and tried to reassure me that you were happy so that I could get on with my life. I know they worried about me. After Ma died, your folks were like my own parents."

"Bill, I have something to tell you. You're going to think I'm crazy, but today, early in the morning, I ran away from home. Nothing's wrong. I have a husband who loves me the best way he knows how." Bill cringed silently. *She deserves so much more than that,* he thought.

"I have three great boys who mostly do all the right things. I love them with all my heart and can't imagine life without them. I live in a huge house in Greenwich, Connecticut, and do a lot of volunteer work. I lunch with friends and get my hair and nails done every week. I get massages from Henrik at the club and play tennis with friends, both at the club and at my house. I go to all the 'right' parties. I am, in fact, living the life most people dream of.

"One day I woke up and realized that I had lost myself somewhere along the way. I'm not the country club wife who has to put on a designer jogging suit to go for a walk and makeup on to go grocery shopping. I'm still the girl who would love to sit on the dock in cutoffs and a T-shirt and dangle my feet in the water. I'd still like to listen to gulls with my eyes closed and smell the sea wafting through my window. I'm the one who likes sailing at sunset and going for picnics on the rocks. I like wearing blue jeans and T-shirts and ratty old sneakers and letting my hair blow in the wind instead of covering it up so that my two-hundred-dollar hairdo won't get mussed up." She paused to see Bill's reaction. His brow furrowed.

She continued, "At least that's who I used to be. I really don't know who I am now. So here I am. It's been too long since I felt like me. I love my husband, and I love my kids, and I'm not looking for anything to complicate that, but I just couldn't continue the way I was. I had to get away, to relax and breathe without anyone needing anything from me, if only for a little while."

Susan looked up and saw tears on Bill's cheeks. He brushed them away and leaned over to her upturned face. He took her in his arms, burying his head in her hair, and whispered, "Suz, what are we going to do? I can't stand to see you unhappy. I could handle it when I thought you were good in the life you chose. But I love you. I've always loved you. And now you're here. We're two adults alone in a deserted house. What are we going to do about it?"

Susan sighed and said, "Bill, I came back here to see if I still belonged here or if it's just a place in my past. You're going to have to give me a little while to figure that out. How about you come over tomorrow and we'll talk? I'm exhausted and scared and really don't want to do anything tonight that I'll regret later."

Bill slowly released his hold on her, stood up, reached out a friendly hand, and pulled her up. Standing there holding hands, he deferred to her wishes, saying, "Suz, I don't want to mess up your life. I did that once before, and I will regret it to the day I die. But I'm not going to lose you twice in one lifetime if there's a chance that we can be together. Figure you've had fair warning that I'm gonna do everything in my power to convince you to stay here with me. I'll see you in the morning." He gave her a friendly kiss on the cheek, dropped her hand, and was gone into the night.

Susan stood where she was for a long while, listening to Bill walk down the steps, get into his car, and head off down the road. She waited for the familiar sound of his VW van, but instead heard the roar of an expensive sedan. When she had recovered, she went out to her SUV, unloaded her bags, and brought them into the house. She then returned to her SUV, unloaded the dry goods she had packed, and brought them into the kitchen. Tomorrow she would stop by the new Hannaford in town and pick up fruit and vegetables and some milk. She'd stop by the Lobster Shack and get some fish from Bill's mom. Then she remembered that Bill's mom had passed away—another passage she had ignored—and wondered who was running the Shack now. Putting the food away in the pantry, she wondered aloud what she might have set in motion by coming here.

Susan began talking out loud to herself. "How am I going to get out of this in one piece? What have I done? I couldn't leave a good thing alone. I had to go 'find myself.' Well, now I've found myself in two places, in two lives. Something tells me that there isn't going to be an easy way out of this." She poured herself a glass of white wine and went back into the living room where she threw a match on the logs in the fireplace. They had been sitting there for a while and caught right away. Soon she was curled up before a roaring fire, missing her children, missing her husband...and missing Bill.

Chapter Twenty-Nine

As the sun peeked through the lace curtains of her bedroom, Susan couldn't remember climbing the stairs the night before. The last thing she remembered was sobbing on the couch in front of the fire and drinking wine. She awoke with a furry taste in her mouth and a headache from drinking a whole bottle of wine. Unfortunately, the wine hadn't made her mind any clearer, but with the light of day, she looked forward to a long walk and time for self-reflection. She trudged into the bathroom and took a long shower, washing her shoulder-length hair until it squeaked between her fingers. After she dried her hair, she emerged from the bathroom and dressed in a pair of jeans and a sweatshirt. She pulled on a pair of old white ankle socks she found in her drawer, tied her Sperry Crest Vibe sneakers, and opened her bedroom door. *Why is my door shut? I'm the only one in the house. Why would I have shut my door?*

As she headed down the stairs, she smiled because her mother was cooking breakfast like she always did. The aroma of sizzling bacon, brewing coffee, and baking muffins wafted up to her from the kitchen. Then she remembered that her mother wasn't there. She had passed away just before Christmas. *There's someone in my house. And they're cooking? What the hell is going on?* She then smelled the unmistakable scent of Old Spice. Pushing open the kitchen door tentatively, holding a poker from the fireplace ready to defend herself against this intruder, she saw Bill.

Bill stood in her kitchen with the sun streaming in the windows, and he was creating these amazing smells. He had a towel tucked into his jeans and was humming to himself as he turned the bacon and poured a cup of coffee for her.

"Good morning, sunshine!" he called out cheerfully. "It's about time you decided to join the day. Have a seat. Breakfast is almost ready."

Dumbfounded, she did as she was told, sitting at the already set table. There was even a bouquet of freshly cut flowers in the center of the table in one of her mother's cut glass vases. She just stared at everything, her gaze roaming around the room—looking first at the table and then at Bill, at the coffee pot bubbling away, the bacon cooking on the stove, and then the basket of freshly baked muffins that Bill was taking out of the warming oven. The whole scene had an air of comfort and home, and she felt as though she had drifted into an alternate universe. She knew that this wasn't her world, that Bill didn't belong in it. But he was standing here all scrubbed clean and smelling so good and making breakfast for her.

Ted sometimes made pancakes for the kids, but never for her. His idea of taking good care of her was to look after the kids for a while. Apparently, he figured that if he fed the kids, she was free to take care of just herself and not them. It never occurred to him that she might want him to do something nice like this for her. In all the years she had known Ted, she had never had the luxury of sitting down at the table and sipping coffee while he cooked and served her instead of the other way around. *Score one for Bill*, she thought and then reprimanded herself, reminding herself that there was no competition. She was just taking a break from her life. She wasn't here to decide which life she wanted.

Oh, who are you kidding? replied the devil on her other shoulder. *That is exactly what you are doing, whether you know it or not. You are trying to decide whether you want to stay here or go back.* Susan's brow furrowed, and she looked up from her coffee cup at Bill who was standing at her side.

"Bill, this is really sweet of you, but what are you doing in my house this early in the morning? And how did you get in? And what makes you think that I want you here? And why did you think you could waltz in here as if you belonged here? And did you come up and shut my bedroom door?"

Susan was getting wound up, and her voice was rising, but before she could continue, Bill swept up to her and, with a flourish befitting a finely trained waiter, placed a plate of fluffy scrambled eggs, sizzling bacon, and crispy hash browns in front of her with one hand while depositing the basket of blueberry muffins on the table with the other.

"Well, if you want me to go, I can take my food and leave," he said with twinkling eyes as he saw how greedily she was eyeing the plate and the basket.

"No, that's okay," she muttered. "Just don't make a habit of breaking into my house and cooking for me. Besides, I wouldn't want all of this to go to waste." And with that, she dove hungrily into the breakfast, moaning as though she had been starved and only now knew what a real meal was.

Susan knew that Bill was thinking that she was there to return to him. She sensed that he was trying to get to her heart through her stomach. Bill just sat across from her and smiled, chuckling and refusing to tell her why he was there. As she ate, Bill kept up a one-sided conversation, bringing her up to date on the comings and goings of the past years in Oceanside.

When Susan had finished every morsel of food on her plate, she felt full and content. She hadn't thought about Ted and the kids for a while. She did think she owed it to them to let them know that she was okay. After all, this was her adventure, but she had left them without so much as a hint that she was leaving for a while. She excused herself, telling Bill that she had a call to make and would be right back.

Upstairs in her old room, she sat on the gingham cushion of her window seat, pulling her feet up and leaning back against the wall, marveling at the view out her window. Through the branches of the maple tree, their leaves fresh and new, she could see the sparkling water of the inlet. The sun made the water dance in a way that was familiar and comforting. She dug her phone out of her Gucci bag and placed a call to the landline at her house in Connecticut. When David answered the phone, she wasn't prepared for the guilt she felt upon hearing his voice.

"Hi, sweetie. It's Mom. How are you?" She figured the kids and Ted would be getting ready to leave for school and work about now.

"Mom?! Where are you? Dad is really worried about you, and we're all scared that you're not coming home. What are you doing? Where are you? Are you getting a divorce from Dad?" As David spoke, his voice rose. Before long the other kids and her husband were on the line also.

Ted gave her a chance to explain to the children that "Mommy is just taking a little vacation and will be home soon. Mommies do that, you know. Remember when Mrs. Lyons went to Florida with her friends? The only difference is that I'm taking this vacation alone. You take care of each other and be good, okay? Now let me talk to Daddy." After hearing the clicks as each child hung up an extension, she was alone on the line with Ted.

"Where the hell are you, and what the hell do you think you're doing?" he ranted in a frighteningly calm voice. "You are certifiably insane. Sane women do not just leave home without any warning! Are you okay? I don't give a damn if you're okay. Just get home. Do you hear me? Get back here where you belong. If you think I am going to allow you to simply walk out and leave us with a bunch of strangers taking care of us, you are crazier than I thought." Each word was hushed, measured, calm...and terrifying. "Susan Goldman, you have a family that is worried sick about you. The boys are scared, and it is all your fault. Do you think that you can just run off without any consequences? When the kids start telling people what you did, there will be consequences. You get right back here where you belong. When can I expect you?"

"Ted," Susan calmly replied, "I am very sorry if I have upset anyone. That was never my intention. I will return when I am ready. I have some things to take care of before I can come back. I arranged for all of you to be well taken care of, and you won't even miss me after you stop worrying about what people will think. As soon as I know what I need out of life, I'll be back. As for where I am, that's my business. As for, am I crazy? No. I have never been less crazy in my entire life. I just needed to do this for me. You understand, don't you? I'll see you soon." Before Ted had a chance to argue, she hung up.

Susan sat and waited for him to call her back, but the call didn't come. She knew that the kids would be confused, and she felt bad about that. She loved them and missed them and wondered if their homework was finished and if their lunches would be packed for them. Ted was mad at her and thought she was crazy. Well, that made sense.

What she had done didn't fit into his plan. He hadn't been the one to decide that she should leave; therefore, she shouldn't have left. He had ordered her to return. That was typical. He always had to be in charge. He hadn't once told her that he loved her and missed her. He hadn't said that he was worried about her. He hadn't asked her what was wrong or why she had to leave. Interesting.

As she was thinking, she didn't realize that she had started crying. She heard Bill's voice from below.

"Hey Suz, I need to run to get on the boat. Do you want to come or should I plan on seeing you tonight? It's up to you."

It's up to me, she thought. *There's a novel idea I could get used to.*

"No, you go ahead, Bill. I have lots to do today," she called down to him. "I'll see you when you get in tonight. Be safe, okay?" And Bill rushed out the front door, the screen slamming behind him. From her perch on the window, she watched him jogging to an old pickup truck. She opened the window and called down, "Hey! Thanks for breakfast!" He flashed his still perfectly white teeth at her, jumped into his truck, and drove away toward the cove.

Susan was surprised to see the truck he drove. She knew she had heard the roar of an expensive car last night. This must be his work truck. It suited him.

As Bill drove out of sight, Susan lazily drifted downstairs and out into the sunshine. It was a perfect, spring day. This early in the morning there was still a chill in the air, but the promise of a warmer day was there. Making a decision, she wandered back into the house, threw an old backpack over her shoulder and pulled on a baseball cap from the peg by the door, thinking how nice it was not to care what her hair looked like. She wore no makeup and didn't care. She really had no place to go and no time to be back. All she wanted to accomplish today was to think and get some fruit, veggies, and fish. Bill had, apparently, brought milk because her coffee had been just the way she liked it. With a book tucked in her backpack and some money in her pocket, she headed off.

As she walked down her driveway, the natural beauty of the town where she had spent her entire childhood struck her. When she was growing up here, it was just home. She never understood why the tourists were always visiting in the summer and taking pictures of everything and saying how they had never seen any place so quaint and beautiful. Artists summered here and painted every nook and cranny of the town, from the little cove to the bay and beyond. She had even seen an artist perched on a stool one time painting her house. She stood now in the road and looked back at it from the artist's perspective. It was quintessential New England with its weathered shingles, black shutters, and big farmer's porch complete with porch swing, Adirondack chairs, and her mother's old rocker still standing guard. The three stone steps leading up from the stone path to the porch had tilted a little over the years, but the imperfection gave them a look of charm. The big maple tree provided shade for most of the house in the afternoon but now simply stood sentry—old and proud. She had never realized how picturesque it was. Her old wooden swing that hung from the maple tree's branches on its twenty-foot-long, thick, weathered ropes added to the picture of homespun serenity, and the gravel driveway that headed out behind the house had an air of mystery to it as though its final destination were a secret. *Hmm,* she thought. *That's why that artist painted my house. I kind of wish I knew who she was so I could get the painting.*

For the first time in a long time, Susan just ambled along, not running or jogging or worrying that she was going to be late. She just walked, excited to see where her feet took her.

The miles and years between her and her hometown had opened her eyes to its beauty. She stood and listened to the sounds—the gentle lapping of the water in the inlet on the rocks at the shore, the crying of the gulls as they circled in the distance, following the lobster boats on their rounds, the chugging of the local boats as they headed for today's catch, and the ever-present whisper of the leaves blown by the sea breezes.

Wow! she thought. *I never really thought about how nice it is here. I missed it because it was home, but I never focused on what made it so special. No wonder my parents never wanted to leave. I wish the boys had a chance to get to love it as I did.* She kicked a stone on the side of the road and remembered one of her childhood games. *Why not?* she thought and, laughing out loud, continued on the road toward town kicking the stone as she went. There are many variations of this game: see how far you can kick the rock, see how many times you can kick it without missing a step, pass the rock to another person like a soccer ball as you walk, or just mindlessly kick it while daydreaming, which will ultimately combine most variations. Since Susan had so much to think about today, she found herself mindlessly kicking the stone as she walked, alternately looking at the dark-green water of the inlet with its reflections of the trees and houses at its sides, and the neighbors' houses she passed.

As she walked, she realized that a sadness she didn't even know she had felt was falling away. Since it was rare for people to leave town, she thought about her old neighbors and wondered if any of them still lived here. She soon got her answer. Over there on the left, Mrs. Ayers was hanging out her laundry to dry. *Look how those crisp white sheets blow in the breeze. They will smell so good when she takes them in this afternoon*, Susan thought. *In suburban Connecticut no one would be caught dead hanging clothes on a clothesline.* It was considered lower class, but Susan suspected it might just be too much work. *Well, they don't know what they're missing.*

Up ahead, a couple of dogs were chasing each other and barking. She didn't see an owner, but that didn't surprise her. There were no leash laws here like you have in the suburbs and cities, and the local dogs were free to roam and play with each other as well as with anyone they met. Everyone in town knew everyone else's dogs and watched out for them. As she approached, she saw first the black lab and then the golden retriever sniff the air, trying to decide whether she was friend or foe. When she tossed a stick into the water for them, they decided that she was definitely a friend and raced off down the rocks and into the water to retrieve the stick for her. The golden was the first to reach the stick, and when he had deposited it at her feet, along with a shake of water that splashed all over her, the black one looked sad, as though he had disappointed his new friend by not being the one to do her bidding. She tossed the stick many times, and each time the two pals rushed to get it. They each had several turns and finally, as they both returned, wet and shaking, she reached out and ruffled their wet fur, talking to them individually, telling them what good boys they were, and sending them off happy. Her T-shirt was now soaked, and she had mud on her jeans where the dogs had jumped up on her in excitement. She simply laughed at the sky because she didn't care.

Farther down the road, she saw a woman riding a bicycle toward her. She looked vaguely familiar, but Susan couldn't place her until the woman looked up when the dogs went running past her. She quickly pedaled her bike, rushing toward Susan, calling out, "Susie? Is that really you?" Pregnant and with a toddler in his seat on the bike, Susan wasn't sure who it was until she got very close and Susan recognized the strawberry blond hair and the grin from freckle to freckle.

"Jeannie! It is you, isn't it?" she exclaimed. "I can't believe how long it has been since I've seen you! You've changed," she said pointing to her pregnant belly.

"Oh, you wouldn't believe it if I told you, but I'll tell you anyway. This is number eight in here," she said, pointing to her belly. "And this is number seven. She rubbed the toddler's back. His name is Harry and he's almost two. The others go from eight to eighteen."

Susan was shocked but tried to hide it from her old friend.

"What are you doing here? How long are you back for? Did you bring your family? I want details."

"Well, why don't you get off that bike and we'll find someplace to talk. It seems as though you have more to tell than I do. Eight kids? Holy crap!" Susan laughed, and Jeannie blushed but laughed along.

"Well, Doug and I do enjoy each other's company," she joked as she dismounted and took Harry out of his seat to let him run. "Harry, you stay away from the water. Mommy is going to talk with her old friend here for a few minutes. You be a good boy and stay close, okay?"

"Okay, Mommy," the little guy answered and sat down to play on the side of the road. Susan giggled, grabbed Jeannie's arm, and they walked off a few feet to some big rocks by the side of the road under the shade of a big old tree. They sat and Susan looked at Jeannie and said, matter-of-factly, "I ran away from home yesterday. I just suddenly decided that I didn't want to be a wife and mother for a while, and I ran away from home. I didn't tell anyone, which by the way wasn't hard since I'm nothing but the staff in my family anyway. I just made arrangements for everything I usually do to be taken care of by someone else, wrote a lot of checks, and ran away." As she spoke, Jeannie gasped and looked at her friend with a combination of admiration, envy, and horror.

"You really ran away? Can a wife do that? No, that sounds really stupid. I just mean, I never heard of anyone over the age of ten who ran away from home before. Did you really? What are you gonna do now? Are you gettin' divorced? What about your kids? How long are you runnin' away for? Where are you stayin'? Does anyone know you're here?" She paused and asked the question she really wanted to ask. "Okay, fine. Does Bill know you're here? He never stops askin' about you. He asks everyone if they've heard from you all the time."

"Yeah, Bill knows I'm here." Susan looked straight at her friend, a smile teasing her lips and her eyes twinkling mischievously, and said, "In fact, he made me breakfast this morning."

"What? No shit!" Jeannie quickly glanced around to see if Harry had heard her swear. "You just got here yesterday, and you already found him and got him into bed? Oh my God! You city types move fast. This is gonna be the talk of the town for years."

"Jeannie! We did not sleep together. And *he* found *me*. He came over last night when I got here because he saw the lights on at my folks' place and was concerned that somebody was breaking in. I told him to come back today, that I didn't want to do something we'd both regret last night, and when I came down from my shower this morning, there he was, making breakfast for me."

"He was making breakfast for you? Oh, my gawd! That is so romantic! I'm gonna die. Doug has never even thought of makin' a meal. Are you gonna get back together with him? I mean, unless your husband makes breakfast for you all the time, you can't let him go again, can you? Oh, I'm sorry. That's not very nice of me. I don't even know your husband. I only met him when you came to introduce him to your folks and then the week of your weddin'. He's probably a really nice guy, right?" Then she thought for a minute and continued, "But if he was such a nice guy, why'd you run away? Oh my God, Susie! Was he abusin' you? I didn't think of that. Are you okay?"

The look of true concern touched Susan. "I'm fine." She felt the need to defend her husband's honor. "My husband is a decent guy. He doesn't make breakfast for me, but he does lots of other stuff. He buys me jewelry and we have a really nice house, and the kids go to a really great private school. He provides for us."

"I don't mean to be rude, Susie, but you mentioned a bunch of stuff he buys for you but nothin' that he does for you."

"Well, he does stuff too. Just last week he left work at seven o'clock so that he could pick up our son from his evening rehearsal and I wouldn't have to go all the way across town to get him. I had a headache. That was nice."

"Susie, don't get all defensive. Most guys don't do nice stuff for us. Face it. That's a one-way street. It's just that Bill had always done nice stuff for you. Us girls was always jealous of you in high school when he would take you out sailin' at sunset 'cause it was your favorite time of day. That was so romantic. All us girls used to die over that. And remember when he would actually make picnics and surprise you with them? Oh, my gawd. I don't think Doug would even know how to make a sandwich for himself if his life depended on it, but I love the old jughead. Who would have me now with eight kids in tow? We're stuck together." She laughed as she watched her little one pile the sand up and see it slide back down again.

"Do you remember the Tiffany plate you gave us for our weddin'? We keep it on a shelf up high so's everyone can see it, but the kids can't break it. It was the nicest thing we got for our weddin', and I think of you all the time whenever I see it."

Susan didn't want to tell her friend that Ted had suggested she give Jeannie and Doug something from Tiffany's so that everyone in her old town would know that she had made it in life. She had thought it a pretty impractical gift, but Ted had convinced her. He always seemed to be able to convince her. Suddenly she realized that Jeannie was still talking.

171

"...and we dated all through high school just like you and Bill. Then he went away to the Army for four years, and I stayed here. When he got back, he looked me up and we kind of picked up where we left off. Before I knew it, I was pregnant with number one, and we got hitched. I don't know why I'm tellin' you that. You know all that." She slapped herself on the head and added, "Pregnancy brain. Anyway, we've been married ever since, crankin' out kids." Jeannie laughed and seemed genuinely content to Susan. "Sometimes I wonder why we stayed together so long, but before I have a chance to think about it, I'm pregnant again, and here we are—an old married couple with eight kids and no chance of ever goin' anywhere."

"Jeannie, I'm sorry. I had no idea."

"No reason to be sorry. Some people get lucky and some people just get laid. I guess I know what type of person I am, huh?" She smiled, and there really wasn't any sadness or regret in the smile. "It's actually okay. The kids are great, and Doug is a nice guy. He's Doug. And it's not like we never go anywhere. Every year on our anniversary his mother watches the kids and we go to Portland. One year he surprised me and took me all the way to Boston for a long weekend. That was our tenth, I think. We stayed in a hotel in a room so high we could see the whole city and even had room service. I'll remember it forevah." Jeannie's eyes glazed over and Susan could tell that she was in Boston on that magical weekend. Susan felt a little guilty for not appreciating all that Ted had given her in life.

Suddenly Harry squealed with delight over a butterfly that landed on his arm and Jeannie was back in reality. Her cell phone buzzed and she saw that it was Doug. "Well, speak of the devil. Just a second," and she answered the call.

"I know. I'm with her right now. Yeah, I know. I know. I agree. Sounds like a plan."

To Susan, she said, "Well, Bill told Doug that you're in town and that he made breakfast for you. He said you were gettin' togethah tonight and Doug thought it would be fun to all get togethah to catch up. He told Bill I wouldn't mind cookin'." Jeannie grimaced but it quickly turned into a smile. "I don't mind. I'm cookin' for so many.

What's two more?" I guess I should go home and clear a path through to the kitchen." She laughed as if she didn't really care that her house was a mess.

Jeannie lumbered up off the rock with difficulty and said, "Well, I know Doug can't wait to see you. He always did think you were the prettiest girl in school. Oh, don't look embarrassed. It wasn't exactly a secret. All the rest of us knew we couldn't hold a candle to you." To Harry, she called, "Harry, come on. Momma's got to get goin' if we're gonna have company tonight." Walking over to her son, she knelt down to his level and told him what a nice house he built out of the rocks and sand. "This one is gonna be my architect, I think," she said to Susan as she picked him up and put him in his seat on the bike, strapping his little Power Rangers helmet on his head. "He's always buildin' houses and bridges and towahs."

"Susie, we eat at six o'clock. We're livin' at Doug's folks' place. His Mom left it to us when she passed last year. It was a lot bigger than our double-wide, so we just moved in and sold our little place. You know where it is, right?" and off she pedaled down the road to the market, not waiting for a reply.

"I'll bring dessert!" Susie called after her retreating back, and Jeannie waved to let her know she had heard.

If I had stayed here, would that be me now? Susan thought. *Bill's a lobsterman and a local guy, even if he does practice law too. He loves it and would never want to leave. If I had stayed here, I'd probably have eight kids by now and look like Jeannie too. No. That wouldn't have happened. Bill wouldn't have let it. I wouldn't have let it.* She looked down at her wet muddy sweatshirt, mud-caked jeans, and dirty sneakers. *Maybe it would have,* she thought. *I've only been back here one day, and already I don't seem to care what I look like.*

Susan realized that she was getting hungry, though she couldn't imagine why. She had eaten a huge breakfast not that long ago. There was something about the sea air, though, that always made her ravenous. Bill used to tease her about how much she ate, and yet she ate like a bird back home. *Home. Is this home or is that home? That's what I need to figure out.*

She picked up her pace because she now had a mission, and soon she was in town. She walked into the Seaside Café, noticing that it hadn't changed a bit since she lived in Oceanside. Someone whistled from behind her. "Weeoh. If it ain't little Susie Wahd. As I live and breathe, it is you, ain't it, Susie?"

She turned to see an old classmate, Walter Haven, sitting in a booth by the door with a couple of buddies, fresh from a construction site. All dusty and dirty, their work boots caked with mud, they leered at her. She felt pretty uncomfortable, even though she knew them, but she wouldn't give them the satisfaction of showing any discomfort.

"Why, hello, boys. I'm just back in town for a few days' vacation. Every once in a while, a girl needs to leave civilization and sit back and relax by the ocean, you know? It was lovely to see you again. Say hi to your wives for me, okay?" She continued on to a stool at the counter, smiling to herself, as they guffawed and went back to eating their lunches.

"I guess you're a girl what can take care of herself, eh, honey?" remarked the waitress, a woman in her fifties Susan had known all her life.

"Helen, it's me, Susie Ward. I was just giving them a hard time. I don't know who they think they are, whistling and cackling at anything that wears a skirt or could."

Helen recognized Susie now and yelled out to "the boys," "Fellas, I think you've met your match. You pay some respect or I'll tell your wives you didn't." She turned back to Susan and said quietly, "That should take care of 'em. For all their bluster, they're all wicked scared of their wives." They both had a good laugh while the men wondered what they were laughing about.

Susan ordered the special of the day, fish and chips, and savored every succulent bit of deep-fried haddock and greasy fries. She soaked the fries with vinegar and dusted them with a snowstorm of salt just like when she was a teenager. She washed it all down with a big glass of ice-cold Moxie, a taste she had forgotten long ago. She giggled a little, remembering when her father had given her a sip of Moxie when she was about three years old. She remembered liking its sweet taste. It tasted a lot like root beer, and she loved root beer. Then she got the aftertaste that is the calling card of Moxie, and her little face had scrunched up in distaste. Full once again with the comforts of childhood and wondering where she was putting all the food she was consuming today, she decided to mosey down to the dock where she had spent so many happy hours. When she turned down the little alley and went behind the Lobster Shack, the dock behind was dirty and smelly and cluttered with old traps and buoys. It wasn't at all how she remembered it. By now the tide was going out, and looking out at the cove, the view was of mud and rocks with just a rivulet of water running through. A few sailboats were sitting in the mud, waiting for a higher tide to lift them up. She quickly returned to Main Street, disappointed, and headed toward the new Hannaford to pick up a few things. Once she had filled her backpack, she strolled back toward her parents' house. After all the good food, exercise, disappointment, and her reunion with Jeannie, she was looking forward to taking a nap when she got there.

Once back at the house, she went inside, put the food away, grabbed a blanket, and sat back on the porch swing to read. She settled down with one of the many books she had brought from home, and before long she was dozing in the afternoon sun.

The sound of gravel flying into the nearby trees awakened her, and as she groggily opened one eye, she saw Bill step out of his truck, go around to the back, and emerge with a basket of lobsters and steamers. He walked right past her, saying, "Dinner will be served, milady, in twenty minutes."

What is happening here? This is way too cozy. And he's being way too nice to me. I left him and married someone else. We've lived a lifetime. I came running back here to figure out why I felt so dissatisfied with my life. Here he is acting as though I never left and married someone else and had a family. If he had his way, we would just pretend that nothing has changed. This is not right. Susie stayed put for a few minutes before getting up off the swing and walking into the house, letting the screen door slam behind her. She walked into the kitchen to see him whistling, throwing lobsters into a pot of boiling water, and getting a salad ready to toss.

"What exactly are you doing?" she demanded to know.

Without skipping a beat, he answered, "Why, making dinner for the woman I love, of course."

"Now, wait a minute," she said. "You can't waltz in here and cook for me and make me feel as though we're married or something. Old times are one thing, but this is really getting creepy. You seem way too comfortable here. It's as though you've been here for years. And besides," she added, "Jeannie invited me to dinner at her place tonight."

"Yeah, I know. Doug told me. They invited me too, but I told Doug I wanted to be alone with you tonight and we'd go over next Saturday night. He totally understood. As for being comfortable here, actually, Suz, I've been here for years. You're the one who left. I used to come over at least once a week and make dinner for your folks. Sometimes I'd come over, and they wouldn't have much in the fridge. I'd go away and come back the next day and pretend that I'd had a great catch and make them a shore dinner or something. Sometimes I'd tell them I'd been hunting, and I'd make them stews and steaks and stuff. I've always loved to cook. I guess you learn to cook for yourself when there's no one to do it for you. Whatever. But the bottom line is that I'm comfortable in this kitchen b́ecause I've been cooking in it for years."

Susan was taken aback. Her mouth hanging open and speechless, she felt guilty that she didn't know that. Worse, why hadn't her parents mentioned that Bill was still a part of their lives, even after he was no longer a part of hers? She felt guilty that she hadn't been here to care for her parents when they obviously needed her. She felt angry that Bill had been there for them. Shaken, she fell into the nearest chair. She sat with her head in her hands just shaking her head back and forth.

This was supposed to be a fun, carefree, fun vacation from my life, she thought. *Now, here I am embroiled in a romance with my past and guilt from discovering how much my folks needed me, and I wasn't there for them. I was just off living the perfect life without a care for what they were going through. I let Ted keep me away way more than I should have. I knew in my gut that I should be here more often, and yet, when he suggested going on a vacation to a resort instead of seeing my folks, I went along with it. How could I have been so selfish?*

Looking up at Bill through her fingers, she thought, *This is way too complicated. Why did I ever leave home? What have I done? What am I going to do?*

Totally unaware of her thoughts, Bill exclaimed happily, "Well, the lobsters and steamers are ready! The butter is melted and the salad is tossed. Should we eat right here in the kitchen or do you want to take it out on the front porch?"

Shaken from her reverie, Susan managed to stammer, "Ah, er, um lobsters are messy. Let's go out on the porch." With that simple directive, Bill grabbed the two platters of lobsters and steamers, tossed on a couple of ears of corn, tucked towels under his arm, and made his way to the front porch. "Suz, bring a couple of beers. They're in the fridge!" he yelled over his shoulder. "And grab the salad."

Numbly, she did as he asked. She grabbed the beers, took an extra one for Bill, picked up the crisp, green salad, tucked a couple of plates under her arm, put some forks in her pocket, and plodded out to the porch.

"Brrr. It's chilly tonight," she said as she stepped onto the porch and saw the porch table loaded with bright red lobsters, golden ears of corn, and a bucket of steamers."

"I thought you might say that, so I brought the old space heater." Bill jumped up and ran to his truck, coming back with the heater which he plugged in on the porch. Soon it was giving off warmth.

"So you did," Susan muttered. She looked down at the floor next to the wicker table at the old heater glowing red in the twilight. "You really do think of everything, don't you?"

A big grin spread over Bill's face as he said shyly, "I try."

"That's just it," she found herself saying. "You try too hard. No one can be as sweet as you have been. Bill, please just be yourself. It's exhausting watching you do everything right. Sometimes the other person wants to do something right too, you know?"

"Sorry," Bill muttered, dejected for the moment. "I just want to make you happy, Suz. I love you, have always loved you, and want you to know what a huge mistake it was for me to send you away. I've dreamed of what my life would have been with you in it. Now that you've come back, I don't want you to ever go away."

"Well, let's forget it, okay? Let's enjoy this meal. It's been a long time since I've had a lobster that someone else didn't open for me. I'd almost forgotten how much fun it is to go on a treasure hunt for the meat." And, as they sat there on the porch, the heater buzzing at their feet, the sweet lobster meat tickling her throat, she felt content.

Soon the two were laughing as lobster juice squirted on them. They got corn silk stuck in their teeth, lost their grip on clam shells as they opened them and watched them fly off onto the front lawn, and talked about the old days until the last bit of food was gone. They moved over to the porch swing after wiping their faces and hands with the lemon-dampened towels Bill had brought out.

As Susan sat on the old swing, full and content, she felt like a teenager again. The toe of her shoe remembered that its job was to push the swing, and it obeyed. Her eyes closed, she floated back and forth, listening to the silence, aware of Bill's presence next to her. She could smell the Old Spice mixed with his manly scent. She could feel his leg pressing against hers. She then felt his arm wrap itself around her shoulders.

"Are you cold, Suz? You shivered," he asked huskily.

"No. I'm fine," she managed. "I guess I was just remembering and marveling that we still fit together perfectly when you wrap your arm around me."

The flannel arm pulled her closer, and she did fit as though she belonged there. It was still familiar, still comforting and warm. His broad, muscled chest was the perfect pillow, and she closed her eyes and let her senses and her memory wash over her.

I shouldn't be sitting here like this. I can't do this. Ted has always tried to be good to me. Even when he had affairs, he tried to keep them from me. Susan remembered the long nights she had spent alone in their bed, knowing that he was traveling on business with *her*. She imagined what they were doing and how Ted must have been laughing at her, thinking that she had no idea. Susan always carried on as though nothing was wrong. *How smug he must have felt to be getting away with it right under my nose,* she thought. *I would never give him the satisfaction of knowing how much he hurt me. He is a good man, though. He has given me a good life, three great kids, a nice house, the freedom to come and go as I please, a credit card to use as I wish. All I have to do is cook and clean and take care of the kids and make sure that when he's at home he can relax. All I have to do is put up with his long absences, his frequent weekends away from home, and the mysterious calls in the middle of the night that he says are business.*

"Suz, you're shivering again," Bill whispered. "Are you cold? Do you want to go in?"

She didn't dare to speak for fear that her voice would give away her inner thoughts. She had never told anyone about Ted's affairs. If she didn't talk about them, they didn't exist. At this moment, though, how she wanted Bill! It would be so easy to get carried away.

There you go again, Susan, she chastised herself. *You always have to think everything to death. Everything doesn't have to be planned. Just go with the flow and do what feels right.*

She lifted her face up to look into Bill's and saw a combination of pain and pleasure. He whispered, "I'm going to kiss you, Suz." And he did—a long, slow, tender kiss. There was no sense of urgency. No obligatory peck at the end of a busy day. There was tenderness. And she kissed him back, long and gently. Her lips were not the only part of her that responded to his kiss. Before she knew it, her body was turning into his and her arms were around his neck. Slowly, without their lips parting and without a word, Bill picked her up off the swing and carried her into the house where he laid her on the carpet in front of the fireplace. He tossed a match into the wood that he must have prepared earlier in the day, and the two of them lay in each other's arms watching the flames grow.

Finally, after what seemed an eternity of silence, he took her chin with his finger and turned it up to his own. He kissed her again, this time harder, more passionately, but still tenderly. His lips were asking her a big question. Was she ready for more? Before she had a chance to answer, he abruptly got up and said hoarsely, "Suz, I love you, but

I'm goin' home now. You have a lot of thinking to do. My life is pretty simple, but yours is more complicated. Before we do something we won't be able to turn back from, I'm goin' home. Good night." And he softly kissed the top of her head as he stood up. He hurried toward the front door, turned, and said softly, just a little above a whisper, "Suz, when you're sure, I'm here. I've waited all these years. I can wait a little longer." The next thing she heard was his truck throwing up gravel as it sped down the road and away from her.

Susan just sat there on the worn carpet in front of a romantic fire with her legs crossed, elbows on her knees, and her head resting on her hands—all alone. *Why did Bill leave so quickly? Was he trying to tease me? Did he think that if he left me wanting him that the next time he saw me I'd pounce on him? No. Bill was being Bill—considerate and understanding. He probably really does want me to be sure before I do something that would complicate everyone's lives. I guess I've just gotten used to thinking of what people's ulterior motives are instead of taking them at their word.*

Susan stared into the flames and started to cry. She'd been doing a lot of that since she made the brave decision to run home. This was supposed to be a carefree break from her mundane life and, instead, it was a confusing and painful trip down memory lane. When she was with Bill, she felt so safe. She felt young. She felt loved. She felt as though nothing could hurt her and that he would take care of her and cherish her forever. But he had broken her heart. He was capable of that. Then there were her children. She missed them and wondered if they were confused and angry that she had left without even saying goodbye or explaining why. If she stayed with Bill, what would become of her children? Bill's life was here in Maine. He would never fit in her other life. Her children's lives were set. They would suffocate in this little town. Then there was Ted. Sure, her marriage had become routine and unexciting. She always knew what to expect and what was expected. She did love Ted. They had a history, memories, almost a secret language. On the other hand, Bill was exhausting because she never knew what he would do next, and although she was pretty sure she knew what he wanted from her, she wasn't sure if he wanted the dream of their past together or the forty-year-old woman she was now.

As she tried to make sense of her folly, she climbed onto the couch, covered herself with her mother's afghan, and fell asleep wondering if she had to choose one life or the other. Maybe she could find a way to have both.

Chapter Thirty

Someone was kissing her forehead. She turned over and snuggled deeper into the couch. Someone was rubbing her back and moving her hair out of her face. "Mmm," she murmured in her half-sleep.

"Come on, you sleepyhead. It's Sunday morning, and I'm not running traps today. You and I are going to spend the whole day together. One way or another, we are going to figure out what we're doing with the second chance we're being given."

Suddenly, she was awake as she smelled strong coffee being placed on the coffee table behind her. She rolled over, and there was Bill, resplendent in a fisherman's sweater and jeans that fit all the right places.

My God he's handsome! He looks like he just stepped out of an Old Spice commercial. He even smells like he used to. Susan inhaled deeply and let out an audible sigh. She also made an uncharacteristic decision to let nature take its course, to be free and happy and not to think about any consequences—if only for a day.

She smiled up at Bill and said, "You have got to stop sneaking into this house. You're going to start all kinds of gossip around town." She smiled coyly, jumped up from the couch, and gave him a big hug around the neck. "Not to mention the fact that you're going to spoil me. A girl could get used to this kind of service." She sipped her coffee and took a couple of bites of the toast slathered with warm blueberry jam that she discovered on the table. She then scampered for the stairs. Not looking back, she called, "Bill, wait right there. I'll be ready in fifteen minutes."

Sure enough, fifteen minutes later she reappeared on the stairs, freshly showered and dressed, an old Red Sox cap on her head. She wore a dark-blue, cable-knit turtleneck that had been in the drawer for twenty years and a pair of well-faded designer jeans she had brought with her. On her feet was a pair of sneakers—not running shoes or cross-trainers or walking shoes—sneakers, her old Keds she had found in the bottom of her closet upstairs.

"Come on, you. Are you going to keep me waiting all day?" she called to Bill as she sprinted to the front door. She began to run, this time away from town and up the road that ran along the inlet. Bill quickly caught up with her and they jogged along in silence for a couple of minutes looking at the water shimmering in the early morning sun. It was going to be a beautiful day.

Suddenly she slowed down and clambered down over the rocks to a flat slab of granite that she had loved as a child. She had spent days lying on this rock, protected from the ocean's breezes and from the view of the road, reading and daydreaming. As a teenager, she had developed her favorite fantasy about this rock. In her twenties, Ted had fulfilled her fantasy on this rock. Now she beckoned Bill to join her in her special place. He effortlessly hopped down, and they tumbled onto the hard surface, laughing and slightly out of breath.

Susan peeked around the jutting rock that obscured their view of the ocean and saw no boats in sight. The tourists weren't here yet, and most of the townspeople were in church or getting their gardens ready for planting. She knew they would be alone. There were no telephones, no family, no friends, and no ghosts of parents watching. And with each thought, she felt her cheeks flush, a thrilling sensation sprinting through her body. She looked at Bill and said, "I need to know something."

Bill listened to her sudden seriousness and said nothing.

"I need to know if you want the eighteen-year-old Susie Ward or the forty-year-old Susan Ward Goldman."

Bill's face told her more than his words, but he answered, "I want you. I've wanted you since we were kids. I've never stopped wanting you. Pushing you away so you would be able to live a good life instead of being saddled with me here was the biggest mistake of my life. I should have given you the choice. I should have known that I could give you a good life, even after my Dad died. And when I saw you at your parents' door Friday night, I felt as though someone had slugged me in the stomach. I looked at you and couldn't believe that you've grown even more beautiful over the years. Suz, make no mistake. I'm not chasing a dream. I'm hoping to live with my dream for the rest of my life."

Bill took a long breath, and before he could continue, Susan leaned toward him and kissed him lightly. As he responded, her kiss became more ardent. Her lips gave him all the information he needed, and he took the lead, moving his hands from her face to her shoulders, then sliding them down her sides. Half expecting that the day would head in this direction, she had not worn anything under the bulky sweater, and as Bill's hands roamed from her waist, she tingled all over.

Bill stopped kissing her and looked into her eyes. He was certain that he saw doubt there. Then she rolled over onto her back, staring up into the crystal blue sky. Bill just stared at her.

"My God, you're beautiful!" he gasped.

She shivered, not from cold but because it had been a long time since anyone had told her she was beautiful. The one thought that she couldn't shake was that she had never been unfaithful to Ted.

"What are we going to do now?" Susan asked.

"I don't know," Bill's raspy voice replied.

Tears trickled down the side of Susan's face and into her ears. "I can't do it, Bill. I just can't." She wrapped her arms around her eyes, blocking out the sunlight.

Without saying anything else, Bill lay back against the rock and Susan nestled into his neck, his arm cradling her head. She was afraid of what might lie ahead.

If she were honest with herself, she had known when she drove into town that she and Bill would end up like this. It was just a matter of time. Although she hadn't planned it, hadn't even thought about it consciously, she'd known deep down that it would happen. Too many unresolved feelings for each other were screaming to be heard. Too many years of wondering what had happened to their love, of idealizing each other, of dreaming of being in each other's arms whenever things were tough with Ted.

For all these years, Ted was her reality, but Bill was her idea of the perfect man—her first love, the one who would always be a teenager in her mind. Well, now she was a middle-aged, married woman who had run away from her life and into her high school sweetheart's arms. She had half expected to be disappointed, all the while expecting him to be unchanged. But she had never expected this. She had never expected to find him yearning for her, still loving her. She had never expected to find him looking so wonderfully masculine and muscular and just plain good.She had never expected that, instead of having her imaginary bubble burst by the reality she would find in her hometown, she would discover a passion she had never known was in her. Now she was more confused than ever. This man seemed too good to be true. Yet, she had known him most of her life in one way or another, and he was what he appeared to be—a good, kind, romantic, loving, passionate, tender, honest, responsible man. A woman could search a lifetime and never find someone like him, and he wanted her. But she had never been unfaithful to Ted and didn't think she could start now, no matter how easy it would be, no matter how much Bill wanted her, no matter how confused she was. She also thought of her boys. She could never do anything that would hurt them. She had loved them from the moment they took their first breaths, and she would love them and protect them until she took her last.

As her emotions leapfrogged, anger set in. She jumped up and scaled the rocks to the road without a word. Once there, she began running toward her parents' house and didn't stop until she got there. Panting and barely able to breathe, she threw herself face down onto the couch in the living room and cried.

Bill had been startled by the sudden transformation. When she bolted, he got up and ran after her, but allowed her to stay a few steps in front of him. He figured she would get tired and slow down, and then they could talk. He was surprised when she ran all the way home. Seeing her throw herself down and cry so violently, he was scared. He assumed that he had rushed her, and she now regretted it. He assumed that he'd read her signals wrong. He knelt by her side and kept telling her that he was sorry.

"Suz, I'm so sorry if I made you sad. I'd never push you to do something you don't want to do. Suz, I'm sorry. I'm so sorry." He didn't know what else to say, so he just kept saying that he was sorry, figuring that her tears were his fault.

After a few minutes, she regained her composure enough to sit up. He was still kneeling on the floor beside the couch, so when she sat up, they were face-to-face. Bill didn't think he would ever get her tortured expression out of his mind. It was too reminiscent of her face when he had told her that he didn't love her and never would and had changed their lives forever.

"Bill, I'm not crying because of what we almost did. I'm crying because you were such a stupid idiot all those years ago. You didn't trust me enough to tell me the truth and let me make my own decision about being with you or going away. You pushed me—no you chased me, shoved me away. You made me believe that you didn't love me, and I was too naïve to see through the words. I believed you. Do you have any idea how much that hurt me? Did you even think that I might be crushed by that? Did you think that by being the macho man you would live a martyred life alone and lonely, and I would go off and find happiness? Did you think that I would ever be truly, completely happy without you in my life?"

As she continued asking questions, her voice grew stronger and soon she was yelling at him. "I cried for years—*years*—over you. I wasted so much time in college grieving our relationship instead of enjoying the college experience. If I hadn't been lucky enough to meet Katie, my roommate, and if she hadn't been the outgoing, empathetic, fierce woman that she is, I never would have recovered. Did you think of any of that?"

"The answer is 'No.' You didn't think of any of that because you were so caught up in being a hero. You were going to protect poor little helpless me from the big old sad life you thought was ruining you. You bastard! You never even gave me the courtesy of facing me with the truth of how much you were hurting after your father died. You were a coward. You never even told me what he said to you when he was on that stretcher. Let me guess. I've had a long time to think about it." She began to quiet.

"Let's see. I'm guessing it went something like this." She lowered the timbre of her voice, mimicking his father, and said with mock sincerity, "Bill, I'm dying, and you have to take care of your mother and your sisters. The money won't be there for college, Son. Just take my boat and make a good honest living for yourself and your family. It's put food on your table and clothes on your back up until now and, if you work real hard, it will do the same for you for years to come. Okay, Son? You'll do it? Promise me you'll do it."

Susie then resumed in her own voice,

"How's that, Bill? Am I close? And then you figured that you wouldn't want me to have to stay in town with you and miss out on going to Smith. You'd sacrifice our love and our happiness. *You'd* sacrifice it. Not *we'd* sacrifice it. No, *you'd* decide that all on your own. You didn't trust me enough to decide whether we could stay together while you were here. Now I come back here to discover that you still love me, still want me—after twenty-two years! Now you don't care what I would have to give up to stay with you." Susan was on a roll and didn't even see the agony on Bill's face or the way he had slumped down onto the floor, his head in his hands. Twenty-two years of pain was pouring from her like lava, flowing over Bill and souring any sweet future that might have grown.

"Now you've decided that I should be a lobsterman's wife after all and live in this dumpy little town with you. I should leave my husband, my children, my home, my friends—everything I hold dear—and just stay here with you." Susan looked down at Bill and now saw that she was hurting him, but she couldn't seem to stop. All the magic of just a few minutes ago was gone—burned out on reentry to her world of what could have been and what was.

"Why is it that back then it wasn't a good enough life for me, but now that I'm used to the finer things life has to offer, you think I'd jump at the chance to live here again? What makes you think I'd do that? I took vows to be faithful to my husband, and I will never break those vows."

She stopped, knowing that she had said the one thing that would make returning to her family the only choice she had left. When she looked at Bill, he was holding his face in his hands, kneeling on the floor before her.

"What have I done to us?" he sobbed. "Suz, I only wanted to protect you and set you free because I loved you so much, and now I see that I have turned you against me forever. I guess I deserve everything you just said. What was almost so beautiful a little while ago on the rocks isn't going to happen, is it? You're not going to stay here with me, are you? You tested yourself and got me out of your system and now you'll go back to your husband and your family without the Bill albatross around your neck. I guess it's true what they say about not being able to go home again. You tried, and look where it got us. What started out so wonderful and full of hope has turned out to be just a sad ending to a sad story." He slowly rose and walked toward the door. "I won't bother you anymore, Suz. I promise." And he walked out the door, got in his truck, and sped away.

"You're a real genius, Susan!" she yelled at herself. "You have a wonderful family that loves you and needs you, and you walk out on them, leaving them to wonder if they're to blame. Then you discover an old love and have the chance to blossom in its sunshine, and you rain all over it. What? Do you enjoy being miserable? Maybe that's it. Susan the martyr. You just told Bill that he was trying to be a martyr. Well, Ma always said that the accuser is more often the offender. Maybe she was right. Yeah. Everyone hates Susan. Woe is Susan. What a terrible life Susan has. Poor little rich girl. Her husband has affairs. Well, what man doesn't? You don't see every other woman running away. I could name half a dozen friends whose husbands have had affairs. They just guilt them into diamond bracelets or new cars. But no. I'd rather play the martyred wife. Well, snap out of it. Figure out a way you're going to fix this mess you've gotten yourself into."

Susan sat down on the couch, blew her nose, and thought. She came up with a plan. Dashing into the kitchen, she grabbed her mother's big wicker picnic basket from the pantry and packed a picnic lunch from the food she had brought with her. She hadn't had breakfast and was hungry. She dashed out to her SUV and tossed the basket onto the passenger seat as she got in. She sped out of the driveway and down the road to Bill's house.

Driving through town, church was just letting out and she had to drive slowly as people crossed the road and waved to her. She plastered a smile on her face and waved back, wanting to get through town and out to the point. Surprised to find Bill's car parked on the lawn instead of in the driveway, she jumped out and began calling his name.

"Bill! Bill! Where are you?" she called as she wandered around his yard. She looked in the back of the house and then noticed his back door was open. She let herself in. After all, he had been doing that to her ever since she got here, hadn't he? She finally found him sitting in an old rocking chair on the sun porch, staring straight ahead at the water, his big old Labrador sitting at his side, its head resting on his knee. When the dog saw her, it recognized her as the new friend who had thrown sticks in the water and ambled over to nuzzle her hand.

"Sic her, Keel," he muttered, and then chuckled, not cracking a smile.

"No, he and I are old friends. We played yesterday."

"Traitor," Bill scolded the dog, no hint of a smile in his eyes.

Susan slowly knelt before Bill's chair.

"Bill, we've got a problem, but we can fix it. We've both said and done a lot of things thinking we were being altruistic when we really were being selfish. We've hurt each other, both without meaning to and on purpose. We've got some making up to do, don't you think? It would be ridiculous to let a lifetime of love go just because we both have quick tempers and even quicker tongues."

She knew that she had nothing else to say until she heard his response. Patiently, she waited, patting Keel who had now lay beside her. Finally, after several minutes, Bill stood up, walked to the other end of the porch, and turned toward her.

"Suz," he began calmly, obviously having given some thought to what he was going to say. "I have loved you most of my life. I loved you from up close and from afar. I loved you enough to send you away when I thought that being with me would be harmful to you and selfish of me. I loved you while you made another life for yourself far away that didn't include me. And I loved you even more when you seemed to have returned to me." Here he paused.

"But I cannot and will not be accused of being a martyr and acting selfishly toward you. I have never done one selfish thing that involved you. I have held you on a pedestal since the day I first noticed you in school and I would never do or say anything to intentionally hurt you." He paused and Susan thought he was finished, but he continued, "But you can't say the same."

This felt like a gut punch to Susan. It hurt even more because she knew it was true. If she were honest with herself, coming back here was selfish. Letting Bill think that she might choose him was selfish. Making him think that she was going to make love with him was selfish. The list was longer, but Bill was talking.

"Just when I thought that you truly loved me too and had chosen me, this morning on the rocks, and I was happier than I can ever remember being, you turned and attacked me. You accused me of some pretty terrible things, and someone who loved me as I love you could never have done that. We had our moment, I guess. We loved purely years ago, if only for a brief time. That's enough for me. Some men never have the woman they love, and I had you, if only briefly. No matter what was and is said now, it was beautiful, and you were beautiful, and I will never forget you as long as I live."

Bill turned and walked out into the yard, Keel at his heels but looking back at Susan as if wondering why she wasn't coming too. She stood, dumbfounded by what he had said. She had come to apologize, but he hadn't given her a chance. It sounded as though he were sending her away again, except that this time it seemed he really didn't want her anymore. Could that be possible? The one constant in her life, always in the background, had been Bill's love.

Whenever she got fed up with her life, she would daydream about Bill. She would imagine what he would have done for her in the situation and how he would have handled it better. She would dream about making love to him on his sailboat or on the rocks or on the beach, even though they never had done any of those things. Many times, though, it was these daydreams that got her through a tough time, like when she found out about her husband's affairs. Then she had returned to this place to discover that her daydreams could be true. He really had loved her for all those years.

Susan followed Bill out into the yard and went to her car to retrieve the picnic basket.

"Bill, you have to eat. Let's have lunch together and maybe we can get past what has happened today." As she spoke, she spread her picnic out on the table in the sun by his big old elm tree. Keel hurried over to see if there was any food for him.

"Again, you're a traitor," Bill scolded him, but this time smiled sadly.

"Come on, Bill. Join me. We don't have to make any decisions. Let's just have lunch. I've got turkey and cheddar with cranberry relish."

Bill couldn't believe that she had remembered his favorite sandwich after all these years or that she had bought the ingredients to have it on hand for him. He gave in and took a seat opposite hers. They ate in relative silence, punctuated by the occasional awkward comment about the weather or the dog or the town. The joy and ease of their relationship was gone. When they were finished, he thanked her politely and told her that had some work to do on the boat.

"Well, maybe I'll see you tomorrow," Bill said pointedly, indicating that she should leave.

Susan packed up her basket, slipped a piece of turkey to Keel, and took the basket to her car. When she turned to say goodbye to Bill, he was gone. She climbed into her SUV and somberly drove back to her parents' house.

Chapter Thirty-One

When Susan called the kids that night, they were aloof. Ben and David said that they were busy and wanted to know if she had anything important to say. If not, they had stuff to do. Crushed, she told them each that she loved them with all her heart and would be home soon. She got the feeling, though, that they didn't believe her. It had only been a few days, and already they seemed to sense that she wasn't telling them the whole truth. The only problem was that even she didn't know what the whole truth was anymore. One truth she was sure of, though, was that she loved her children fully and completely, and she would not let them think otherwise.

When it was Sam's turn to talk, he blurted, "Mommy, Daddy said that we shouldn't tell you that we miss you and that we should be big men, but I'm not a big man. I do miss you—a whole lot. Pleeeeeeeeease come home now. Ben and David and me won't fight anymore, and we'll say thank you every time you do something for us. We promise."

Hearing the pleading tone in his little voice and realizing that he thought it was their fault that she had left, she thought her heart would break. How could she have done such a thing to her children? How could she have thought that she could just walk out like that? This wasn't a movie or a book. This was her life. They were her children, and she had hurt them deeply. They were probably all thinking what Sam had bravely said. They probably thought it was their fault that she had left. How could she ever explain to them that her running away had nothing to do with them and everything to do with her own selfishness?

"Sammy, tell your brothers to go pick up extensions." When she was sure they were on the line, she said, "You listen to me, guys. Mommy had some problems to work out that had nothing to do with any of you.

She needed some quiet time to think about her life and get everything straight in her head. You know how sometimes when you have some big decision to make, Ben, you go into your room, close your door, turn your music up loud, and just lie on your bed and think? Well, that's what I felt like. Only I had to go away to do my thinking because when I'm at home everyone needs something from me all the time and I don't get a chance to think much. Sam, you know how when someone teases you at school you come home and build Legos all by yourself and think about what to do about it? Well, that's what I'm doing now."

"You're building Legos, Mommy?" Sam asked innocently.

"No, you moron," David interrupted. "She's trying to decide whether to leave all of us or just leave Dad, and she can't decide while she's here with us because she has to be away from us to think about it."

"No, David!" Susan exclaimed. "I am *not* thinking about divorcing your father or leaving you. I love you with all my heart. I simply needed to get away. I needed a vacation. I needed to go someplace quiet where I could be alone with my thoughts and relax and be myself. I wake up in the morning without an alarm and eat what I want whenever I'm hungry. I don't have to get dressed up or put on makeup, and no one needs anything from me. I now realize, though, that the way I left was very mean and very wrong. I am so sorry if I hurt any of you."

"So you went back to your folks' place in Maine, huh?" she heard her husband interject.

"Ted, I didn't know you were on the line. That was pretty sneaky... and I didn't say I went to my folks' house. I didn't say where I went." She started to get angry with him for tricking her.

"Well, it doesn't take a genius to figure out where you'd be where you could 'be yourself,'" he snarled. "You're always saying that you miss the carefree atmosphere of that town."

"Boys, would you mind letting Daddy and me talk alone for a few minutes?" she asked as nicely as she could. "Daddy and I have to make some decisions, and they're really just between the two of us."

"You're in trouble now, Dad," said David.

"Okay, Mommy," said Sam.

"Whatever," added Ben.

193

"I love you guys, and I really will see you soon, okay? Trust me. I've never lied to you and I'm not starting now.

"Sure Mom. Whatever you say," answered a sullen Ben. "Get off the phone, guys. Let Mom and Dad fight in private." And with that, she heard three clicks.

"How dare you...?" Susan began.

"How dare I?" Ted quietly roared. "How dare I what? How dare I try to figure out where my wife has run off to? How dare I try to figure out what I possibly could have done to cause her to up and leave me and the boys without even telling us where she was going or why? How dare I wonder why I have complete strangers in my home at all hours of the day and night doing the things we have come to rely on you for? How dare I care enough about you, about us, to worry and wonder if there even is an *us* anymore? How dare I wonder if you have run off with someone else? How can you say, 'How dare you?'"

Susan was stunned. Ted really sounded scared. He missed her and the things she did for him and the boys. He was hurt that she had not even talked with him before she left. She didn't think he would have cared. She had this romantic notion that running away from home would be great fun. Well, it certainly had its moments, but it had not been the reflective, calm, relaxing adventure she thought it would be. All she had done since she had left was worry and cry and say the wrong things to Bill and to the kids and to Ted.

"Ted," she began softly, "I'll be home in a few days. I just have a few things to wind up here. You're right. I'm at my folks' house. I was feeling guilty because I wasn't there for them all those years. I wasn't here when they died, and I wasn't here to take care of them when they needed me. I really should have been here, but I always listened to you when you said I shouldn't go to them. You always seemed to have a good reason why I shouldn't go. Lately, I started resenting you for that and I needed to come back to make my own peace with a lot of things."

"With Bill too, I suppose," said Ted, much to her surprise.

Susan didn't know how to honestly answer that, but given the events of the past afternoon, she decided to answer him honestly and let the chips fall where they may.

"Yes, with Bill too," she said softly.

"Well, it's about time," answered Ted sadly. "We've been living with his ghost for too many years and, quite frankly, I was getting a little tired of competing with him in your mind all of the time. Have you seen him?"

Susan was flabbergasted. "I, er...yes, I have," she stammered. "We've spent some time together talking about old times. I've told him all about you and the boys."

"And?" Ted asked.

"And?" Susan echoed.

"Are you coming home to us or are you staying there with him?" Ted inquired bluntly.

Susan didn't know what to say. She had no idea that Ted knew how much Bill had haunted her all these years. He had no idea how close she almost came to staying with Bill. She asked Ted, "What do you want me to do?"

Much to her surprise, Ted answered, "It doesn't matter anymore what I want. It's what you want that matters. I don't want you and Bill in my bed. I only want you. If you can come home to me and commit to me, I want you to hurry home. But I'm getting too old to compete with a memory. I'm in my forties, and your idea of him is still in its teens. I just can't deal with that any longer. Did you realize that when you fall asleep on the couch and I come down to wake you up, half the time you're muttering his name in your sleep? How do you think that makes me feel after all these years? After all I've done for you? I work damned hard to give you a good life. I have never deprived you of anything you wanted. I think I've been a good father. But that was never quite good enough for you. No, you had to run away from home like some childish brat trying to defy its parents. I don't want to be your parent. I want to be your husband."

Ted had never spoken to Susan like that. She had no idea that he felt that way. She could never get him to talk with her about his feelings. She always had to guess and interpret what he meant and how he felt. She now realized that she often interpreted incorrectly. She had no idea that Ted felt threatened by Bill. It was so long ago. But, if Susan were honest with herself, she would realize that she had kept Bill alive by comparing Ted to him. Any time Ted disappointed her or didn't react in the way she wished he would, she found herself thinking that Bill would have done it differently. That really wasn't fair. Once she made the decision to marry Ted, she should have left Bill in the past.

"Ted, I'll be home soon. I promise. When I get there, we need to sit down and talk like this face-to-face. Please? You've never talked with me about feelings, and I need to hear these things. I didn't think that you loved me anymore. Life had become so monotonous. I really felt like the hired help."

Susan hesitated for a second and continued, "And, Ted? I love you. I also love this place. I really wish that the boys had gotten to know it here. I mean really know it, not just a day here and there over the years. It's beautiful and calm and gives you room to breathe. I can put on a pair of old jeans and a sweatshirt and just go for a walk by the water. It fills my soul. I know that sounds corny, but it really does. Just sitting on the porch swing going back and forth aimlessly, smelling the salt air, and feeling the breeze, looking out at the sparkling water, playing with a neighbor's dog.... All of these things are comforting. They're relaxing. They make me feel like me."

Before Ted had a chance to answer, or to say anything else, she calmly hung up the phone before he heard her cry.

Chapter Thirty-Two

For the next few days, Susan walked, read, and sat by the ocean, appreciating its beauty. Her evenings were spent with Bill. They quietly came to understand that they would not have a future together that was anything other than friendship. They slowly made peace with the horrible things she had said to him the day they had almost made love on the rocks. She hoped that someday he would truly forgive her. Although he kept telling her it was okay, that he understood, she could sense a difference in the way he looked at her, the way he spoke to her, even the way he gave her a soft peck on the cheek when he left to go home each evening. Somehow it now was easier for her to forgive him for sending her away years ago because if he hadn't, she never would have met Ted or had her wonderful sons.

For him, though, forgiving was hard. He had spent so many years with her on a pedestal, his teenaged Suz. He had berated himself for making a dumb decision when life threw him a curve, a decision that sent Susan into someone else's arms. When she returned to Oceanside, he thought that she had come back to him. And when she not only allowed him to kiss her, but kissed him back so hungrily, he thought he was right. When she had taken him to the rock and given him clues that she wanted to make love with him, he knew he was right. His world suddenly was brighter. The years washed away, and he saw a bright future with her by his side. That dream didn't last long enough. She crushed him. He now knew what she must have felt when he pushed her away.

Over the past few days, out on his boat working hard, Bill had time to think. It never would have worked to have her move back here with him. As much as he wanted her, she wouldn't have been happy, and that would have killed him. He couldn't have done that to her. Having her wasn't enough if she felt guilty for leaving her husband or missed everything he provided for her that Bill couldn't.

And what about her kids? He hadn't even been thinking of them. She would never move her kids here. They were getting an amazing education in their private school. Jeannie had told him about it, and when he looked it up online he was astonished at what it offered. They were probably participating in activities the local school had never heard of. They loved their dad, and it wouldn't be fair to move them so far away from him. Plus, Bill knew what it felt like losing a father when he was still a teenager. It was hard not having him around to talk with, to learn from, to lean on. Her sons were not his and never would be. He could never have taken the place of their father, nor would he have wanted to. They didn't belong to him, and they didn't belong with him. He knew that under different circumstances he would gladly accept her sons as his own, would cherish time spent with them, would relish teaching them about the ocean and even letting them help him out in his law practice. But the circumstances would never give him that chance.

So what had started out with heat and romance and the memory of lost love had become something comfortable. Susan wasn't sure if she had hurt Bill so deeply that he didn't love her anymore or if he was, once again, trying to make it easy for her to make the right decision.

She told him about her life, and he told her about his. Although he still believed that a part of him still loved her and wanted her to choose to stay with him, she knew he understood the only decision she could make. She told him all about her life with Ted. She told him how they had met and how he had saved her when she was drowning in missing Bill. She talked about her home, her sons, and her husband as if she were talking with a girlfriend. She shared intimate thoughts with him and thoughts she didn't even realize she had until she began relating the past twenty-two years. She shared the telephone conversation she and Ted had, and he told her that she was very lucky. Her husband was right to expect her to love him and him alone. Secretly, though, Bill was touched that she had thought about him as much as he had thought about her all these years.

Bill told her how hard it had been when he had been expected to take over his father's boat and to give up his own dreams and love. He explained why he had made the choices he had made and how painful they had been. As he spoke, she realized that he was a truly remarkable, selfless man. She wished that she had not been the one to cause him so much pain. When she told him that, he said something that surprised her. He said, "Suz, I'm a big boy. If I had ever found anyone who loved me and who I loved, I would have settled down. But the truth is, I never did. You know me. I'm the one who has to be reliable and responsible. Any woman I met had to understand that and appreciate it. No one ever did. I met girls who wanted to have a good time, and don't get me wrong, I had a good time with them. But in the end, I was still alone.

"Once, when I was in law school, I thought I had met a woman I could settle down with. Actually she reminded me a lot of you. She was pretty and smart and could hold her own in any argument. We went out for a while, but when I told her I was serious about her, she told me she was serious about being a lawyer and she wasn't about to settle for hanging out a shingle in some rinky-dink town. She wanted to work for the government and make a difference. I don't know how I could have been so blind as to miss her ambition.

"After that, I graduated and came back here for good. Except for an occasional fling with a summer resident, I've been pretty much alone. You know how it is in this town. By that time all the girls my age were married and had a few kids. I kind of resigned myself to living alone. It's not so bad. I have good friends, and whenever I feel sad about not getting married, I stop by Doug and Jeannie's, and I get cured real fast." Bill laughed at the image of Doug and Jeannie's house overflowing with kids and toys and noise.

"It's not your fault that I'm alone, Suz. I could have moved away when Ma died. By then my sisters were married and taken care of. It was my choice to stay put. If I held onto a hope that someday you and I would get together again, it was only a hope. I never really expected it to happen. Then when I saw you, though, I believed that maybe it was a real possibility, and I guess I started moving kind of fast. I gave you the impression that I'd been pining for you when, in fact, I've had a full, busy life. Plus, I've got Keel. He's a good boy and lots of company. In the summer, he picks up women for me. You saw how he picked you up." Bill laughed again.

Susan liked the way his face crinkled when he laughed. It looked kind and familiar. She then realized that it was his dad's face. She hadn't noticed how much he looked like his father until this moment. When she did the math, she realized that she and Bill were now about the ages their parents had been when his father died. *Where has the time gone?*

Just when she thought she had Bill all figured out, he surprised her. Susan felt somewhat vindicated by Bill's telling her that he had made the choice to live the life he lived. It wasn't something forced on him. It wasn't her fault because he loved her and pined for her. She felt somewhat relieved and not quite so guilty.

Chapter Thirty-Three

With only two days left until her self-imposed return-to-sender date when she would go back to her family, Susan figured that it was time to pack up her parents' things and finally get this house ready to sell. Ted had willingly paid the taxes and utility bills long enough. It was time for her to sell the house. First thing in the morning, she would begin. She called Ted.

"Hi, Ted. First of all, thank you for understanding that I needed this time alone. I really feel that I have come to peace with myself and have a new appreciation for you and the boys and my life. I'll be home in a couple of days, but first I need to pack up my folks' stuff and get the house ready to put on the market. It's time to sell it. I also need to take a look at the shop in town and talk to a realtor about someone else leasing the space."

Ted heard the sadness in her voice and knew that she shouldn't have to do this alone. It would be hard for her, and he wanted to help. To Susan, he said, "Susan, I've been thinking. It's Thursday night. How about if I pick the boys up early from school tomorrow and we head up there to help you pack? It would be good for the boys to be able to spend some time rummaging in the old house and to see a part of you they don't really know. We live in my parents' old house, for God's sake, but they didn't really get to see your folks or Oceanside as much as I know you would have liked. Frankly, I hated to go there because I felt the ghost of lovers past with me whenever I was there." He chuckled at his own joke. Susan just listened and didn't respond because she couldn't believe what she was hearing. When Ted was finished, she quickly answered.

"Ted, that would be amazing. They could decide if they want any of the old stuff, and we could go to the beach for a picnic, and I might even get you to eat a meal at the Lobster Shack."

"Well, let's take this one step at a time," Ted ventured. More quietly, he asked, "Um, Susan? Have you resolved things with him?"

Susan decided to tell Ted the whole truth, or most of it.

"Ted, we have spent almost every evening together talking—just talking. We have come to be friends. In fact, when you and the boys come up, I'm going to invite Bill over for lunch, and you'll see. There's no reason why we can't all be adults about this, and you might even like him."

Again, Ted replied with, "Well, as I said, let's take this one step at a time," but Susan noticed that he didn't say no. She really couldn't believe what she was hearing. He was going to leave the office early and pick up the boys. Then he was going to drive five or six hours and then help her pack up the house. Wow! She felt a warmth start in her toes and work its way up to her face. She really did love this man. They had a life, a history, and now they seemingly had a future.

The next morning, Susan arose as the sun was just beginning to peek up over the ocean. She made a quick pot of coffee, drank a couple of cups, nibbled on some toast, and told herself it was time.

"Susan Ward Goldman, stop procrastinating," she said out loud. "You have to do it sometime. You may as well start now."

As she was giving herself this little pep talk, she heard the sound of tires on the gravel driveway. Knowing that Bill wouldn't stop by in the morning anymore, she wondered who it could be. Before she even made it to the front door, in came her screaming brood.

"Mom, I'm hungry!"

"Hi, Mom. Surprise!"

"What's for breakfast?"

"Mom, this is the awesomest place I've ever seen in my whole life," enthused Sam as he gave her a big bear hug. "There's a big swing on a tree out front. Did you know that?" Susan smiled.

"Sam, my father, your grampy, put that swing up there for me when I was about your age. It's been there a long time, and you're right. It *is* awesome. You won't believe what a big, long swing you get on it." Sam's eyes opened wider. "Ben has tried it. He can tell you." Sam's eyes widened in awe as he turned to look at Ben.

"Can I go try it out?" he asked, turning to his mother.

"Come on, squirt," Ben offered. "I'll push you."

Off they ran.

"It really is a neat house, Mom. It's got a cool swing on the porch too. Grammy and Grampy were real swingers, huh?" Ben asked as he headed to the front door. Susan laughed out loud again.

"Oh, Ben. Only you would think of that."

"Can we go out on the rocks by the water, Mom?" asked David. "This place is unreal! There's all kinds of things to do here. Dad told us on the ride up during the night that this whole town is special, but he didn't say why. How come you never told us about it? How come when we came here, we just sat in the living room and talked and then went back home? We passed a place that looks just like the picture in our kitchen back home. And Dad says that even kids can sail here, actually take boats out on the water all alone. Is that true? That sounds awesome."

"Well, David, if you go out to the barn in the back, you might find a small sailboat called a Sunfish that needs a lot of work but probably still floats." David's eyes opened wide. What was his mother saying? She had a sailboat? "There's also an Old Town canoe and a couple of paddles."

"How come we never knew, Mom? There really are boats in your barn? Can I go see?"

"Sure, go ahead." Ben decided that a potential boat in the barn was too cool a thing to miss, so he and David headed out the back door toward the barn.

Ben called out the front door to his little brother, "I'll push you later, Sammy!" Sam stuck out his tongue at his brothers and decided he'd push himself.

When the whirlwind that was her children had scampered off to find treasures and great adventures, she looked and saw Ted standing on the front porch, not coming in. He was facing the water across the road and she couldn't see his face. Opening the door, she wrapped her arms around him from behind and said, "Ted, I am so sorry to have scared everyone. I really didn't mean to. I was feeling unappreciated by everyone, and I was having trouble talking with you about anything. I now see that it was my problem, not yours. When I left, I didn't even know I was coming here. The car headed north and before I knew it, I was here." She stammered and gushed and tried to explain to him in sixty seconds what had taken her days to figure out. As she was still talking, Ted turned around, placed his mouth over hers, and kissed her longingly. She opened her eyes wide and kissed him back, not knowing that he could kiss like that. She had known him a very long time and never had felt anything like that when he kissed her. Wow!

"Eeeeeeeeewwwwwww! Go inside. I don't want to see that," they heard from Sam who was swinging out front.

Laughing, Ted said, "Do you think you could invite me in, or should we make a spectacle of ourselves right here on your front porch and mar our son for life?"

Susan laughed.

"Would you like to enter, kind sir?" She punctuated her formality with a curtsy.

Ted smiled. He liked this woman. She was fun.

"By the way, I thought you were coming this afternoon. You must have driven all night to get here this morning. You're missing a day of work." Susan had never known him to willingly miss a day of work.

"Imagine that," Bill replied. "Something must be very important for me to miss a day of work. And the boys are missing a day of school too." He opened his mouth wide and placed his hands on either side of his face, mimicking the boy from his sons' favorite movie, *Home Alone*.

Susan laughed again. She liked this playful Ted.

Suddenly, playful Ted was gone. Serious Ted returned. He walked her to the living room couch and pulled her down next to him, the same living room couch where.... *Don't go there, Susan. Stay in the moment.*

"Mrs. Goldman, I have a proposition. Well actually, the boys and I have a proposition. We discussed it on the way up here and decided unanimously that we should have a summer house. Of course, Ben thinks it's unfair because he's almost grown up and won't be able to enjoy it as much as the little guys. I assured him that one day he will have a family and they can use the summer house too. He liked that.

Anyway, we decided that we should have a summer house in Maine. I've been a real ass about not letting them spend the time they should have spent here over the years. I let my own insecurities stand in the way of them getting to know the place and your folks as well as they should have. I want to make amends now.

"What would you think of keeping this house and spending every summer here? I could come up for long weekends or maybe even for a few weeks. You could teach them how to sail and how to do whatever it is that you do that makes you love this place. They could discover a side of you they've never known…and maybe I could too. I know you work really hard for us. Believe me, after seeing all of the strangers in and out for the past couple of weeks I know you work really hard for us." She grinned and he returned a crooked smile. "Susan, I guess what I'm saying is, you could get away from it all every summer."

She couldn't believe what she was hearing. Did he really just say that she could keep this home, and not only could she spend time here, but her boys and he would too? It was something she had always wanted. Just as she thought she was about to cry from happiness, Sam came bursting through the screen door.

"Mom! I just saw a big black dog out front. He's not on a leash. I figured I'd better come in."

"Oh, Sammy," she cooed. "You don't have to be afraid of him. That's Keel. He's a great dog, and he loves little boys." She had an idea. "And you know what else he loves? He absolutely loves to have little boys throw sticks into the water for him to go fetch. You want to give it a try?"

"By myself?" Sam was unused to heading out and doing things without supervision.

"Yep," she replied. "By yourself. You'll find that the rules are different here. Keel will be your best buddy if you play with him.

"Wow!" Off he went to make a new friend.

Back to the idea that they could keep her home and use it as a summer house, Susan said, "Ted, we could make some changes here to make it more comfortable for you. We could renovate the kitchen and bathrooms, add some carpeting, and replace those lace curtains with some nice draperies. We could get some leather furniture for this room...."

"Susan, stop. Shhhhhhhh. Don't change a thing for me, Susan. This house is you, and it's high time I learn who you are, lace curtains and all." He cringed jokingly. "If you want to change anything for yourself, by all means, go ahead. But this is going to be your retreat from now on. It needs to reflect what you want."

"Have I told you lately that I love you, Mr. Goldman?" she asked.

"Why no, Mrs. Goldman. You have not," he replied formally, and they both laughed. *We're laughing again. It feels so good to be laughing again.*

Ted was looking around. He had never paid much attention to the place whenever he felt forced to briefly visit Susan's folks.

"This place is charming," he said. "It's right on the water and has a large yard. The barn is incredible. I can't wait to go through it and see what treasures are out there. Maybe I could even build a small office out there and spend more time here than I thought. I could work long-distance for part of the summer and take some as vacation...." *He's thinking that he might want to spend more time here too.* Then he added, "But, if you want this as your escape place, I could just visit once in a while."

"You silly, silly man. I would love to have you here." Susan kissed him again.

"Hmm. I guess you would," and he kissed her back.

"We could moor a sailboat across the road in the inlet, couldn't we?"

"Yep," Susan answered, and a smile spread from ear to ear. "A small sailboat. It would have to have a mast that goes down so it would fit under the little bridge on Main Street. Or, we could get a mooring in the cove and have a bigger boat. I could teach the boys to sail and they could have summer romances and take their girlfriends sailing at sunset."

"Who said the sailboat would be for their romances?" Ted asked, smirking. I just might have to learn to sail myself so that I can take my best girl out on a moonlit night for a little hanky-panky under the stars. We may be forty, but we aren't dead yet, right?"

"Right again, Mr. Goldman. I don't know what you did with Ted, but would you please leave him locked up wherever you put him? I like you better. But don't tell my husband," she added with a giggle.

They began groping each other on the couch like two lovesick teenagers. As they were entangled in each other's arms, in burst three boys—two from the back and one from the front—screen doors slamming all around.

"Yuck!" exclaimed Sam.

"So you two are back together, huh?" asked David.

"Get a room, will ya?" said Ben.

Susan took off a sneaker and threw it in the general direction of her sons.

"You guys are old enough to know that there are times when a couple just has to be alone! And this is one of those times!" Then she had a thought. She turned to Ted and whispered, "Come with me." Then, in a louder voice she said, "Boys, there has always been a rule in this house for as long as I can remember. There is a master bedroom upstairs, and it is off limits. If you are bleeding and have a leg hanging by a nerve, you may knock on the door and ask one of us to come help you. But, under no circumstances are you ever allowed to enter the room. Do you understand? Your grandparents were married for over forty years, and they never let me in that room. I am almost forty years old and to this day have never been in the room. From now on, whenever we are at this house, it is your father's and mine. Understood?"

"Yeah, I guess," muttered Ben with a knowing look of disgust.

"Okay," answered David, not liking it but agreeing.

"But Mommy, I might need you—" Sam began.

"Don't worry, Sammy. I will always take care of you, but you can't come into that room. It's Daddy and Mommy's clubhouse, and we are the only members. But I tell you what," she suddenly had a brilliant idea. "How about we all build a clubhouse in that big old elm tree in the backyard? You guys go take a look and work up some plans for what you want it to look like and what materials we'll need."

Ben took the lead. "Come on, guys. They want to be alone." All three boys trooped out the back door, Ben picking up a pad of paper and a pen from the kitchen table on his way out.

Susan took Ted's hand and began to walk slowly toward the stairs. "I guess there's no time like the present to get started on packing up Ma and Dad's things."

"You know, Susan, we headed out to come here because when you said you were packing your folks' stuff up and putting the house on the market, you had the same sound in your voice that you had at the football game a million years ago. All I wanted then was to put a smile on your face and, when I heard that sadness again, I knew we had to come help you. It was kind of a spur-of-the-moment thought while I was driving that we could actually keep the house. You should have seen the boys when I woke them all up in the car and talked with them about having a summer house. They were half asleep, but even so, they loved the idea."

"You have no idea how much I appreciate that, Ted. You've never really been there for me when I needed you in the past few years. Maybe I never let you know how much I needed you to be."

As they talked, they continued up the stairs, hand in hand. Susan couldn't remember the last time they had held hands. Soon they were standing in front of the closed door to her parents' bedroom.

"I haven't even been in here since I've been back. I've been sleeping in my old room. I guess there's no time like the present."

Susan bit her lip as she opened the door and gasped as she entered the room. It was lovely. While the rest of the house was functional and tidy, decorated in an Early American style, this room was like something out of a magazine. It truly was an escape. The large room was papered in a bright floral print that coordinated with the ruffled comforter on the queen-sized, dark cherry, four-poster bed. On the matching nightstands stood two antique blown glass lamps with fabric shades. At the foot of the bed was a quilt rack that held three of the most beautiful handmade patchwork quilts that Susan had ever seen. As she looked at one of the quilts, she recognized fabrics, and as she looked longer, she realized that each square was a piece of a garment she had worn as a child. She saw her first recital outfit when she had played "My Pretty Maureen" on the piano. She saw Halloween costumes, her first party dress, Easter dresses, favorite jeans, the blouse she had worn on her first date, and a tiny piece of her wedding dress. There were many fabrics she didn't recognize, many that looked like baby clothes, and she knew that they had to be all ones she had worn at one time or another that had provided her mother with fond memories.

Susan picked up another quilt and spread it out on the bed. She recognized her father's old work shirts, her mother's "Sunday-go-to-meeting" dress, and bits of pajamas and robes. The quilts were living memories of her family's life!

Looking across the room, Susie saw a reading alcove with two coordinating upholstered chairs and ottomans. They faced the windows that looked out over the water. Next to each chair was a cherry pie table with a lamp for reading, and on each table were her parents' favorite books. Next to what must have been her father's chair was a worn copy of Edgar Guest's collected poems. Her father had loved Edgar Guest's homespun poetry. He would quote the poems whenever appropriate, having memorized dozens of them. They spoke of honesty and courage in the face of life's everyday trials. And they praised the beauty in life's simple pleasures. Next to her mother's chair sat her table, laden with books: Jane Austen, Nicholas Sparks, Elizabeth Strout, and Sarah Blake all sat waiting to be read. Her mother always admired strong women who didn't bend to a man's every wish. She always had a mind of her own and wasn't afraid to speak it. When she read, she liked to read of women like herself who could handle whatever life threw at them—with or without a man.

On the floor of this room was thick, light green carpeting that, combined with the floral walls, gave Susan the feeling of being in a beautiful garden. Then her eye caught the photos on the dressers. Ted stood in front of them, smiling as he looked at dozens of photos of her. In each frame, Susan saw herself at a different stage of her development, smiling for the camera and for her parents.

Entering the bathroom attached to this bedroom, something that was in itself unusual in an old farmhouse, Susan got another surprise. She felt as though she had entered a Roman bath. Stone tiles adorned the walls and surrounded the oversized claw-foot tub. A separate stall shower was lined with stone tiles, and on shelves were busts and vases reminiscent of ancient Rome. Over the door hung a large stone frieze of a chariot race. Towels in beige and rose still hung from the towel racks, and candles still stood guard on their tall golden pedestals surrounding the tub.

This was a world she had never suspected. Susan couldn't believe her eyes. She had grown up in this house yet had never known that such a haven existed. When she had peeked in one stormy night, the room was dark, and she had not been aware of the opulence that resided within. Amazing!

Ted looked around with admiration.

"As I said before, I wouldn't change a thing," he said jokingly. "I had no idea your parents had this kind of taste. They certainly didn't seem to, did they?"

While her first instinct was to get mad at him for insulting her parents, instead Susan had to agree with him. The rest of the house was clean and nice, but certainly not like this.

"Well, I guess we'd better get busy," she said, reluctantly. "I really don't want to do this, but I know we have to."

Ted leered at her and began striding toward her with a tiger walk.

"I agree," he huskily said. "We should definitely get busy." The implication was obvious. "You said yourself that we have to."

Susan laughed.

"Are you serious?"

"Woman, I have never been more serious. You see, my wife has been gone for a while now and I have to admit that it has been a long time since we 'got busy,' if you know what I mean."

Susan laughed at his tone of voice, low and deep, sort of like Marvin Gaye. At that thought, she laughed again and then, in mock sexiness, she lowered her voice and sang as she danced for him,

Let's get it on
Ah, baby, let's get it on

Ted stood, mesmerized by this woman before him. He had never seen this side of Susan and liked it a lot. As she sashayed toward him, his grin told his joy. With the door securely locked and the boys busy in the yard, in the middle of the day with the sun streaming in the windows, Ted and Susan got it on.

"Well, that was interesting," Ted began. "Where have you been keeping that Mrs. Goldman?"

"Well, Mr. Goldman, when I am happy and feel that my husband understands me, when he is being nice to me, I have all kinds of desire to please him." Susan winked as she jumped up off the bed and ran to the shower.

As she was starting to wash her hair, Ted appeared.

"Mind if I join you? I'm thinking we need to conserve water when we're using a well.

"Well, that's the most eco-friendly thing you've ever said to me, Mr. Goldman," Susan purred in a southern accent.

Dressed and very clean, Susan said, "Well, I guess we'd better really get busy. I don't want to pack up Ma and Dad's things, but I know we have to. Would you mind going downstairs and getting the boxes I picked up yesterday? We'll just empty out the closets and drawers and take everything to the church. They know who can use the stuff."

When Ted went downstairs to retrieve the boxes, Susan noticed a hope chest tucked against the wall in the corner of the room. It had a tiny gold lock with a tinier key inserted in it. Curious as to its contents, she turned the key and the lock popped open. As she opened the cover, an old, yellowed envelope appeared on the top of the pile of linens that was inside. Not recognizing the handwriting, she shivered as she opened the envelope, though she didn't know why. She sat down in the slipcovered chair by the window and began to read:

Dear Mary,

So it was a letter to her mother.

As I write this, you are a grown woman about to have a baby of your own. I know that my days are numbered, but before I go, there are a few things that you have to know. When you read

211

this, I hope that you will already be a proud and happy mother because then you will understand what I am about to say.

Mary, when I was a little girl, it was a different world. I had lots of brothers and sisters and my parents struggled to make ends meet so that we would be fed and clothed and have a roof over our heads. Your grandparents didn't hope for more than that. They felt that if their children were clean and dry and well-fed that they had done their job as parents. They plodded through life, never seeming to 'enjoy it—simply putting in their time on this earth. With ten children, they couldn't afford the luxuries that make life easy. Theirs was a cold and harsh life. I believe that somewhere in their hearts they did love all of us children, but they hardly ever showed it. We didn't get the hugs and kisses that children deserve. Maybe they were afraid that they didn't have enough time to show affection to all of us so they never showed much to any of us. I don't know.

One thing I learned from them, though, was that if I ever had children, my children would know that I loved them and would have happy, fulfilled childhoods. I wanted so much for you. I wanted to hold you and hug you. I wanted to kiss you and tell you how much I loved you. I wanted to laugh and cry with you and buy you everything your heart desired. But old habits die hard.

As much as I wanted to, I just couldn't find the strength to overcome a lifetime of learning and actually do them. It tore me apart that you never really received the kind of affection and demonstrations of love from me that I wanted to give and that you deserved. I watched you grow up laughing and crying and throwing tantrums and, believe it or not, I especially liked the tantrums. You had a fire in you. Whenever you were mad at your father or me, you would storm into your room, slam the door, and cry your heart out. It sounds strange for a mother to say, but a part of me loved that. I never could have done it. I never could have released emotion so freely, and I celebrated that you would not be emotionally handicapped like I was. Somehow, even though I didn't show you much emotion, you had learned how to handle it yourself.

Mary, you're a strong woman. You've always had an inner strength that I have admired. You never followed the crowd or took the easy way out. You would argue endlessly that the sky was green if you really believed it was. But I've watched you these past few months as I've gotten sicker. You have put a wall between yourself and the rest of the world. At a time when you should be rejoicing in your impending motherhood, you have shut down your emotions. I am so scared that you are doing this because you think it's what I want. Why can't I talk with you about this? I am failing you. All I can do is write this letter to you and hope that you read it in time to not lose out on the pure joy that can be yours in life.

After I'm gone, I hope you have the strength to read this and to get on with your life. You've a great husband in George. You will have a wonderful baby girl to love. I just know it will be a girl. I lie here in this bed staring out the window at the water and I dream of what she will be like.

Oh, how I wish I could be around to see her grow up. She will be the lucky one. She will get the hugs and kisses I couldn't freely give you. You will sing her praises, laugh with her, and cry with her. You and George and your daughter will lead the life I always wanted for us. I know you thought of me as cold, Mary, but I was never cold. I reveled in your accomplishments, and I cried myself quietly to sleep when you were sad. If only you could have known that. Then you would have understood how much I loved you.

Dear, dear Mary. If you are reading this letter, then I am gone. Oh, I said that already, didn't I? I'm so sorry that I couldn't tell you these things while I was alive. I guess I didn't want you to think I was weak. By being stoic, I thought I was showing strength for you. In reality, I was a coward. I never could face emotion head-on. It's probably what will kill me in the end. I bottle everything up inside and one day I'll just explode. I know I'm being melodramatic, but it's not healthy to keep anger and happiness and sadness inside.

Live a long, healthy, happy life, my dear Mary. Shower both your wonderful daughter and husband with hugs and kisses,

laughter and tears. Allow yourself to FEEL and to SHOW IT. If you loved me as much as I loved you, do this one last thing for me.
    Love,
    Mother
    P.S. The enclosed key fits my hope chest. I have left some things for you to give to your daughter. On the bottom of the chest is a very special gift for you. It has given me many hours of joy and I hope that you enjoy it as much as I have.

Susan couldn't believe what she was reading. It was a letter from her grandmother to her mother, written before Susan was born. What remarkable insight it provided to her grandmother's heart. She wished that her mother had shared it with her, and she felt sad that she had never known her grandmother. She did remember receiving gifts that her mother said were from her grandmother. To a little kid, the mittens and hats, nightgowns and pajamas didn't seem like much, but now, remembering as an adult, they were priceless. As she was thinking this, she realized that another letter was in the same envelope. She carefully opened its brittle folds and read:

My dearest granddaughter,

"Oh my God!" she exclaimed out loud. "This letter is to me from my grandmother. I wonder why I never saw it. I think I remember my mother reading it to me, but I had forgotten all about it." Susan read on:

You don't know me, but I'm your grammy. Before you were born, I got a very bad disease that made me very sick. I knew that I wasn't going to get better, although I wouldn't let the doctors tell your mommy that. Since I knew that I probably would never meet you, I wanted to make sure that you knew me and thought about me once in a while and knew how much I loved you. In this trunk is a very old photo album. In fact, your mommy didn't even know about it. In it are pictures of me when I was a young lady, a new wife with your grampy, a new mommy, and pictures of your

mommy when she was a little girl. Your mommy was a beautiful little girl just like I'm sure you will be. (If I'm wrong and you turn out to be a little boy, I apologize to you, but I am just sure you will be a little girl.). Hopefully, this album will be something that you and your mommy can look at together and laugh and cry about. I never could do that with your mommy but I bet that she and you will. Enjoy it. It is my gift to you.
   Love,
   Your Loving Grammy Susan

Susan hurried back to the hope chest and quickly found what she was looking for—the photo album her grandmother left to her and to her mother. As she looked through it, Ted arrived in the room carrying empty boxes. One look at her tear-stained face, the agony and joy behind the tears, and he dropped the boxes and ran to her side.

Kneeling on the floor in front of her, Ted tentatively asked if she was okay. She just looked at him. Looking at the album in her lap, he asked her what it was, a note of concern in his voice. Susan couldn't respond. She simply opened it and showed it to him as she looked at it. She did remember sitting in her mother's lap when she was little, looking at these pictures and thinking they were pictures of herself. She really did look an awful lot like her mother had looked at her age. It was remarkable. After studying the photos for quite a while, Susan looked up at Ted, tears stinging her eyes.

"In all these years, I had no idea that treasure was buried in this room," she whispered. Carefully placing the album back in the chest, she returned the tiny key to the lock. Still holding the envelope, she sat back down and looked inside. There was a smaller note. She read:

Dear Mary
   I apologize for hitting you with so much so fast, but these presents are my final gift to you and your own little girl. If you have a boy, my name will be mud and this won't be very meaningful. I'm sorry. The thought made me laugh. It isn't a problem. I know you'll have a girl.

*Since I will not be there to spoil her like any good grand-
mother should, I need a little help from you. It has been difficult for me to get out these past few months, as you know. But
I have managed to do what I love best. I have used my time to
create a legacy for my granddaughter. Inside this chest are enough
gifts for you to give to her from her grammy on every birthday
and Christmas for the next few years. I wish that I could have
done more, but the good Lord chose otherwise for me. By the time
she's older, though, maybe she will understand that although she
doesn't have a grandmother like other kids, she can still feel the
love I had for her when I was making these things. Please wrap
them for me and give them to her with all of my love.*

Love,

Mother

Susan gasped. To Ted she said, "That's why my mother insisted on
saving all of my hats and mittens and scarves and dresses and even my
pajamas. She glanced across the room at the quilt resting at the foot of
the bed.

"Ted! The pajamas in the quilt are the ones my grandmother
made for me before I was born as she was dying! I bet a lot of those
things are things she made. They've been here all this time and I
didn't even know it. My mother used to hint that I had a great legacy
and someday I would realize what it was. This has to be what she was
talking about. She was always so cryptic about it, as though to tell me
would spoil the surprise."

Ted could see that she was overwhelmed. "Listen, Susan," he began.
"Let's call it a day for this room and go out and enjoy the sunshine
with the boys. We can get to packing things up tomorrow. If we have
to stay an extra day or two, we could do that. We also could come up
next weekend. It's really not that far. I just need to call the office, okay?
Agreed? Good. Let's go downstairs."

But Susan didn't want to leave this room. She had discovered a
treasure trove of family memories and hadn't realized how her heart
had longed for these memories until she found them. Reluctantly, she

allowed herself to be shepherded from the room, down the stairs, and out into the bright sunshine.

When the boys saw them coming, they ran toward them, all talking excitedly about their plans for the promised clubhouse. Ben figured that he could build the structure. David could make a list of materials they would need. And Sam could be their gofer and plan all kinds of activities they could do when it was finished.

"Guys," started Ted. "This is all going to have to wait a bit because your mother and I have decided to take a walk into town for brunch. Come along. We'll have great fun! It will be an adventure! Who knows what we'll discover on our way."

Susan looked at him with a smirk and asked, "You really want to walk? It's about a mile."

"Well, I may be over forty but I'm not dead," Ted joked. I think these old bones can make it," and as he spoke he hunched over and took on the posture and gait of an old man. As he shuffled along, the boys laughed and urged him to keep it up. After a couple of minutes, he tired of the joke, however, and began walking quietly beside Susan, who wore a Mona Lisa smile.

Every so often, Susan would call out to a neighbor and introduce her family. Bill's dog and its friend appeared out of nowhere and remembered that she had thrown sticks in the water for them. They each brought her a stick and she dutifully threw them. When the wet dogs returned to beg her to do it again, Ted shied away from them and the boys whooped.

"It's just water," Susan scolded him. "If you're going to hang around here, you'd better get used to getting wet and dirty." She grabbed the slobbery sticks out of the dogs' mouths and tossed them far out into the inlet. The excited dogs bounded toward the water, plunged in, and quickly retrieved the sticks. This time when they returned, the boys hurried to meet the dogs and Susan offered proper introductions and then told the dogs to play with the boys. As if they understood English, they dutifully trotted off with the three boys and the five of them continued their game all the way into town.

Arriving at the Seaside Café, Susan advised the boys to go to the men's room and wash the water off their hands. Little Sam piped up,

"But Mom. That doesn't make any sense. You want us to go wash the water off with water." Susan had to laugh at his logic but insisted that he do so anyway.

"Your brothers will explain," she said to him as she affectionately patted his fanny and sent him on his way.

"Hi, Helen," she called to the woman behind the counter.

"Hi, yourself," Helen called back. Just then she realized that Susan was here with a very good looking, strange man. He was a city type and looked as though he was going to ask her to clean the seat before he sat down. Susan noticed him standing next to the booth and pulled him down onto the seat.

"You're going to insult Helen," she whispered.

Helen moseyed over to the table, her order pad and pen at the ready.

"So who are you?" she asked Ted bluntly.

"Um, I'm Susan's husband," Ted answered, surprised by the bluntness but then remembering that he was now in Maine, the land of no-nonsense straightforwardness and honesty.

When Ted said he was Susan's husband, all the heads in the café turned toward them. There weren't too many people here at this time of day. It was late for breakfast and still a little early for the lunch crowd, but Susan was sure that within a couple of hours, every single person in town would know that her husband was in town. The gossip mill would really start to churn now. All she had to do was to keep Ted from hearing any of the old gossip. It seemed that Bill had told Doug in strict confidence that he and Susan had almost made love. Doug couldn't stand being the sole proprietor of such a juicy piece of gossip and had told Jeannie in strictest confidence. She, of course, had told Beth in strictest confidence, who had told Mavis in strictest confidence, and so on and so on until the entire town knew that Bill and Susan, high school sweethearts who had found each other again, had almost made it on the rocks at the end of the Coast Road. Now she had to make sure that Ted didn't become part of the chain until she had time to tell him in her own way. She told him she'd be right back and scooted off to wash her hands.

Just then the boys came out of the men's room with the same quizzical look on their faces and jumped into their seats at the table. David was the first one to speak.

"Dad, who's Bill?" he asked out of the blue. Ted whipped his head around to look at the boys and Susan arrived just in time to see his perplexed expression. When he didn't answer, David turned to his mother. "Mom, who's Bill? Susan plopped down on the bench of the booth and sat with her mouth wide open. Regaining her composure, she asked innocently,

"Why, honey?"

"Because it says on the bathroom wall that Bill loves Susie forever. We figure this is a small town and Susie must be you. So who's Bill?"

David had always been the persistent one, so Susan figured that there was no time like the present for little truths. She looked at each of them, avoiding Ted's eyes, and said, "Well, Bill was my high school sweetheart. We dated each other all through high school, and everyone thought we'd get married. His father died and he had to forget about going to college, and I went away and met your dad and fell in love with him. We got married and had you monkeys, and I never saw Bill again until I came back here. Now we're just old friends."

"Oh," said David.

"Sure," smirked Ben.

"Okay," agreed Sam.

"Really?" asked Ted.

"Really, truly," answered Susan. "In fact, you'll probably all meet him tonight because he was planning on coming over for dinner after he got back in with the boat. He's bringing lobsters, so you'll have a chance to sample a real New England shore dinner with lobsters fresh out of the ocean. Does that sound cool?" *I'd better text him and let him know there are four more people for dinner.*

Everyone except Ted thought that sounded cool and every ear in the café was tuned to his frequency. They were not going to miss a word of this. Gossip this juicy didn't come along very often and it would sustain them throughout the long Maine winter.

"He's coming over tonight?" asked Ted. "When were you going to tell me that? If we hadn't arrived unexpectedly, you and he would have had a nice quiet dinner for two, I suppose." Ted's jealous nature was rearing itself. Susan realized that it was probably time to tame it.

"Ted, our old high school friends, Doug and Jeannie, are coming over too. It was just going to be an innocent evening with old friends. If you want me to cancel, I will, but you'll have to tell Jeannie because she has seven kids and is pregnant, and when she gets a chance to get a babysitter and have a night out, I wouldn't want to be the one to tell her she can't do it after all." Susan laughed nervously. She hoped that Ted wasn't going to make a scene here in the café.

After a moment's pause, Ted replied cheerfully, "Well, that sounds like fun. I'll finally get a chance to get to meet some of your old friends. You know all of mine, but I don't know yours. I bet they have all kinds of fun stories about your teen years." With that, he summoned Helen back over to take their order, and everyone in the diner returned to their meals.

Chapter Thirty-Four

After they finished eating, Susan asked them if they would like to see something very cool. David piped up, "Mom cool or really cool?" "Wise guy. This is really cool and Mom cool."

Susan led the way out of the diner, down the street to the lobster pound where she ducked down the alley between it and the general store next door.

Ted was hesitant to follow. "Where are you taking us?"

"Just follow me. The tide is in, and this is my Oceanside. In fact, I think if you look closely, you'll all recognize it."

Susan hurried down the ramp onto the float and plopped herself down on its edge. As she sat, her focus changed. At first, she saw the cove, the irregular shape of it, the rocks at the shoreline, the houses perched above, pine and oak and maple trees with the occasional brightness of birch. She saw the green water, reflections of the trees along the shoreline giving it that deep green appearance she had come to love. She saw boats bobbing at their high tide moorings—lobster boats, old and dirty, worn by the weather and the waves. She saw sailboats feeling sorry for the working boats. The sailboats were shiny and unmarred, their hulls painted brightly in blues and reds and white. The lobster boats, on the other hand, were worn. Paint was missing. Raw wood ached for a coat of paint to make it new again. The lobster boats looked tired while the sailboats were energetic and lively. They only went out a few times during the summer, enjoying leisurely day sails loaded with happy families. The lobster boats worked every day dragging tired lobstermen and women from trap to trap and waiting patiently while the traps were hauled up onto the deck, dripping water and seaweed. When the traps were emptied and refilled with smelly bait, they were lowered again and the lobster boats dutifully moved on to the next trap. No wonder that, as a native Mainer, Susan looked out over the cove in awe of the lobster boats. They were hardworking, sturdy, and reliable. The sailboats, by contrast, were luxury playthings that never worked a day in their lives. They were the playboys of the boating world.

She explained all of this to her family, who thought her descriptions were, in fact, cool. When she told them to think of the painting hanging in their family room over the fireplace, each face, in turn, lit up in recognition.

"I told you this was a cool place," she said as she turned on her heel and headed back to the road. "It used to be a lot nicer, but time takes its toll on everything." As she spoke, she wondered whether the dock had changed or she had.

On the walk back to their new summer house, Susan had a chance to talk quietly with Ted. The boys were running up ahead and climbing on the rocks. She figured that she'd better get it over with.

"Ted, there is something I should probably tell you," she began.

"Oh?" was all he said.

"Yes," she continued. "When I came up with the idea to teach all of you a lesson about taking me for granted, it was because I was feeling trapped. It didn't seem as though anyone appreciated what I did for them. I ran myself ragged from dawn until midnight, and all I got was criticism and lists of more things that had to be done. I seemed to be going through the motions of life without enjoying it. When it occurred to me that most of what I did for the four of you could be done by hired help, I decided to give it a try. It was really a sort of social experiment, I guess. But then it took a strange turn.

"When I got here, I planned to just rest and relax and think about ways to make things better at home. I figured with some peace and solitude, I'd come up with some brilliant solutions to everyone's problems. All I seemed to get, though, were bigger problems."

At this point, Susan hesitated and looked at Ted to gauge his reaction. She couldn't tell from his face what he was thinking. She forged on. She figured that he wouldn't make too big a scene right here in the road.

"You see, when I got here I didn't realize that Bill had been keeping an eye on the place for my folks and then just kept on keeping an eye on it after they were gone. The night I got here, he saw lights on and was worried that someone might have been breaking in, so he stopped by. Nothing happened, I swear, but I admit I did have feelings for him when I saw him again. He was my first love, and I got all confused about what I was feeling. I'm sure you still have feelings for your first love, too, even though you don't talk about her.

"Well, here I was faced with a dilemma. I could either slam the door in his face, or we could become friends. I decided that it would be childish to run away from him, so we became friends. Bill and I have spent time together since I've been here, but as friends. I've spent some time with Jeannie and Doug, too, but you're not jealous of them, so you don't care.

"But, Ted, even if something had happened between Bill and me, it wouldn't have meant anything because my life is with you and the boys."

At this point, Ted's honesty meter was moving. He turned and looked at Susan, trying to understand what she was really telling him. Was she trying to tell him that something happened but that it was meaningless, or was she saying that if it had happened, it would have been meaningless? He decided to calmly confront her. Without raising his voice, he asked, "Susan, do you think I'm an idiot? You left home without a word. Where did you go? Back to your childhood home, a place you have wanted to go for as long as I have known you. You had unfinished business here. I knew that. I guess that's the real reason I never wanted to come here. I was so afraid of losing you if you saw him again that I figured I'd just make sure you didn't see him."

Susan was astounded. She had no idea Ted felt that way. He really did love her. In fact, he loved her so much that he didn't even want to take the chance that she might prefer Bill over him. He had always seemed so in control of everything, so secure. Now she saw him as an insecure man, afraid of losing his wife.

"Susan, what happened here? I don't really want to know, but if we're going to keep this place as our summer retreat, everything has to be out in the open. What you say and what you do are important to me. I love you and I need to know."

Susan hesitated. She looked at Ted as they stood on the side of the road. The kids had gotten far ahead of them by now, enjoying their freedom. Susan figured that she had two choices. She could tell Ted the truth and hope for the best, or she could lie.

She did love her life, and she had a new outlook, having gotten Bill out of her system, as Ted had said. She saw no upside to hurting her family. She was so glad that she hadn't done anything she couldn't come back from. If she had made love with Bill, she would have been risking her marriage, her family, her entire life for a few moments' pleasure. Ted had hidden his affairs over the years, and she had accepted them. It was her choice. She knew, though, that if she had given herself fully to Bill, Ted would not have been able to forgive her. It might be a double standard, but it was the way it was. Even if they did stay together, he would always look at her differently. They had promised to love each other until death do they part, and they did. That promise didn't preclude minor indiscretions that had nothing to do with their love for each other. She looked up at Ted and decided to tell him the truth.

"Ted, I was very vulnerable when I arrived here. When I saw Bill, all the old feelings came rushing back, and for a brief instant I felt as though I was a teenager again, and it felt good. We sat on the porch swing and talked about old times, and he kissed me. I kissed him back." Susan saw the hurt in Ted's eyes just from her kissing Bill. She continued.

"Bill and I had a lot of history together, but it's ancient history. It's childish history. It's the stuff friendships are made of, not great lifelong loves. Ted, you and I have that. We have almost twenty years of joy and pain, facing trials and overcoming obstacles. We've built a good life and have three wonderful sons. We have the kind of history that matters. We have a love that will never diminish. I love you with all my heart."

Susan saw Ted's face soften and relief spread across his features. He reached out to her, and she went into his arms. From a neighbor's porch, they heard a song drifting out to them, and they both smiled. Susan began singing along,

If I could put time in a bottle,
The first thing that I'd like to do
Is to spend every day like a treasure and then
Again I could spend them with you.

Ted smiled. "You are so corny. Everything is a song cue for you, isn't it? It always has been." He wrapped his arm around her, and they began walking again, secure in the knowledge that they would love each other differently from now on. She did love him. He knew that. If she had needed to get Bill out of her system, Ted didn't have to like it, but he understood it.

Ted walked along silently for a while. He was trying to decide whether he should be honest with Susan and tell her about his indiscretions. On the one hand, if he told her, he wouldn't have to carry the guilt with him wherever he went and whenever he looked at her. On the other hand, if he told her, he would hurt her, and that was something he didn't want to do. The affairs had meant nothing to him. They were just convenient, in-the-right-place-at-the-right-time occurrences. He had seen Susan wrapped up in being a good mother and seeming not to have time for him, and he had found women who had all the time he wanted and who made him feel virile and masculine. They dressed sexy and smelled sexy and looked sexy. They welcomed him, and he walked right into their embraces. After being without Susan for the past couple of weeks and doing a lot of thinking about her and about their life together, he knew that he would never let himself stray again. Maybe the price he should pay was to shoulder the guilt alone. He decided not to say anything.

Susan had been watching Ted's face out of the corner of her eye as they walked along hand in hand. The boys were far ahead now, laughing and playing together like they used to when they were little. Ted looked tortured, but she didn't think it was because she had kissed Bill. She thought she knew what it was. He was trying to decide whether or not to confess his own dalliances. Since Susan had come to terms with them long ago, and since she wanted their relationship to move ahead free of lies or secrets, she stopped walking. She tugged on Ted's hand and moved him over to a big rock on the side of the road where she sat down. She pulled him down next to her.

"Ted, since I just told you about how Bill has haunted me my entire adult life and now will be a friend, I need to tell you something else I have been keeping secret from you."

Ted turned abruptly, looking at her with eyebrows pulled together and eyes like slits, his head tilted to one side. He said nothing.

"Theodore Michael Goldman," Susan began in a gentle voice, "the secret I've been keeping is that I know all about your affairs. I knew when they were happening and I've come to terms with them. I've had a lot of time to think up here, and I've done some soul-searching and self-reflection and am finally able to be honest with myself. When we had the boys, with each one, I became more involved in their lives and their needs. I'm not apologizing. They were tiny beings who depended on me for everything. You were an adult who should have understood that. But, if I'm honest, you came home to me after long days of work to find me wearing a sweatsuit with traces of baby food on it, my hair pulled back in a ponytail, and no makeup. I immediately started complaining about my day without even bothering to ask about yours."

Ted's eyes glistened with tears, but still he said nothing.

"Contrast that image with the women in your office who admired you, dressed for success, discussed the things you cared about, and met you on a level intellectual playing field. Heck," Susan tried to smile. "I probably would have been attracted to them."

"Susan, I am so sorry. I never meant to hurt you. I never loved you any less. You are the love of my life, the mother of my children. I always have and always will love you."

Susan's lips smiled, although her eyes refused to join in. "Ted, that is why I forgave you long ago."

Ted reached out and pulled her close. He knew that this woman was one in a million. He knew that he would love her for all his days and would never stop trying to be the husband she deserved. Suddenly, he stood, pulling her up with him. He then got down on one knee, holding her hands in his and spontaneously asked her a question.

"Susan Elizabeth Ward Goldman, would you marry me—again? I want to renew our vows before our sons and let them know that they can always count on us. I want you to know that I love you with all my heart and that I will spend the rest of my days proving that to you."

Surprised by this turn of events and seeing her sons running back toward them, questions on their faces, Susan simply said, "Yes."

Chapter Thirty-Five

Six weeks later, Susan was a bride—again. She stood in the gazebo in the center of Oceanside, wearing a long white sleeveless dress, flanked by her childhood friend Jeannie, her college friend Katie, and her Connecticut neighbor friend Raye, each wearing a pretty summer dress of their choosing. With their sons in new navy suits with sailboat-adorned neckties and Ted standing resplendent in a matching navy suit and tie, Susan and Ted renewed their vows. They promised to love each other forever, to never again take each other for granted, and to listen to each other, not just hear each other.

Seated in rented white chairs on the freshly mown lawn were friends from home, childhood friends, new friends, townspeople, and a few tourists who wanted to be a part of this happy day. Ted's mother sat proudly in the front row, happy that her son looked so content, though she couldn't understand why this ceremony had to once again be held in this tiny town. Since Katie was in the wedding party, Prince Richard sat with Ted's mother, making her feel special.

Following the brief service, everyone adjourned to the Goldman summer home where they feasted on lobsters provided by Bill, sweets provided by Jeannie and her friends, and all of the fixings prepared by Susan and Ted before they had dressed for their day. At one point, Ted looked up at the now-finished clubhouse, supported by both the big old tree and wooden beams, and saw all three boys laughing together at some joke. He pointed it out to Susan and she smiled, happy that her sons were once again getting along as brothers should.

When the last guests had left and the boys were asleep—Ben in his bedroom and David and Sam in sleeping bags in the clubhouse—Susan and Ted took glasses of wine to the front porch swing.

"Well, Mrs. Goldman, I have a little surprise for you."

Susan couldn't imagine what surprise Ted could have.

"You may not believe this, but my mother has agreed to come and stay at our house for two weeks in October." Susan had thought he had a nice surprise, but this one meant a lot of work for her. She caught herself before she said anything, though. It would be nice for the boys' only grandparent to spend more time with them.

"She's coming to stay because you and I are going on a second honeymoon. For two weeks we will forget that we have children and will bask in the Mediterranean sunshine enjoying a cruise. We will delight in casual luxury as we sleep late, dance into the wee hours, visit ports of call, sample delicacies, and you, Mrs. Goldman, will be responsible for absolutely nothing except enjoying yourself."

Flabbergasted, since they had never taken a vacation without the boys, Susan didn't know what to say. She simply hugged him and whispered in his ear, "Mr. Goldman, maybe we can try for that daughter you've always wanted." Ted was shocked that she would suggest it but could see that she was serious. Wow! What Ted didn't tell her was that Katie and Richard would be hosting them on the royal yacht. He left that as a happy surprise for her to discover later.

Chapter Thirty-Six

When the family returned from Maine to their home in Connecticut, everything went back to normal. Ted worked long hours. Susan drove the boys all over town every day. But something was different. They all seemed to have a new appreciation for each other. The boys argued less. Susan enjoyed doing things for the men in her life. She felt needed again—especially after she saw how the house-keeper had reorganized her pantry, purchased brands her family didn't like, and cleaned around everything instead of doing things thoroughly as Susan herself did.

Once Susan had her house in order, and since it was school vacation, she decided to use the time when the boys were engaged with their friends or at tennis lessons or swimming in their backyard pool to start writing again. She and Ted had discussed her aspirations on the drive back from Maine while the boys slept in the backseats. She had attended one of the most prestigious graduate writing programs in the country but had never published any of her writing. She had files on her laptop and a box in the attic filled with stories she had begun during the past twenty years. Maybe it was time to take another look at them and polish them up.

She was determined to finish something she had started writing. She went to the attic, brought the box downstairs, and organized it, putting each story or story idea under a separate heading in a binder. Using her trusty three-hole punch, she prepared each story and placed it in its appropriate place. Once she had them all organized, she read through them carefully to see what triggered her imagination. She settled on two of them and set aside time each day for writing. She was going to work on them interchangeably, the one about her first trip abroad one day and the one about her hometown the next. She figured by doing that, she would never be bogged down with one, and both would get finished.

Once all three boys left on their bicycles to meet friends at the club to go swimming the next day, Susan was excited and ready. Finally, she was going to be doing something she had always yearned to do but for which she had never made time. She sequestered herself in Ted's home office, sat at his desk, and stared at her laptop. All the male energy seemed to block her ideas, so she set out to find a more inspiring writing location. She sat on the couch in the family room, but every time she looked up she saw dust on the bookcase, toys on the floor, and a carpet that needed vacuuming, breaking her concentration. She tried sitting at the kitchen table, but found herself thinking about what she would make for dinner or what she needed to buy at the grocery store. Soon, the only thing she was writing was a grocery list.

Undeterred, Susan decided to leave her house and find a suitable place to write. The boys were occupied for several hours. She wanted a cup of coffee, so she drove to the local coffee shop. This seemed promising. She got her coffee and settled herself at a small table in a corner of the shop. For a while, she wrote with abandon. Soon, though, because she lived in a small town and knew many of its residents, people kept interrupting her to say hello and to ask what she was working on. As nice as it was to chat with folks she knew, she decided to move on and find a spot where she wouldn't be interrupted as much.

Susan drove from the coffee shop, through town to the park where she set up shop at a picnic table. *Hmm,* she thought. *This just might work.* After writing for a few minutes, she noticed a mother pushing a carriage and was taken back to her early days of motherhood when she had stalked similar women in order to make friends. *I should write about that,* she thought, and off she went in another direction, writing about her adventure in the park all those years ago. Whenever she looked up from her writing, she was distracted by the pretty flowers and the birds chirping and the children playing on the playground nearby.

Beginning to feel as though she would never find the right place to write, or the focus to stay on task, she returned to her car where she sat in the passenger seat with her laptop wedged between her knees and the dashboard. *Look what I've been reduced to,* she thought with a laugh. She wasn't angry, just frustrated.

Since she was already out, Susan decided to go to the grocery store and pick up something for dinner that night. Back at home, unloading her groceries, she realized that she had been trying to write for four hours and had only five pages to show for her efforts, two of them on a totally new story about the park. Determined, she tried sitting at the kitchen table again, telling herself that she would focus and not be distracted by anything else, but every time she looked up from her screen, she saw dishes to be washed or papers to be put away or dust on the floor or a blanket to be folded in the adjoining family room. She remembered that there was laundry to be done or the telephone rang or the dog needed to go out, or she got up for a drink of water and realized that she had to go to the bathroom. This was ridiculous.

Sooner than she had expected, the boys came bounding in, each asking if he could go to a friend's house. Since she knew all of their friends and, lucky for her, they all lived in the neighborhood, she told them to get lost. Happily, they took off, leaving her with the afternoon to herself.

She began wandering through her home. It really was lovely. She strolled through the kitchen to the family room. Off the back of the family room, looking out over the backyard, was the sunroom. Its French doors were open, as they always were, and Susan thought again what a pretty space it was. She strolled out and sat in one of the slipcovered chairs, looking out the windows across the pool to the pond visible through the trees. She was always at peace in this space. It felt like her room. Ted and the boys had never liked the frou-frou (their word) way she had decorated it. A pale-green carpet provided the grass, and floral slipcovered chairs and a coordinating striped sofa were the flower beds. *Oh my gosh,* Susie thought. *I decorated this room just like my mother decorated my parents' bedroom before I even saw that space.* Looking out the paned windows on three sides, she could see the sky. It was like her secret garden in the house. *Mmm. I feel at peace here,* thought Susan, her eyes closed.

Suddenly, her eyes popped open and, closing them to observant slits, she evaluated the room. She could move the two chairs closer together over there. She could put the couch over there. She could add low, sill-height white bookcases all around behind the furniture. A writing table could go right there, facing the backyard. Voilà! Susan knew that this would be her writing office. By closing the French doors, it could be her retreat. Her men didn't like it anyway.

Not even waiting to discuss her decision with Ted, Susan called each of the homes where her sons were playing, asking if they could stay for a couple more hours. The moms readily agreed since the boys were having fun with each other. She then hopped into her SUV and drove to the nearest furniture store where she purchased a writing table and chair. She also found the low, white bookcases she wanted. Much to her surprise, she was told that the furniture was in stock and could be delivered later in the afternoon. She then drove to the office supply store where she purchased a printer, paper, pens, and other office supplies.

Once back at home, Susan moved the furniture in the sunroom to accommodate her new furniture. She set up her printer on the corner of the desk, put some of her supplies in the single drawer and the rest on the bookcases. She went upstairs to the library and pulled her writing books from the shelves. It took her several trips, but she carried them down and put them on her new bookcases. She then placed the binder with her unfinished writing on the bookcase closest to her desk. Grabbing her laptop from the kitchen table, she set it on the desk. She closed the French doors and surveyed her new office. It was perfect. She sat down in her new desk chair and began to write. The words flowed, and she was lost in their world. She never heard the boys return home, one by one, until they started banging on the doors and calling out to her. She opened the doors with a flourish and enjoyed their surprised expressions as they saw her new office.

"I'm not putting a "Do Not Disturb" sign on the door, but this room is going to have the same rule as Daddy's and my room in Maine. You are not *ever* to enter this room. Understood? It's mine."

"No problem," replied Ben. "It's too girly anyway."

"Okay," said David.

"But what if I need you?" asked Sam.

Susan smiled. Their reactions were always so predictable. She really loved these guys.

"Sammy, if you need me, you knock on the door, and I will always be here for you."

That seemed to satisfy Sam, who ran off to play downstairs in the game room. The other two sauntered off as well. Susan realized that they were growing up. She could write even when they were at home because they could now entertain themselves. She shut the doors again, sat in front of her laptop, and returned to London.

As she wrote about a knock on the door of her London apartment, Susan actually heard the knock. She then realized that she was in Connecticut, and the knock was real. She rose, shook the kinks out of her hands from writing furiously for hours, and opened the doors to find a surprised Ted standing there, looking over her head at the new office.

Susan giggled and asked him what he thought of it. He was shocked. In all their years of marriage, they had always discussed furniture purchases and decorating ideas. She had always asked for his opinion. As he stood there looking at the transformation of the sunroom in a single afternoon, and at his wife, glowing with pride, he simply pulled her into his arms and hugged her.

"Susan, it is absolutely you. What a great idea! This room has been wasted space. You should have taken it over years ago." Susan was a little offended by the comment, but she knew what he meant. He and the boys didn't like it. "It's the perfect office for you. Now we each have our own space. Now I know why Sammy told me I'd better knock instead of just opening the doors." Susan laughed out loud at that, and Ted grimaced playfully. Noticing the laptop and the open binder on the desk, he asked, "What are you doing, anyway?"

"I'm finally writing the novel I had planned to write when I came back from London. It's about a naïve country girl who travels to London for the first time. It portrays her experiences and reactions to the city."

"That's fantastic!" Ted enthused. Then he jokingly added, "I thought you were probably writing about a mom who runs away from home to find herself but ends up finding herself running back home."

Susan smiled and said, "That's my next book."

And then....

- Susan did write her novel about her adventures in London, and it made it to number seven on *The New York Times* Best Seller list. She received critical accolades about her debut novel, and reporters asked her when they might expect her next book. Susan told them it was already in the works and that it was about a middle-aged woman who, feeling unappreciated, runs away from home, only to discover that she had a pretty good life. A reporter asked if it was autobiographical and Susan simply smiled and said, "Maybe a little...." She also told them that it would not be published until she had given birth to her daughter.
- Ted relaxed his hours at the office and left promptly at six each night. He did bring work home often but tried not to let it interfere with his family time. When his daughter was born, he learned to give her a bottle and even changed a few diapers, so enamored was he of his auburn-haired beauty.
- Ben graduated from high school and followed in his father's footsteps, attending Harvard where he met the girl who became his wife following graduation. Susan found it amusing that she was from a small town in New Hampshire and fell in love with Oceanside and the house there.
- David and Sam became protective big brothers to their baby sister, although they didn't think she was much fun for several years.
- Rebecca Mary was the apple of her parents' eyes. She was the baby, the last child they would have, and the only girl. She was eight years younger than her closest sibling, almost a second family. By the time she began kindergarten, Sam was a teenager, David was in college, and Ben was thinking of proposing to his girlfriend. Ted and Susan tried hard not to spoil her, but they lavished attention on her.
- Jeannie and Doug stopped at eight children and stayed in touch with Susan and Ted, enjoying summers together but never venturing as far as Connecticut to visit their home.

- Katie gallivanted around the world with her Prince Charming and their daughter, Alice, who was the spitting image of Katie. Whenever Katie and Richard were in New York, they made a point of visiting with Yankee and Dimples, happy that everyone's lives had turned out exactly as they each wanted.
- And then there is Bill. What became of Bill? After he realized that Susan was never going to be his, he opened his heart more to other opportunities, and within two years, he married the woman who had gotten away during law school. She was practicing in the state capitol in the attorney general's office, and their paths crossed when Bill went to Augusta to lobby for the lobstermen. The two law school classmates hit it off again, and interestingly, she was at a point in her career when she was looking to move to a small town and hang up a shingle. She and Bill opened a law office in George Ward's old jewelry store space and handled the legal work for people who lived for miles around. Bill sent Susan and Ted an announcement of their civil wedding and on the back wrote,
- "Sometimes running home is just what you need to do in order to know where that home is."

And they all lived happily ever after....

Book Club Questions

1. If you felt unappreciated, could you see yourself running away from home?

2. Have you ever thought about a high school sweetheart and wondered what your life would be like on the road not taken?

3. Have you ever had a friend like Katie, someone who pulls you out of your shell?

4. Do you have unfinished dreams that you could (or did) return to someday like Susan returned to her writing?

5. What did you think of Bill when he pushed Susie away after his father died?

6. Did you want Susan to get back together with Bill, or were you hoping that she would return to Ted?

7. Were you surprised when Ted suggested they keep the Maine property as a summer house?

8. When Susan refers to people commuting to New York City as living significant lives compared to her new role as a mother, what was your reaction?

9. Thinking about your responsibilities, could you hire someone to take care of them like Susan did?

10. Were Ted's reactions when Susan left realistic? Did you expect him to be angrier? Did you expect him to be more understanding?

11. What did you think about Susan's tactic when she wanted to make new friends after she had her first child? Have you ever done something similar?

12. What did you think of Susan's decision to leave her career behind and be a stay-at-home mom?

13. Could you envision going to a restaurant or bar with five other mothers and six babies?

14. Did you think Katie and Richard would end up together?

15. What did you think of Susan not writing for so many years when it was her passion?

16. Did you want more for Jeannie and Doug, or were you happy they stayed small-town folks?

Acknowledgments

Writing a book is thought of as a solitary pursuit; however, as with most endeavors, it takes a village. *Running Home* is no exception. I am grateful for the careful first readers: Rick Robison, Linda Andersen Jessen, Raylene Matheny, and Sally Lyon. Their comments improved the manuscript. I am always thankful for the support of my sons, Robbie and Andy, and daughters-in-law, Leah and Katie. Their encouragement and positive reinforcement sometimes have me asking when the children became the parents. I could not have completed this book without the folks at Maine Authors Publishing. Christina, Nikki, Molly, Michelle, Dan, Nadia, and Jane were always available to assist, direct, and encourage. As a co-op publisher, their support throughout the publishing process with editing, design, printing, distribution, and marketing was a huge help.

If you enjoyed *Running Home,*
here is a sneak peek at the next book,
tentatively titled *GEEKDOM.*

AVAILABLE FOR SUMMER 2023

Prologue

Jacqui Parker is a genius. Ask anyone. That's what everyone will say. They won't tell you that she is kind and compassionate. They won't tell you that she is tortured by her brilliant mind. They won't tell you that her pink hair is a plea for people to see her as something other than the smartest person they know. They will tell you that she is a genius.

When Jacqueline Elizabeth Parker came screaming into the world, seven pounds, eight ounces of her parents' joy, no one knew what life had in store for her. Her mother and father held her proudly and promised that they would love her forever, protect her, and give her a happy home. People should never make promises they cannot keep—especially to children.

Chapter One

Jacqui sat in her corner office staring at the bay out her window, grateful that she had made the decision to drop out of MIT and start this company. After years of being "a good little girl," she could finally be herself. She was the boss of GEEKDOM. Of course, deep down, she was still a good little girl, but now she was free to run with the big boys, to challenge the system, to speak out for injustice in her own way, to finally find happiness—maybe even fall in love.

The idea for GEEKDOM had come to her when she was thirteen years old. She and three other geeks from her school had just finished playing a video game she had created, and they were debugging it, helping her to make it better. They liked the fact that it allowed them to become the characters they had always loved, to do magic with Harry, live on the prairie with Laura, or enjoy hijinks with Pippi. Jacqui's game was a video interpretation of those choose-your-own-adventure books she and her friends liked, only she had created adventures they could see instead of just imagine. Her imagination and all the hours she had spent in other worlds in order to escape the boredom of her own had led her to create this game. It was like nothing on the market, and she knew that children like her would love it. When she had a prototype completed, she had asked three kids at school to play it with her. For months, they holed up in her basement, her parents happy that she finally had friends over to play, and oblivious to what they were doing. Every hour or so her mother would bop down the stairs with a plate of cookies or a bowl of pretzels. She would smile as she saw her daughter playing games with other children and go back upstairs, relieved that finally Jacqui wasn't all alone.

Jacqui sent each of her friends on a different adventure and welcomed their input to make the adventure better. By the time she was fourteen, the game was ready.

Chapter Two

Jacqui's reverie was interrupted by loud knocking on her door, followed by three people bursting in, charging across to her desk, and yelping that today was the day. Oblivious to her cues that she wanted to be alone, they opened a bottle of champagne and poured four glasses, handing one to her. She laughed at their exuberance in spite of herself, for she felt it too. Butterflies in her stomach and bees in her ears gave way to excited laughter. Where would she be without these three goofballs? Then she laughed, thinking that her mother finally had her wish. Jacqui truly had friends.

When she had decided to start this company instead of finishing her junior year at MIT, she knew she couldn't do it without the three amigos. Steven, Phillip, and Leah had gotten her through her teen years. Without them, she shuddered to think what she might have done. From the first time she gathered them together in her basement to be the beta testers of her first game, she knew they would stay friends forever. Now, here they were running their own company together. Of course, it meant that Steven had dropped out of Stanford, Phil had left Carnegie Mellon, and Leah had abandoned her studies at RPI. Actually, Jacqui was surprised at how easy it had been for all of them to make the decision to leave school—not only because they thought the video game development company was a worthwhile endeavor but also because their parents would never understand. How could such bright kids just decide to drop out? That didn't make any sense to their parents and families. But it made perfect sense to them. School had never been challenging. Academics were a bore. Teachers who repeated and repeated themselves ad nauseum. Kids who cared more about gossip and bullying each other than truly caring. Classes that covered material at such a basic level that it was laughable and far from interesting.

For their entire lives they had listened to variations of the following:

"Jacqui, pay attention! Why must I always interrupt class to ask you to pay attention?"

"Steven, I have just about had enough of your questions. The other children in the class are not interested in all that. If you keep asking so many questions, I'm afraid the others will start making fun of you, and you won't have any friends."

"Leah, Ben is having trouble with this assignment. Why don't you be my helper today and give him a hand with it? That's a good girl."

"Phillip, you have to show your work. Why do you never show your work? Are you copying the answers from someone else?"

When Jacqui had called them and told them that she was leaving MIT to start a video game company with a social conscience, creating games for people like them, her friends didn't hesitate to join her. They just wanted to know where and when. Within weeks, Jacqui, unbeknownst to her parents, had written a business plan, approached investors, raised the seed money, found the perfect building on Massachusetts' North Shore, summoned her troops, and quit school. She had never been happier.

Now here she sat with her three musketeers and partners, about to launch GEEKDOM's first game. Not yet old enough to legally drink, they toasted their success and optimistically looked forward to the future—a future they would create for themselves. Now the hard work would begin. This first game was the one Jacqui had created at thirteen and together they had perfected it. Now they would need to follow it up with others. Among them, they had several similar games in various stages of readiness. They weren't worried...

For more information or to contact the author

Website: www.NancyAreyCohen.com

Facebook: @Nancy.Arey.Cohen-Author
@Readers and Writers

Email: NancyAreyCohen@gmail.com

Instagram: nancyareycohen

Twitter: @NancyC2012

Running Home is available on Amazon as well as directly through www.NancyAreyCohen.com. You will also find it in many of your local bookstores.